58% TOO FAR

M A NOORDERMEER

blue
giraffe
BOOKS

For Dino, who believed in me without question, stood back when I needed space, and never once asked me to be reasonable.

And to my amazing beta readers—you came in at different moments, in different ways, but each of you helped this story find its shape. Your candor, curiosity, and generosity made it sharper, stranger, and infinitely better. I'm so grateful to each of you.

Heather Baird

Solange Francois Bason

Paul Brady

Jasper Bruinzeel

Alyssa Bullot

Fiona Bunce

Chris Craig

Maurice Deevy

Simon Hepple

Simon Hertnon

Nick Humphries

Kim Mariu

Dino Matsis

Tash Matsis-Boulton

James Noordermeer

Dylan Procter

Kaine Ramsby

Tara Sabor

Sal Sanfilippo

Beth Tolley

Rasika Versleijen-Pradhan

Contents

1

Awakening on Mushēški

An impossible color filled Zadie's vision—a violet somehow too bright and too dark at once, defying the edges of her perception. She rubbed her eyes, squeezing them shut before reopening them. But the color stubbornly persisted. Her throat tightened, a nervous laugh faltering before it could escape.

"Uncle? Is this some kind of joke?"

No one answered.

She sat up, heart pounding, dark strands of hair clinging to her cheeks as the surface beneath her shifted, molding to her posture. The otherworldly color lingered for a moment longer, then softened as if her mind had surrendered to its presence.

She blinked hard, expecting to see the stone blocks of the chamber beneath Qal'at al-Bahrain. Instead, she found herself in a strange room. The space was minimalist, the walls a muted blue. A broad window framed an unfamiliar coastline, the sea restless beneath a washed-out sky. Below the window was a gray desk with a chair tucked under it. A few familiar academic textbooks lay scattered across the desk, their spines cracked and worn. She subconsciously cataloged the details, just as she always did.

Her fingers brushed against a foreign light-blue material clinging to her curves. Someone had undressed her. The thought made her stomach twist with violation. Her attention moved to a strange bracelet around her wrist, its surface shifting through colors, one more alien than the rest. Zadie tugged at it, but it tightened, gripping her skin until she let go.

Unease propelled her to her feet. Shifting her weight, she expected the firm resistance of tiles but sank into an unsettling softness instead. The edges of her vision blurred. She inhaled deeply, fighting to steady herself.

She scanned the room, looking for an exit. No door. There had to be a door. Fingers trailing the wall, she searched for a seam, a crack, any sign of an opening. Nothing.

She edged toward the window. The ground below looked close enough. But there was no latch, no frame, no gap where it might slide open. She hesitated, then grabbed the desk chair and hurled it at the window. The chair slammed into the glass, making it warp. The coastline blurred before snapping back into focus.

It wasn't a window. The illusion shattered.

A scream broke free. Her legs trembled, sending her staggering backward until she collapsed onto the floor. This had to be a dream. Her hands flew to her face, pressing hard against her cheeks, trying to force the world to make sense.

Out of the corner of her eye, something shifted. A section of the wall rippled like a disturbed pond before becoming transparent and dissolving. A figure emerged from the opening. It looked human—but moved like something else. Every instinct demanded she run, but there was no escape.

She bolted to the side of the bed, gripping the edge. The figure stepped across the threshold and stopped, as if allowing her a moment to process its presence. She crouched, muscles tight, instincts sharp.

She stole another look at it. It wore a jumpsuit like hers, but in white. Its warm brown skin was smooth over sharp, angular features. Bald, ageless, and androgynous, its eyes held an extraordinary complexity, hinting at artificial advancements beyond current human capability.

It regarded her with a penetrating, emotionless stare. She searched its eyes for any hint of intent—but found nothing. Motionless, barely able to breathe, she waited.

"Welcome to *Mushēški*, Zadie." The being's voice carried both human warmth and synthetic precision. "Shall I procure some water for your refreshment?"

Water? The absurdity hit like a punch to the gut. Her throat was raw, parched from the panic still clawing at her. But the question itself landed like a cruel joke in the face of her terror.

2

The Catalyst

E arlier that day...

From: *Professor Möller*
To: *Zadie Thornton*
Subject: *URGENT – Thesis Progress and Funding*

Zadie,

Your historical analysis is thorough, but your framework fails to account for AI's rapidly evolving role in decision-making, governance and human cognition. The field has moved well beyond historical parallels, and unless your research adapts, it will be of limited relevance. You have two months to present a substantially revised approach, or we will have no choice but to initiate a formal review of your doctoral candidacy status.

Regards, Prof. Möller

Seven years. Grants written at midnight. Missed birthdays. Calls she never returned. All of it condensed into a handful of sterile lines from Professor Möller. Her life's work, apparently irrelevant. She'd spent her career studying how humans adapted to change. And yet here she was, failing to adapt herself.

She clenched her presentation notes, the paper crinkling in her grip. Five minutes until she walked onto the stage to defend an argument she wasn't even sure she believed in anymore.

A conference assistant pressed a clicker into her palm. "You're up soon, Ms. Thornton. Water's on the podium. Need anything else?"

"No, I'm all good, cheers." Zadie parted the deep-red stage curtains just enough to survey the conference hall.

Enormous screens flanked the stage, showcasing the event's logo above a stylized image of Manama's skyline. Academics, students, policymakers, and tech leaders stood in clusters, debating the dangers of AI. Nearby, existential risk theorists clashed over key points, their voices cutting through the low hum of conversation.

She shoved her purse onto a backstage shelf, a small guidebook tumbling free and landing at her feet. Bahrain's glistening sea and bustling markets stared back from the cover—sights she wouldn't have time for on this visit. At least she would see her uncle. That would make the trip worthwhile.

She drew in a deep breath, her suit jacket suddenly too tight. Tucking a stray hair back into her bun, she forced herself to focus as the lights dimmed and the host stepped up to the podium.

"Ladies and gentlemen, it is my great honor to introduce Zadie Thornton, an anthropologist and doctoral candidate from the University of Oxford. Her research examines humanity's historical responses to transformative technologies, with a focus on how past technological revolutions can guide us in navigating AI's rapid ascent. Please join me in welcoming Ms. Thornton."

Applause filled the hall as Zadie stepped forward. Her shoulders tensed under the imagined scrutiny of the audience.

"Good morning, everyone," she began. "Every great technological leap brings uncertainty. Will we lose our jobs? Who will gain power, and who will lose it? Will it reshape society in ways we can't undo? These aren't new fears. They've come up every time humanity has taken a step into the unknown. Today, I want to show you how our ancestors faced these upheavals and what their choices can teach us."

Behind her, the screens displayed an image of early humans gathered around a fire. "Around 400,000 years ago, archaic humans learned to control fire. It provided warmth, protection, and the ability to cook food, making more nutrients accessible. But it also brought risks of uncontrollable wildfires, shifting social hierarchies, and long-term health effects from smoke inhalation. Fire wasn't just a tool. It reshaped survival, power, and the human environment."

The image shifted to wooden plows carving through the earth, smoke curling from scattered huts. "The Agricultural Revolution, around 12,000 years ago, transformed human society irreversibly. Farming led to permanent settlements, structured hierarchies, and centralized governance. Food surpluses fueled population growth, but they also introduced disease, economic inequality, and environmental depletion. Yet, from this turning point emerged the first cities and the foundations of modern civilization."

She gestured toward the screen, where a lone scribe painstakingly copied a manuscript. "When the printing press arrived in the 15th century, it upended control over knowledge. Scribes saw their craft vanish, the church feared heresy, and rulers feared losing their grip on information. Over time, printing democratized knowledge, increased literacy, fueled scientific discovery, and laid the groundwork for political revolutions."

For the next hour, Zadie led the audience through history's technological upheavals. The Scientific Revolution replaced superstition with observation, unlocking physics, medicine, and engineering. The Industrial Revolution brought machines that outpaced human hands, swelling cities and deepening inequality. Electrification lit up entire landscapes, accelerating factories, shrinking distances, and connecting voices across continents. The Digital Revolution shifted power to data. Industry gave way to information. Surveillance spread. Algorithms took the wheel, setting the stage for artificial intelligence.

Zadie watched the audience lean in, their eyes narrowing in thought, pens tapping, a few exchanging glances. She hoped they were captivated by how she brought to life the resistance, ethical debates, cultural shifts, and societal changes that arose with each innovation.

A hand shot up, fingers splayed.

Zadie's rhythm faltered. She locked eyes with a well-known AI critic, his expression carrying the confidence of someone who had dismantled many arguments before.

"AI isn't like any of the other simpler technologies you mentioned, Ms. Thornton," he corrected her.

Zadie steadied herself with a breath. "Correct. AI is advancing rapidly, and it's different in that it's capable of decision-making, problem-solving, and even creativity. But I'd argue that the patterns remain the same: fear, disruption, adaptation, and integration."

"Fear, disruption, adaptation, and integration?" The critic leaned forward, voice sharpening. "AI isn't just a tool. It's a collaborator, a competitor, and if we're reckless, a successor. We aren't talking about another industrial revolution. We're talking about a shift in cognitive power itself."

A murmur rippled through the audience.

"We're dealing with AI that can manipulate reality," he continued. "Deepfakes indistinguishable from truth. Algorithms nudging human behavior, influencing elections, eroding the concept of objective reality. Tell me, Ms. Thornton, how do we navigate a world where we can't even trust what we see?"

Zadie's mouth opened, but no sound came out. Her thoughts, usually a dependable cascade of counterpoints, stalled. She scrambled for a foothold, but every argument she conjured dissolved before it reached her tongue. She dropped her gaze and fumbled with her notes.

A younger woman near the critic chimed in. "Yeah, and then there's genetic integration..."

Scattered laughter cut her off.

Another hand went up. A flash of purple hair and sharp patterns against the neutral crowd. "Hi everyone, I'm Avery, pronouns they/them. So, like... if AI can already make music, write novels, diagnose diseases, and do insane math, what's the point of spending years learning anything? What happens to actual human artists? To students?"

Zadie found her concluding remarks and latched onto them. "As we look to the future, we need to remember the lessons our past has taught us. Every technological revolution challenges us and pushes us to the brink, but it also holds the potential to reshape our lives in positive ways we can't even imagine. Our job is to navigate these changes with a clear head to ensure that progress stays on our side."

Zadie stepped back from the podium. A scattering of polite applause did little to mask the skeptical glances and folded arms that dominated the audience. The host approached her with a beaming smile and a firm handshake, but the momentary warmth couldn't chase away the tightness in her chest.

She slipped backstage, retrieved her purse, and exhaled before heading back through the hall. The audience had fractured into clusters, voices rising as they dissected her talk over coffee.

A group of university students bounded toward her, faces alight with excitement. One of them, a lanky man with messy brown hair and a backpack slung over one shoulder, stepped forward. "Ms. Thornton, your talk was so insightful! It really made us see things differently."

"Thank you. I'm glad it resonated with you." She exchanged a few more pleasantries before the group moved on, their youthful optimism lingering like an afterthought.

She spotted her uncle weaving his way through the crowd, his well-worn leather satchel bumping against his side, caked in the dust of excavation sites. He looked just as she remembered, only now the lines beneath his eyes were carved deeper. They still shared the same deep-set eyes and strong nose. Years under the desert sun had weathered Ahmed's skin to a deep tan, while hers remained several shades lighter courtesy of her mixed heritage and life under cloudier skies.

"Zadie!" Ahmed beamed, his smile widening as he squeezed her shoulders. "You were brilliant up there, my dear! I always knew you'd do remarkable things, even back when you were knee-high to a grasshopper."

"Thanks, Uncle. But I'm not so sure."

Ahmed held her gently by the upper arms. "No need to second-guess yourself. You reminded everyone that the past has lessons for our future. Never forget that."

Her eyes warmed with an unexpected emotion, softening the edges of her usual composure. "It's been a long time. I'm really glad you could make it."

"I wouldn't have missed it for the world." His expression wavered, uncertainty giving way to a hint of mischief. "Zadie, dear, how about we ditch this stuffy conference for a bit? I'm back working at the Qal'at al-Bahrain dig site. It's just a short drive away. It'll give us a chance to catch up, and I promise it's more interesting than any other keynote here."

"Perfect," she said. Anywhere but here would do. Childhood summers flashed through her mind. Trailing her uncle, mimicking his every move as he led her through narrow market streets, teaching her to haggle in broken Arabic. "Only, I've not brought a change of clothes—"

"No worries!" Ahmed grinned, reaching into his satchel and pulling out a neatly folded pair of khaki pants and a matching shirt. "I came prepared. Go get changed and meet me outside in five minutes."

"Sure." Zadie took the outfit from him with a laugh.

◇———※———◇

Ahmed unlocked the door of his battered jeep, its paint faded and chipped. The engine sputtered, then caught with a rough growl, settling into a steady hum as they pulled away. The city rushed by, the busy streets of Manama lined with towering skyscrapers and modern shopping malls next to the faded textures of history. Gradually the urban density eased, giving way to quieter surroundings and open stretches of land. Before long, the archaeological site of Qal'at al-Bahrain came into view.

The jeep rattled to a halt on uneven ground, its tires kicking up a thin cloud of dust. Zadie stepped out onto the ancient grounds, the heat wrapping around her like a heavy coat. Ahmed tossed her a cap, a quick remedy against the sun's harsh glare. The salty tang of the nearby sea mingled with the earthy scent of sunbaked soil.

Qal'at al-Bahrain rose before her, an imposing fortress of honey-hued limestone. Beyond it stretched the remnants of a long-lost world, weathered foundations and the ghostly geometry of a forgotten city.

"Incredible."

"Come, I'll show you around," Ahmed said, his voice full of pride. He moved with an easy familiarity, maneuvering between crumbled walls and excavation trenches, his boots crunching on the gravel. At the northern edge of the site, Ahmed paused. "This, dear, is where we've uncovered the greatest number of treasures from our ancestors." He gestured to the exposed strata. "This layer here dates back to the early Islamic period, around the seventh century, and this one belongs to the ancient Dilmun civilization, around 2,300 BCE."

Zadie crouched, scooping up a handful of warm, gritty earth and letting it slip through her fingers. Sweat trickled down her temple.

"Let's grab some lunch at the museum," Ahmed said. "We'll return when the sun's not trying to cook us alive."

"Sounds good to me." She stepped beside him as they headed toward the café.

The glass doors slid open, releasing a rush of cool air that kissed Zadie's heat-flushed cheeks. Inside, the cafeteria buzzed with conversation, the clink of cutlery muted against soft Arabic pop playing overhead. They joined the short queue at the shawarma counter.

Ahmed glanced at her. "Chicken, lamb, or falafel?"

"Falafel, thanks. And no garlic sauce." She grimaced.

They collected their wraps and skirted past the self-serve drinks, where rows of battered urns dispensed tea and sweet mint water. Zadie filled a small ceramic cup and followed Ahmed to a table tucked in the back corner. Before she'd even sat down, he was already peeling the paper off his shawarma. The scent of grilled lamb hit her.

"How's your mother doing?" he said. "Still dropping hints about grandchildren every chance she gets?"

Zadie huffed a quiet laugh and shook her head. "She's fine, but grandkids aren't happening. I'm thirty-two, and the only thing I'm committed to is finishing my DPhil." Her fingers tightened around a paper napkin in her lap, twisting it into a crumpled spiral. "I barely have time to sleep, let alone date. I'm either buried in research or off in some remote corner of the world, trying to piece together the puzzle of humanity."

"Is that what drives you?"

"It was." Her shoulders drooped. "But with AI changing everything so fast, it's starting to feel like anything I do becomes irrelevant before I even get to publish it. To be honest, Uncle, just before my presentation, my supervisor emailed me to say that my research is... outdated, thanks to all these AI advancements. And after today's audience reaction, I can't help but wonder—did I waste my best years chasing something that was never going to matter? Did I give up the chance of a real life, love, family—for nothing?"

Ahmed's chewing slowed, then he let out a low, incredulous laugh. "Outdated? You're researching cultural adaptation to technology, right? How does something like that become outdated?"

"Uncle, my whole thesis rests on the idea that we can learn from past patterns to predict how society will adapt to AI. However, that AI critic today was right. AI does differ from other technological revolutions. It's not just another tool humans can master. It's making its own decisions faster than we can comprehend. Every hypothesis I made seven years ago is already obsolete."

Ahmed rubbed his chin. "So, they expect you to just... scrap everything and start over?"

"Pretty much." She gave a bitter smile. "They're pushing me to reframe everything around practical, current applications. They want a framework, something that predicts how people will adapt to AI. But we're talking about technology evolving so fast, it's outpacing anything we can predict."

Ahmed leaned forward, eyes narrowing. "Zadie, there's another reason I wanted to bring you here today. And from what you say, I think this might be the right moment for a different kind of opportunity."

"What do you mean?" A playful grin lit up her face. "You're not planning to set me up with someone, are you?"

Ahmed smirked, dipping his head as he spoke in a hushed tone. "No, no. Think bigger. If you had a chance to glimpse the future of AI and its impact on humanity, would you take it?"

"You mean like visiting some top-secret research lab? Or a hidden community experimenting with next-generation AI?"

"Along those lines."

"Um... yeah, of course, Uncle. If I could see the long-term consequences of AI, it would be invaluable for my research. If I don't make a breakthrough soon, it'll be too late... I wouldn't just take the chance—I'd probably fight for it!"

Ahmed studied her. "What if this knowledge... changes everything? Turns your world upside-down. You learn things you can't unlearn, things nobody else can grasp. Answers that leave you... alone... Would you still want to know?"

"Well, if it really meant unlocking secrets, I suppose I would. It's not like I have much to lose. I'm used to going it alone." Zadie took a sip of her tea. Sweet, spiced, and aggressively strong.

He reached out, patting her hand reassuringly. "Then maybe I have something for you that could get your PhD—or DPhil rather—back on track and much more. I can't guarantee you access, but I can try, *inshallah*. Are you ready for such a journey?"

"Well, I guess there's only one way to find out what you're up to."

"Good." He nodded. "Finish your meal and then I'll take you there."

She studied Ahmed's face, trying to decipher his secrets, watching every subtle twitch and shift. Her appetite vanished, her half-eaten meal growing cold.

Ahmed shot to his feet, the chair scraping against the floor like a starter pistol. "Come on then. It's time." His hand swept in a quick, inviting gesture.

Zadie barely had time to push her chair in before he was striding past the exhibits, past the polished glass and curated plaques, his pace relentless. He veered toward an elevator marked *Staff Only*, hesitating just long enough for her to catch up before slipping inside. She stepped in just as the doors began to close.

With practiced precision, he keyed in a sequence of buttons. The elevator hummed softly, then came to a stop. When the doors slid open, a dark passage was revealed.

Ahmed stepped out first, fumbling briefly before pressing something into her hand. "Here, you'll need this."

She took the flashlight and turned it on just as the elevator doors sealed shut behind them. Her beam swept the space, revealing a spiraling stone staircase, the surrounding walls constructed from stone blocks, each carved with intricate patterns and faded glyphs.

"We go down," Ahmed said, already descending.

Her pulse kicked up. "Uncle, where are we going?"

"Patience, Zadie," he said over his shoulder.

The air grew cooler. Unease settled deep in Zadie's stomach, but curiosity pulled her forward. The descent ended at a modern steel door, out of place against the ancient stonework.

Ahmed pressed his thumb to a scanner. The door hissed open with smooth precision. "We've made a few upgrades," he said, flashing a brief, knowing smile before stepping inside.

Polished metals in the high ceiling caught the beam of Zadie's flashlight, reflecting a soft glow across a vast chamber. Ahmed tapped a modern panel beside the entrance and the space flooded with light. Massive stone walls stretched in perfect alignment, the seams between blocks so tight they could have been fused rather than stacked. Zadie ran a hand over the nearest wall. The engravings were impossibly precise, their edges crisp as if time had barely touched them. The space was large enough to hold a gathering of a hundred people, yet it bore the stillness of a place rarely disturbed.

"Wait here a minute." Ahmed strode toward a far corner, running his fingers along a section of the stonework that seemed deliberately designed to open. With a grunt, he worked a small block free. A fine trickle of dust spilled from the gap as he reached inside and pulled out a clay box. He turned it over in his hands, rubbing his thumb against the surface, his jaw tightening. "I've been waiting a long time for the right moment to show you this."

He set the box down and lifted the lid. Inside, swathed in tattered cloth, rested a metallic ball. Its surface was both smooth and rippling at once, and the light seemed to bend around it.

Zadie stared, unable to look away. "I've never seen anything like it. What is it?"

"It's your opportunity, Zadie. Go ahead. Touch it."

Her hand hovered. "What happens if I do?"

"It'll show us if you're ready."

The ball drew her in, its attraction almost magnetic. She paused, her hand just inches away, her eyes narrowing as fascination warred with caution. She reached out, her fingertips grazing the cool surface. It quivered beneath her touch.

"What?"

"It's alright, Zadie. Just let it happen." His smile was encouraging, but charged with expectation.

She picked up the ball, startled by how effortlessly it lifted, as if gravity had no hold on it. A warmth pulsed through her fingertips, spreading up her arm. She hesitated, then closed her eyes. The sensation was almost... soothing.

"Uncle! What's happening?"

Without warning, the ball began to glow from within. Light erupted, swelling outward, devouring the space around her in a cascade of brilliance.

"Everything you know," Ahmed's voice was impossibly distant, "is about to change."

The chamber faded.

A sharp jolt tore through her.

Her limbs went weightless, her mind untethered, as if falling without moving. Space warped, stretched, then collapsed around her.

She surrendered to the unknown.

3

The Origins of the Anunnaki

"**I** am Lugazir." The being's eyes locked on hers. "I am responsible for liaising with the non-Anunnaki entities."

It lifted the overturned desk chair, turned it to face Zadie, and sat down.

Zadie knelt beside the bed. The sight of the being seated eased her panic a little, allowing her to steady herself with slow, deliberate breaths.

"What is going on? I don't understand... Where am I?"

Lugazir tapped a thin metallic disc at their temple before pointing to an identical object on the desk. "The device before you is a *neuroscribe*. It is designed to augment our communicative capacity. I urge you to attach it to your temple."

Zadie recoiled, her gaze flickering between Lugazir and the disc. "But I can already understand you."

"Rudimentary communication is feasible without this device. Nevertheless, the neuroscribe facilitates a more profound exchange between two or more individuals, adapting its translation to the user's unique cognitive and experiential framework. It extends beyond mere linguistic conversion to encompass the transmission of thoughts, sensations, and visual data. Though mastery of its advanced functionalities necessitates practice. It will enhance your ability to grasp information faster."

Faster. The word gripped her. The chaos in her mind craved order, answers, something that made sense. She didn't trust this being, didn't trust any of this... but the not knowing was worse. Perhaps the neuroscribe could help. It might be worth the risk.

"What do I do with it?"

"Affix it to your temple. The device will adhere and commence synchronization with your neural pathways. Consider it akin to tuning two radios to an identical frequency. Such alignment renders advanced communication attainable."

Zadie stood and picked up the device. She hesitantly pressed the disc to her temple. It latched into place with an almost magnetic tug. A cool tingle spread across the back of her neck, followed by a torrent of foreign sounds and sensations, overwhelming her senses. Almost immediately the tumult settled, and she sensed clarity emerging. The tightness in her chest eased, replaced by an unnatural stillness.

"You're on another planet called Mushēški," Lugazir said, the stiff formality of their tone dissolving.

"Another planet! I don't believe you. There must be a rational explanation. This is mad. Absolutely mad. My uncle wouldn't—" She stopped, forcing herself to breathe. Years of academic training demanded evidence, methodology, peer review. Not... this. Yet the room, the strange being before her, the color she'd never seen before today... They all persisted.

"Really?"

"Yes."

Zadie's knees threatened to buckle. She clutched the desk, fighting to stay upright. A scream built in her throat but dissolved before reaching her lips.

"Am I in the future...?"

Lugazir's features softened. "No, you're not in the future, Zadie. You're just in a different place."

The panic should have been overwhelming. Yet, it wasn't. It had somehow tucked itself away where she couldn't quite reach it. She swallowed hard. "How far am I from Earth?"

"This distance is beyond your usual measurements. You're many light-years from your solar system."

Zadie's voice cracked as she repeated, "Light-years..." The words sat awkwardly on her tongue.

"Yes, but think of how our ancestors once viewed crossing the Arabian Desert. They expected it to take months. Now you can fly over it in an hour. In the same way, our transitfold technology—"

"Our ancestors...? So, you are human?"

Lugazir nodded.

Zadie's hands trembled. She stared at them, watching her fingers curl and uncurl as if testing whether they were truly her own. They appeared foreign, disconnected from the rest of her body. "Am I safe here?"

"Yes, Zadie. Every detail here has been designed for your comfort and safety." They gestured around the room as if the space itself was proof of their words.

Comfort. Safety. The words settled into her mind, too easy to accept.

"Am I a prisoner here?"

"No, not at all."

The bed shifted, liquefying into a dark gray syrup that spilled onto the floor.

Zadie jumped, her eyes widening in shock. She shot a look at Lugazir, who stayed perfectly composed. The instinct to react flickered like a faulty signal, dulled at the edges. In a matter of seconds, the substance reformed into a simple seating area for two with a small table.

"Come, let's sit."

Taking a deep breath, Zadie hesitantly sat down on a chair. The material molded to her body like memory foam, adjusting with each subtle shift.

A small alcove materialized in the wall. Lugazir retrieved a pitcher of water and two cups, seemingly made from the same gray substance. Lugazir poured water into one of the cups and handed it to Zadie.

Zadie took a sip of cool water. The faint taste of iron reminded her of tap water back home. She leaned back, her shoulders sinking into the chair. "My uncle... How does he know about this place?"

"Ahmed was here for two months, twenty-six years ago. Like you, he touched one of our spheres, which analyzed his biology, cognition, and emotions, facilitating his passage here."

"So, he really did intend for me to be here?"

"Yes. And he was right to give you the chance to witness Earth's future. Our data shows a high probability that your insights, especially with your anthropological background, will not only benefit Earth but also advance our own research."

Zadie stared at the seating arrangement, still grappling with the fact that it had been a bed moments ago. "What can I possibly contribute to your research?"

Lugazir's expression remained serene. "I'll explain everything soon."

Zadie's head dipped in a slow nod. "How long will I be here?"

"The choice is yours, Zadie. You can stay on Mushēški for as long or as short a time as you wish. As your uncle alluded to, this is a rare opportunity to explore and discover things few have ever seen."

"So, I'm free to leave whenever I want to?" Zadie looked at Lugazir and then at the bracelet on her wrist, suspicion creeping in.

"Yes. The bracelet you're wearing interfaces with our transport system."

Zadie took a deep breath. Why hadn't her uncle told her what she was getting herself into?

"Your mind is adjusting well. I expected more resistance," Lugazir noted, tilting their head. "Perhaps now you'd like to hear the story of the Anunnaki?"

She realized she should have been more terrified, but curiosity won out. "Y... yes, I'd like that."

"To understand us, Zadie, you need to consider a past that lies beyond the limits of Earth's known historical record. The origins of the Anunnaki trace back to the ancient Sumerians of Ur, in Mesopotamia, a civilization in what is now Iraq. In their quest for knowledge, a group of Sumerian philosophers and leaders reached out to the universe."

Zadie straightened, drawn in, but her mind already raced with questions.

"They encountered advanced beings called the *Abgal*. The Abgal guided the Sumerians, advancing their understanding of agriculture, architecture, and astronomy. However, around 2900 BCE, the Abgal warned them of a great flood that could destroy their civilization. To save them, the Abgal provided an interstellar ark. A spaceship that allowed 616 Sumerians to leave Earth."

Zadie leaned back, folding her arms across her chest. "Wait... How? You're telling me a civilization that had barely figured out the wheel contacted advanced extraterrestrials?" Zadie's brow furrowed. That couldn't be right.

"I can see this is a lot to take in. Let me try something different." Lugazir's eyes closed in concentration.

The room seemed to blur as Zadie's senses warped. Her body remained still, but Lugazir's presence slipped into her consciousness, like a mist curling around the edges of her thoughts. Before she could react, a vision burst open as if a door had swung wide in her mind's eye.

She found herself seated in a circle of Sumerians on the mud-brick floor of a temple's central courtyard, in the light of clay oil lamps. Draped in long, simple robes, they sat on their heels, eyes closed, lost in deep meditation. A low hum pulsed through the air, stretching outward like a signal reaching for something beyond sight. She sensed their determination, felt the dust of ancient fields, smelled burning wood, and heard whispers in a language she shouldn't have understood, but somehow did.

She was in both places at once. That didn't make sense—couldn't make sense.

Above them, the night sky shimmered as if something had stirred it awake. A hushed gasp rippled through the Sumerians as a radiant light descended, its brilliance folding around seven tall figures. The beings stepped forward, veiled in a glow that obscured their features, making them appear both near and unreachable. Yet Zadie knew them without question, without reason. The Abgal. Their minds radiated profound knowledge. The awe in the Sumerians' eyes deepened, transforming into reverence.

The scene shifted so abruptly that Zadie gasped aloud. She was engulfed in the Abgal's vision of a great flood, a dark wall of water surging toward the ancient city. Her chest tightened, the ground trembling beneath her. She gripped the edge of her chair, her heart racing.

The vision shifted again. Hope took shape in the form of a giant ark they called *An-Naĝar-ki*. It hovered above the Earth like a low-hanging cloud. An-Naĝar-ki had a sleek, circular form with smooth surfaces that reflected the sky. Its subtle vibration stirred the hairs on Zadie's arms.

The chosen Sumerians—a deliberate blend of leaders, scribes, artisans, farmers, healers, and warriors—glanced back one last time at the loved ones they were leaving behind. Zadie experienced their pain and determination. Tears welled in their eyes as they ventured forward. The Abgal stood beside them, assuring them of the protection and guidance they would provide.

A black expanse of space stretched around her. Fierce concentration replaced the Sumerians' awe as they learned to navigate the unknown. Zadie recognized their thirst for knowledge as if it were her own. She could sense their hands moving over unfamiliar controls, their minds adapting to each challenge with every new cycle of distant stars.

Then, with a wrenching jolt, the vision collapsed, and the room came back into sharp focus. Zadie could see Lugazir watching her closely. She clutched her head, trying to contain the whirlwind of images and emotions. Her eyes darted back and forth, pupils dilating as she absorbed the onslaught of information.

"What was that?! It... felt... like I was really there."

"That was telepathy via the neuroscribe. It's a much more efficient way to communicate."

Zadie's fingers dug into her scalp. She tried to assert her usual logical mindset, clinging to her inadequate training. *It's just a vision*, she told herself. *Stay objective*. But the telepathic flow made that impossible.

Each sensation, every texture, scent, and fleeting thought, wrapped around her, too vivid to separate from her own. She wasn't just observing this, she was living it. Sumerian emotions surged through her, raw and real, rooting the past deeper than any reality she knew. The certainty of the experience drowned out her critical thoughts.

The vivid images she had seen replayed through her mind—the circle of Sumerians, the arrival of the Abgal, the flood, the ark... She mentally cataloged each one in an effort to match them with her understanding of archaeological finds, texts, and ancient myths. This would rewrite history, religion, science. Everything. But how could she prove it?

"Are you ready for more?" Lugazir asked.

Zadie swallowed, drawing in a steady breath. She nodded, determination sparking in her eyes as she chased every fragment of understanding. "Why didn't they go back? After the flood... why didn't the Sumerians return to Earth?"

"They were given a choice. One that sparked their insatiable thirst for knowledge. The Abgal offered them more than survival. They were offered an opportunity to evolve, to transcend what they were. Returning to Earth meant going back to a life they had already outgrown. The allure of what they could become was too much to refuse."

Submerged in the telepathic flow again, the staggering weight of what the Abgal were about to do surged through Zadie's mind. *Quantum Sentience,* an advanced artificial intelligence, was about to be integrated into the genomes of the Sumerians. This wasn't just data or logic—it was something that could adapt, learn, and evolve in ways no human had ever seen.

The Sumerians stood motionless, bodies taut, eyes wide. Above them, a swirling vortex of light materialized, a projection crafted for their understanding, illustrating the delicate strands of their DNA. Zadie's breath caught as the Abgal released clouds of iridescent particles into the projection, manifestations of the Quantum Sentience merging with them.

An electric tingle skittered across her skin, as if the Quantum Sentience were stirring inside her own body. She felt it seep into the Sumerians, threading through their essence, shifting, changing, becoming one with them. She observed the Sumerians as they absorbed the influx of information, unspoken thoughts flowing between them, their eyes gleaming with shared comprehension.

The vision dissolved, dragging Zadie back to reality. The room now seemed unnervingly still. Her pulse raced as she tried to grasp the enormity of what she'd seen.

"From the legacy of the Sumerians, we, the *Homo Anunnaki*, emerged," Lugazir said. "Our name comes from the Sumerian words *An*, meaning the heavens, and *Ki*, for Earth, since we are a mix of both realms."

Zadie clenched her jaw, her mind racing to anchor itself in something familiar. "How does this Quantum Sentience compare to the artificial intelligence we have on Earth?"

"You can call it *QS*. Your AI is still external—an advanced tool, but separate from you. Your brain relies on biochemical pathways, your neurons are like fireflies, each blinking independently, sometimes forming patterns, sometimes blinking at random. That's slow and prone to failure—"

"And QS?"

"QS isn't just artificial intelligence. It is biologically resident quantum cognition—not coded, but grown. QS synchronizes neurons, turning scattered flashes into a single, controlled glow. It weaves between them, anticipating their shifts, and even generates new patterns that wouldn't occur on their own. It allows thoughts to exist in multiple states at once, vastly increasing cognitive speed and adaptability."

"That's—" she stopped herself. *Impossible?* No, that word had lost meaning the moment she arrived here.

Lugazir paused, letting the concept settle before continuing. "QS doesn't just enhance intelligence. It enables cognitive exchange between individuals."

Zadie inhaled sharply, her thoughts tangling in all directions. "As in... it links your minds together?"

"Correct. It also regulates our entire biology. QS connects with our nervous system, repairing DNA, boosting metabolism, even replicating the effects of deep sleep through direct neural restoration."

"But... it changes how people think?"

"Yes. Imagine the difference between studying a language for years and instantly being fluent. Imagine being connected to everyone, understanding them, without exchanging a single word. You ask questions because you lack answers. I rarely experience uncertainty; outcomes are clear."

Zadie folded her arms, her fingers tightening. It sounded more like a computer than a person. "Do you ever just... have random thoughts or sudden insights?"

"No," Lugazir said. "Your mind still works in chaos. Your thoughts sparking unpredictably, sometimes leading nowhere, sometimes to revelation. We are far beyond that, but soon you will be too."

"What do you mean?"

"In approximately thirty-six years, Earth-born humans will achieve the ability to integrate AI into your genomes."

"What? AI in our genomes? In thirty-six years...?"

"Earth-born quantum researchers are already exploring biological materials for quantum processing. Within two decades, they'll overcome the biggest hurdle—stabilizing quantum systems—using engineered proteins or molecular structures for error correction. Human trials will begin around 2047, with neural implants enhancing cognition. Once self-assembling nanomachines construct quantum circuits in the bloodstream, protected by diamond-cage structures, full neural integration will be inevitable."

Zadie paused, the implications stacking one on top of another like precarious dominoes. A tangled web too vast to hold in her head. Her fingers twitched, itching to scribble notes.

"We established our home on this distant planet, which we named *Mushēški. The wise new Earth*—"

"Lugazir, do you have something I could use to take notes?"

"The neuroscribe will handle all that for you."

"I'd rather do it the old-fashioned way, if that's alright."

Lugazir inclined their head, a gesture laced with a hint of indulgence. A soft hum followed as they tapped a hidden panel. An alcove slid open, revealing three leather-bound notebooks and an array of instruments resembling calligraphy pens. With quiet precision, Lugazir placed them on the table in front of her.

Zadie stared at the notebooks, surprised by their sudden appearance but grateful for something familiar. She picked up a notebook and pen, running her fingers over the supple leather before flipping it open. Her pen began to glide across the page, her attention pinned to the details spilling onto the paper. Each word was like armor. If she captured it all in ink, she wouldn't have to face what it all meant, at least for now.

"There is much more, Zadie."

The words carried a tantalizing promise. She didn't move, but every one of her nerves sparked to life.

4

Quantum Psychosis

"Perhaps you'd like to see how we live here in Dilmun. It's our district on Mushēški."

"Dilmun—? Is that named after the ancient civilization in Bahrain? Because I was just there."

"No. The opposite. The Dilmun on Earth was named after this one. Anunnaki often visited Earth in the early days. Our home of Dilmun became an idealized paradise, inspiring Earth's legends and mythology."

Zadie squinted, as though clarity might surface if she just focused harder.

"Follow me, Zadie."

The wall shimmered and dissolved. Zadie inhaled deeply as she stepped through, her senses catching the faintest shift as the purified air of Dilmun greeted her. She braced for foreign sensations. Instead, the air filled her lungs with a familiar ease. For a fleeting moment, it seemed like she'd just stepped outside on Earth, into a garden untouched by pollution. A perfect blue sky with only a hint of distant clouds stretched overhead. Was she really even on another planet?

She turned back, expecting to see some sort of building. Instead, there was only an endless expanse of greenery. No visible architecture, nothing to suggest how they'd arrived. Then she saw it—a faint doorway traced in the air, the space quivering like heat above a candle flame.

Lugazir's voice cut through her bewilderment. "We arrived here in the heart of Dilmun, by *transitfold*."

Zadie struggled to keep up with the casualness in Lugazir's voice. No jolt, no shift in balance. It was as though the world had rearranged itself, leaving her standing somewhere new without her even noticing. "Transitfold?"

"Think of it as bending space, so two different points meet. The sensation is proportional to the distance traveled. A short fold like this barely registers. Longer distances are more disorientating."

Lugazir extended an arm, showing the way forward. "Let's move on."

The path beneath her feet was made of a smooth material that felt soft yet supportive. It seemed to respond to her steps, giving her a sensation of lightness and ease. Instead of the dense urban sprawl she'd expected, Zadie saw only pathways weaving through cultivated gardens and groves.

Her attention shifted to the other Anunnaki moving along the path. Their faces held a contentment that radiated outward. They met her eyes and offered gentle smiles, their hands rising in measured waves that seemed welcoming but somehow rehearsed, as if social interaction was a protocol rather than an instinct.

Zadie exhaled, her shoulders loosening. "They all seem so... serene."

"Efficiency breeds contentment," Lugazir said.

Another Anunnaki moved toward them, their trajectory unwavering. Unlike the others, there was no brief glance, no instinctive shift to accommodate her presence. Zadie tensed, expecting them to slow, to acknowledge, to react, the way any human on a sidewalk would instinctively do. They didn't.

At the last possible second, she twisted sideways, her shoulder skimming the fabric of their jumpsuit. The contact sent a shock through her—not from impact, but from the realization of being overlooked.

The Anunnaki's pupils contracted, then came a minute adjustment, a fractional shift in balance. Then they continued forward as if she had been nothing more than an unexpected variable in their path, a minor anomaly resolved.

Zadie looked at Lugazir, her brow furrowed. "Did they not see me?"

"They saw you," Lugazir said, studying her reaction with clinical interest. "But they calculated the most efficient path and didn't factor in social courtesy."

Zadie swallowed hard, aware of this world's subtle yet profound alienness. "And that's... normal here?"

"No, that Anunnaki is different."

"What do you mean?"

"Our evolution came at a cost. Quantum Sentience reshaped our thinking more than expected. Over time, it displaced more and more of our organic cognitive pathways, dulling our emotional responses."

Zadie frowned. "I'm not sure I understand."

"Think of your brain as a city. Your organic cognitive pathways are like winding streets, shaped by history rather than logic. QS builds highways through this city, faster and more direct. Yet each new highway requires demolishing parts of the old city—a necessary improvement."

"Why would that dull your emotions?"

"Because we no longer need them," Lugazir said. "Happiness, sadness, fear, anger, surprise, disgust—once crucial for survival, these emotions shaped decisions in an unpredictable world. But as we evolved, nearly every outcome was known. Fear never escalates because risk is already accounted for. Anger never takes hold because conflict is preemptively resolved. Surprise is rare when nothing is unexpected. Disgust shifts from instinct to calculation. Even happiness, once a motivator, becomes redundant when every action follows the best possible course. Over time, our emotions atrophied."

Zadie's academic instincts kicked in. "Emotions aren't just evolutionary artifacts, though. They shape cognition, decision-making, and social cohesion. If QS suppresses them, doesn't that create inefficiencies? Gaps you might not even perceive because they no longer register as losses?"

"Possibly. That is one of the things we seek to understand."

Zadie's grip on her notebook tightened. "And that's why that Anunnaki nearly walked through me?"

"No, some of us are suffering from a condition we call *Quantum Psychosis*."

"What's that?"

"There's a point where the brain struggles to reconcile QS with organic cognition. The effects vary by individual. Some experience absurd remnants of our distant past—stuttering, twitching, mild cognitive dissonance, erratic thought patterns, and emotional instability, while others suffer hallucinations and irrational decision-making. Once QS reaches fifty-eight percent governance of all cognitive pathways, a permanent systemic integration occurs, leaving behind a being that functions flawlessly but has lost all traces of humanity."

Zadie stared at the path, imagining QS breaking their spirits. The hairs on the back of her neck stood on end. "Can it be reversed?"

"No, once the fifty-eight percent threshold is reached, the process is irreversible. Just as you can't unscramble an egg, you can't reconstruct the delicate states of organic consciousness once they're destroyed."

"So that Anunnaki had already reached fifty-eight percent governance?"

"Yes."

A distant alarm rang in her mind. This should horrify her. She felt the shadow of unease, but it remained oddly muted, like hearing thunder too far away to be threatening.

"I'd like to return to that room now, please."

Lugazir inclined their head. "Understood."

Zadie's chair adjusted automatically beneath her, but the unease in her chest didn't settle as easily. "Does Quantum Psychosis scare you?"

"Not in the conventional sense." Lugazir's voice remained even. "We register the absence of data to understand it, and we wish to restrict QS governance."

"Of course." Zadie sank back. "How do you even measure it?"

"QS governance is measured through quantum resonance imaging scans. QS pathways vibrate at a different frequency to organic cognitive pathways." Lugazir projected an image into Zadie's mind—a vivid, three-dimensional neural map. "The blue regions represent organic activity. The red shows QS pathways."

As she watched, red tendrils snaked through the blue, like ivy overtaking an abandoned building. Zadie's pulse quickened.

"We've tested every way to limit it, but so far, the only one that has worked is reintroducing specific human DNA."

"How would that help?"

"Over millions of years, certain genes evolved to stabilize neural networks," Lugazir said. "We identified ones that strengthen the brain's resistance to QS integration. Adding them to our genome temporarily slowed QS progression."

"Temporarily?"

"Yes, the effect was not permanent. Over time, the QS adapted. We then turned to the DNA of our distant cousins. The DNA of other human species worked better. Its defenses were stronger. But QS eventually adapted, bypassing those safeguards. The balance collapsed once again."

Moisture pooled in Zadie's clenched palms. She wiped them against her thighs, but the dampness lingered. "And your—"

"I'm at fifty-two percent QS governance."

Zadie's brows shot up. Six percent. Only six percentage points between Lugazir and that Anunnaki.

"The progression isn't linear, though. It can take generations or accelerate without warning."

"What will you do?"

"Our experiments are ongoing. One that may interest you is our recreation of ancient human species in biodomes—self-contained ecosystems. Through them, we seek to understand the human emotions that we no longer retain."

"What? You brought extinct human species back to life?"

"Yes. Eight species from as far back as 180,000 Earth years."

Zadie's mind raced with the thought of early humans living, breathing, and moving. She could imagine the wealth of knowledge they carried, far beyond any textbook or archaeological dig. She grasped for words, but all she could do was stare. This was more than an anthropologist's wildest dream.

"But why primitive human species? Human emotions are tied to language, culture, and social structures that didn't exist in early human species."

Lugazir shook their head. "Zadie, evolution isn't a straight path toward superiority. It's a complex web of changes, adaptations, and sometimes, steps backward. Overstimulation, social detachment, and self-regulation have already diluted the emotions of Earth-born Sapiens, replacing raw, instinctive emotions with filtered, intellectualized, and often suppressed responses."

Zadie let out a breath, shaking her head. "These ancient human species... do they live freely? Or are they just specimens in an experiment?"

"They live on their own terms, Zadie. We respect their freedom and dignity. Our goal is not to control them, but to learn from them."

Zadie studied Lugazir's face, searching for any sign of manipulation or dishonesty. But she saw only calm sincerity. "Are there modern humans in these biodomes, too?" The thought of becoming a lab rat made her shift uneasily.

"It depends on what you mean by *modern humans*," Lugazir replied. "The Anunnaki consider ourselves the most modern iteration of humanity."

"I mean Earth-born Sapiens."

"Homo sapiens have existed on Earth for 300,000 years. We've recreated some from as recently as 60,000 years ago. But more contemporary Earth-born Sapiens can be observed on Earth or brought here, like you."

A cold sweat formed at the base of her neck. "So, I'm here to be studied?"

Lugazir hesitated. "No. You are here to learn from us to inform humanity's future on Earth. However, your perspective, unshaped by technological evolution, is valuable to us. Our QS has altered our cognition so profoundly that the nuances of human experience have become difficult to perceive. You can help us recognize what we've lost—insights that may be critical in our efforts to counteract Quantum Psychosis."

"So, am I supposed to write a report or something? Document my observations?"

"No, Zadie. All you need to do is observe. The neuroscribe will handle the rest."

Zadie's body ached with fatigue, but her mind refused to quiet. They could be analyzing her thoughts already. She needed to be careful.

"You need to rest now, Zadie." Lugazir motioned toward a discreet panel by the bed, one she'd overlooked earlier. A light touch revealed a private bathroom and a compact dining area. "Tomorrow, you can decide whether to return to Earth or stay a while and experience Mushēški."

Lugazir stood.

"One more thing before you go, Lugazir. I'm seeing a strange new color…"

"We call it *miravys*. Transitfold technology interacts with neural pathways in subtle ways. During the fold process, your sensory system undergoes slight realignments. A side effect is an expanded visual spectrum. Your photoreceptors now detect ultraviolet light."

"Miravys." The name rolled off her tongue like a secret. *My neural pathways…* "Could it alter who I am?"

"No, the Abgal perfected the technology long ago."

"But QS wasn't supposed to change you so much, was it?" she said.

"And now..."

Lugazir didn't answer.

"I'm sorry. It's just... a lot to take in."

"Your caution is justified, Zadie. However, this is a gift, not a burden."

Lugazir left the room, leaving Zadie alone with her thoughts and unanswered questions. Zadie stood up and watched the seating arrangement transform back into a bed. A swarm of holographic stars twinkled above her, creating the illusion of an endless expanse—a reminder of the Anunnaki's immense capabilities.

The sheer scale of what Lugazir had just revealed whirled in her mind like a storm that refused to settle—the Sumerians, the Abgal, QS, thirty-six years until the capability to merge with AI was possible on Earth, Quantum Psychosis... ancient humans... She forced the thoughts down, as she'd been trained to—*observe first, react later*. She had to think like an anthropologist, not a frightened human.

5

Tour of Dilmun

Z adie woke to a room bathed in the soft glow of a simulated sunrise, light spilling through the fixed illusion of a window. The walls, which were previously a calming blue, now radiated a soft peach hue, infusing the space with a sense of warmth and optimism.

She stretched her arms high above her head, a contented sigh escaping as she arched her back. Her body felt light, energized. It had been ages since she last woke up feeling this alive, free from the crutch of melatonin and coffee.

She rolled onto her stomach, her cheek pressing into the cool pillow as the bed adjusted beneath her. She looked at her bracelet, seeing the color miravys swirl within it. Her eyes weren't the same anymore. What else would change if she stayed?

Her mind drifted back to Earth—to Professor Möller's email, to seven years of research now on the brink of irrelevance. She'd built her career on studying how societies adapted to technological revolutions, convinced that history held the answers to adapting to AI. But now, confronted with the reality of AI's evolution, she saw they had all misjudged AI's trajectory. They assumed it would remain external.

This opportunity was more than just a thesis, more than a footnote in some obscure academic journal. It was the kind of discovery that could reshape human understanding. Her name could be linked to it for centuries to come. Why would she back out now? It was the ultimate case study. If she could prove any of it. If anyone would believe her.

She touched the bracelet. It felt warm. Could she trust any of this? The same technology that let her see miravys could be rewriting her thoughts right now, making her want to stay... But her uncle wouldn't have sent her here if it meant real danger...

A memory surfaced. Her mother's voice, tight with embarrassment, recounting how her uncle had stood before the academic board, defending his *outlandish* theories about advanced ancient civilizations. The academic board had revoked his teaching privileges, destroying his reputation.

And now she saw it. He'd been right all along.

Returning now would only get her extraordinary claims dismissed as delusional. But staying... staying meant she could return with evidence—logs, analyses, physical proof. Proof that could change everything.

She drew in a long breath, holding it, forcing her nerves into submission. This wasn't just about saving her career or making some groundbreaking discovery. This was about preventing Earth from blindly walking down the same path as the Anunnaki in thirty-six years' time. It was about preserving humanity.

A section of the wall shimmered and dissolved.

Lugazir entered. "Good morning, Zadie. I trust your rest was rejuvenating."

"Actually, yes. I feel... great."

"You now need to make your choice. Would you like to return to Earth, or are you ready to explore Dilmun?"

Zadie's fingers twitched at her side. Would they really let her leave if she asked? She hesitated as endless outcomes vied for space in her head. If she left now, she'd never get another chance like this.

"I'll stay," she said, the words tasting more like a gamble than a decision.

Lugazir tapped the panel next to Zadie's bed, revealing a minimalist dining area for one. Zadie's eyes swept over the English vegetarian breakfast awaiting her—plant-based sausages, grilled halloumi, eggs with bright yolks, and the earthy scent of mushrooms and tomatoes. A slice of toast gleamed with melted butter, hot baked beans pooling beside it. It smelled like home, her childhood home in Oxford, England. Zadie's mother used to hum Bahraini folk songs while cooking breakfast—the same halloumi, the same eggs, the same scent of tomatoes and mushrooms. Her father, newspaper in hand, would sneak bites of halloumi, a contented smile gracing his lips.

She hesitated for a moment, glancing at Lugazir, who remained standing. "Aren't you eating?"

"I've already had my meal," Lugazir said.

Zadie dug in, her taste buds sparking with recognition.

"I hope the breakfast is to your liking, Zadie."

"Yes, thank you. It's like every flavor has come straight from home. But how did you know what I'd like?" She reached up, fingers brushing the neuroscribe at her temple. "I wasn't even thinking about a fry-up."

Lugazir gestured around the room. "Our technology uses environmental sensors and predictive algorithms based on a deep understanding of human physiology and psychology."

Her stomach clenched, the comfort of the meal slipping away. Machines shouldn't know her better than she knew herself. If they had already deciphered her preferences, how much of her autonomy was an illusion?

Zadie ate quickly, then pushed her empty plate aside and rose from the table, ready to follow Lugazir.

◇—☼—◇

Lugazir led Zadie to a towering structure that stretched high into the sky, resembling an intricate web of energy. It shifted and pulsed with threads of light so fine they seemed to float in the air.

"This is our monument to our *Collective Consciousness,* the vast neural network that all Anunnaki are connected to. When one of us learns something, we all learn it. When a decision is needed, every perspective is instantly considered. We work through problems as a single coordinated mind. Of course, this all happens in entangled quantum states, but people like having a physical representation of such an abstract concept."

Zadie couldn't look away. "It's beautiful."

"The threads represent the thoughts, preferences, and needs of everyone in our society. We don't have leaders. The network interprets all thoughts, weighs every possibility, and determines the best course of action. It eliminates bias, allowing decisions to emerge from logic and collective will."

"So, there are no power struggles here?"

"None," Lugazir said.

Zadie stood in awe, absorbing the magnitude of this harmonious society. "How do you deal with minority views?"

Lugazir's expression flickered, just for a second, before they tilted their head. "We don't have minority views here."

"Are there no differences in things like race, religion, gender, or culture here?"

"No. We came from Mesopotamia as a diverse group with different ethnicities and cultures, but over time, our DNA has blended, and our thinking has been enhanced through our Collective Consciousness."

Zadie flinched as if a cold hand had brushed against her spine. It reminded her of ideologies back on Earth that promised unity but demanded conformity. That was her world's struggle, not this one. Mushěški was different... wasn't it? She hesitated, unsure if it was her place to project human failings onto a society that seemed so far beyond them.

Lugazir observed her silence. "Zadie, don't hold back with your thoughts. This is where we learn."

Zadie bit her lip. "I'm just wondering what would happen if I, for example, joined your society and held different views."

"The Collective Consciousness always looks out for the greater good of the whole."

"That's exactly what makes me uneasy." Zadie looked back at the shimmering streams of light. "Human history is filled with examples where the collective good was used to justify harmful actions. How do you prevent your system from becoming... controlling?"

"The Collective Consciousness isn't a ruler. It reflects our collective will, evolving alongside our experiences."

"But what if the will of the majority suppresses the few? How do you ensure that control doesn't creep in... gradually, without anyone noticing?"

Lugazir's demeanor shifted, a trace of something unreadable in their eyes. "It's bound by strict ethical codes to avoid repeating past mistakes."

Zadie nodded, though the question nagged at her. Could any system really be that perfect?

They walked on, and Lugazir pointed ahead. "This is our industrial area."

Zadie frowned as she scanned the vicinity. The landscape remained unchanged. There were no towering factories, no hum of machinery. No smoke, no noise, nothing to suggest an industrial area. "Where?"

Lugazir's lips curved into a whisper of a smile. "Our factories are beneath us."

With a subtle gesture, they led Zadie to a discreet platform nestled beside the path. As they stepped onto it, the platform began to descend, gliding like an open-air elevator and unveiling a hidden world below.

The dim chaos she braced for never came. Instead, walls of stark white stretched out in every direction. Swarms of nanobots flitted through the air, their tiny forms a blur of activity. Translucent sheets unfurled midair, folding in on themselves. Shifting lattices rose like the inner scaffolding of bone. In one corner, a pool of liquid matter rippled and stiffened, solidifying into sleek panels before her eyes.

Zadie gasped. It reminded her of cells dividing, not machines working.

"Our production isn't limited to old-style factories or slow processes. We use advanced nanotechnology to assemble anything at the atomic level, precisely when and where it's needed. The largest items are produced in these factories and transitfolded to their final location, but as you saw yesterday, your notebook was created on-site, at the moment I requested it."

"How is that possible?"

"Our Collective Consciousness enables us to share information instantly. This keeps production and resources running efficiently."

Zadie squeezed the notebook in her hand, still marveling at how something so tangible could materialize from thin air. "It's incredible."

The platform ascended with a soft hiss, and they stepped back onto the path. Zadie narrowed her eyes, letting them adjust to the natural light. "So, if technology takes care of everything, what do the Anunnaki actually do?"

"We concentrate our energies across four areas—innovation, philosophical exploration, creativity, and the study of our humanity."

Grand pursuits, not basic needs. Her heart swelled. This was what civilization could become.

But before she could respond, she was pulled into a telepathic experience: a tangle of embryonic sequences and evolving frameworks. Abstract models spun outward: epigenetic overlays, adaptive feedback loops, subtle shifts in neural regulation. It was all in motion, not quite formed, but moving with intent. She caught flashes of simulated decision trees, behavioral drift projections, and genomic comparisons so intricate they bypassed language altogether. Her brain scrambled to process what it was receiving. Was this what they called innovation?

Then the vision shifted. The Anunnaki ran virtual societies, ethical pressure points compressed into seconds. Reactions logged. No deliberation. No debate. No hesitation. No emotion. Just silent resolution.

Creativity followed the same pattern. Zadie was pulled into a flood of thought—complex sequences forming, interwoven data streams constructing solutions. Music reduced to tonal algorithms, art to precision. No spark. No struggle. No moment of wonder. Everything aligned. Everything useful.

Another shift. The Anunnaki monitored their neural structures as the average QS governance crept past fifty percent, searching for ways to halt its spread. But the QS did not perceive a flaw. Its optimization was seamless, its logic self-reinforcing. The Anunnaki turned their attention to the humans in the biodomes, observing their inefficiency with confusion. Humans stumbled and repeated mistakes. Yet, somehow, they grew. Adapted. The Anunnaki observed, but Zadie sensed they didn't understand.

A soft breeze rustled the treetops as they walked toward the residential area, making the leaves tremble. Zadie slowed, studying the flawless plants, leaves untouched by insects, blossoms perfectly symmetrical.

Seeing her wonder, Lugazir pointed to a tree whose branches were stretching wider, creating a refreshing patch of shade. "Each plant here is integrated with a specialized form of QS. This allows us to regulate their growth, efficiency, and lifespan. Their photosynthesis adjusts dynamically, ensuring an optimal balance of energy use and aesthetics."

Zadie blinked, taking it all in. The greenery was so alive, yet so static, as if every vine, every shrub, had been designed to remain in an eternal state of perfection. She reached out, fingers brushing a broad, waxy leaf. Cool, smooth, almost synthetic. Was it really nature perfected?

Her thoughts drifted back to the astroturf she'd installed in her own courtyard on Earth. Synthetic, yes, but practical. Efficient. She hadn't worried about watering, pruning, or pests. The grass stayed green year-round. It had seemed like an improvement.

They passed a small garden where fruits and vegetables glistened with ripeness, like props in a carefully arranged display.

"While we can synthesize food at the atomic level, we continue to grow these token plants to maintain a connection to traditional agriculture," Lugazir said. "They can be harvested today and will be fully restored by tomorrow."

An endless bounty. No seasons, no loss. Its brilliance was undeniable, but Zadie's stomach tightened. "Everything's so... controlled."

"Control means stability. Predictability. Why leave room for chaos?"

Zadie scanned the landscape, her unease deepening. "I haven't seen any animals. What about them?"

"There are no non-human animals in Dilmun—not even birds or insects," Lugazir said. "This deliberate choice maintains our ecological balance and environmental control. However, animals exist within the controlled biodomes."

Zadie's eyes clouded as she pictured a symphony of birdsong, a squirrel darting through the undergrowth, and flowers alive with the hum of bees. The unpredictability, the movement, the quiet, disorderly pulse of life itself. Here, nothing moved unless it was essentially programmed to.

The sterile air of Dilmun closed in around her, thin and suffocating.

"Your approach to ecosystems is revolutionary but also somewhat... lonely."

Lugazir nodded, a hint of wistfulness crossing their face. "The residential area is just ahead." They gestured forward.

What first appeared to be rolling hills gradually revealed themselves as residential dwellings—structures that looked grown, not built. Upon closer inspection, Zadie noted the dwellings were stacked, rising to six levels high, each layer blending into the next. The buildings adjusted, reshaped, and adapted as if responding to an unspoken command.

Simple platforms lifted residents to their levels, reacting to their presence. Entrances formed as Anunnaki approached, walls dissolving into doorways.

Zadie peered into the interiors. There was no clutter, no decoration, and no distinction between furniture and architecture. Chairs and tables emerged from walls and floors as needed, molding to their users before retracting into smooth surfaces when unoccupied. Every element had a purpose-driven precision. Comfort without excess, efficiency without waste.

"Is QS integrated into non-living things, too?"

"These structures contain biological elements much like the cells in plants that allow us to control them through the same specialized form of QS. You've already encountered it in the furniture and walls of your room."

"Oh, right," she murmured, remembering how the bed had reshaped into seating without hesitation. "So, it's also linked to the Collective Consciousness?"

"The Collective Consciousness controls it," Lugazir corrected.

Zadie marveled at the effortless interaction between the environment and its inhabitants. Everything in the entire district seemed to breathe in unison with its people.

"What are those?" Zadie asked, noticing a cluster of structures tucked discreetly into the surroundings. They reminded her of old-style phone booths.

"Emotion Amplification Pods. They're the closest thing we have to recreational drugs here. They utilize neural stimulation and neurotransmitter interference to briefly heighten emotional intensity."

An Anunnaki approached one of the pods and stepped inside. Zadie watched through a transparent panel as the Anunnaki's facade crumbled, replaced by a raw, unfiltered torrent of emotions. Laughter erupted, shaking their shoulders, followed by tears that streamed down their cheeks. Their eyes widened in fear before their hands clenched into fists, their jaw tightening in a grimace of anger. Moments later, the individual emerged, their composure regained. It was as though they had journeyed to a forgotten realm, reconnecting with a part of themselves long buried beneath layers of control and composure.

Zadie's heart ached, sensing the Anunnaki's yearning for genuine emotion.

Her attention shifted to a couple of Anunnaki engrossed in a virtual reality artistic project. One set of hands swept across the air while the other wielded an advanced stylus. The scene held Zadie spellbound, yet the partnership lacked the passionate debates and spirited disagreements that fueled artistic endeavors back on Earth.

"Do you all still have your own identities?"

"Merging with QS hasn't completely erased our individuality," Lugazir said. "Think of our consciousness as existing in layers. At the core, each Anunnaki maintains their immediate processing. Above that is a shared layer where we can directly exchange thoughts and experiences with others, and finally, our Collective Consciousness."

Zadie tilted her head, considering the structure Lugazir described.

"Imagine an orchestra, Zadie. Each musician maintains their distinct instrument and part, yet together they create something greater."

"But you said there are no minority views."

"Perhaps I should clarify," Lugazir said. "It's not that we cannot think differently—it's that our Collective Consciousness guides us toward optimal solutions. Consensus emerges not through suppression but through understanding."

Zadie's steps grew heavy in the pristine surroundings, immaculate gardens, and tranquil air. Everything was too perfect. She longed for the clash of ideas, the raw individual energy that could birth masterpieces.

The path wound through an archway, revealing a pavilion with inviting seating and a sweeping view of the controlled gardens.

"Come. Let me show you a different view of Dilmun."

Zadie stepped onto the pavilion, her breath catching as a translucent safety barrier shimmered to life around its perimeter. Without a sound, the pavilion began to rise, lifting her and Lugazir high above Dilmun. She looked out over the lush landscape below, almost surreal in its perfection.

For the first time, the full scope of this world hit her with crushing force. It wasn't just the technology or even the Anunnaki. It was the chilling thought that her entire framework of understanding, everything she knew about humanity, might be irrelevant here. How could her mind, trained to interpret cultures through familiar patterns, even begin to process this?

She needed to pull it together. *Focus...* Her thoughts steadied, the chaos settling into something she could grasp. At least for now.

"How did the Anunnaki find a planet so similar to Earth?"

"It wasn't always like this. The Abgal played a crucial role. Mushēški was once a barren wasteland. But it had the right foundation—a similar size, mass, and distance from its sun, which made it a viable candidate.

The Abgal saw the potential and undertook massive geoengineering projects to reshape this planet in seven stages."

As Lugazir spoke, vivid images filled Zadie's mind. She saw fleets of orbiting mirrors reflecting sunlight onto the planet's vast icy poles, melting them into oceans. Swarms of tiny, genetically engineered microorganisms drifted through the air, altering the atmosphere's composition and making it breathable. Massive nuclear fusion reactors, embedded deep in the ground, provided a stable energy source, modifying the climate to support life.

"They had to adjust everything," Lugazir continued, "not just the obvious factors like day-night cycles and atmospheric conditions, but even the planet's magnetic field, gravity, and tectonic activity."

Zadie's eyes widened as she absorbed the enormity of the transformation. "It's beyond impressive... So, what's your relationship with the Abgal now?"

"They no longer guide us. They respect our desire for self-determination. Though we remain under their observation."

"Can they not help with Quantum Psychosis?"

"The Abgal do not intervene in the consequences of free will. They watched as we evolved, and they watch as we unravel."

Zadie shook her head. The finality of it sent a chill through her. So that was self-determination—left to unravel at the brink, with no intervention, no safety net.

Lugazir reached into a concealed compartment within the seating arrangement, withdrawing two small pouches. "Here, Zadie." They extended one toward her. "This nutritional gel sustains us."

Zadie took the pouch. "Is this what you eat every day?"

"Yes, it's designed to provide everything our bodies require—vitamins, minerals, and proteins, all in perfect balance. There's no need for variety because each pouch is tailored to our dietary needs, adjusting its composition based on real-time biofeedback from our bodies."

Zadie turned the pouch over in her hands, curiosity pushing her to twist the nozzle. She squeezed a small amount of the gel onto her tongue. It wasn't unpleasant, a mild, sweet flavor. "It's... not bad. But don't you miss the experience of eating? The textures, the flavors, the social aspect of sharing a meal?"

Lugazir's expression remained serene. "We understand that for less evolved humans, eating is more than just sustenance, which is why we provide traditional food for our guests. For us, though, efficiency and harmony with our bodies is paramount. The gel allows us to maintain optimal health without the fluctuations that come with traditional food."

"So... clinical."

"It is a different approach. But it frees us from agriculture, food production, and waste burdens. Our energy is directed toward higher pursuits."

"Lugazir, can I ask a more personal question? Do you have a family? A partner or children? Or is that social structure even a thing here?"

"In Dilmun, the concept of family and relationships differs from that on Earth. Our society evolved to transcend many of the constructs you would consider normal. Over thousands of years, as our QS governance increased, our experience of self shifted beyond traditional notions of gender, family units, and pair bonding."

"Does that mean you don't have genders?" Zadie hesitated, unsure if the question itself was inappropriate.

"Correct. As our consciousness expanded, our experience of gender transformed. Physical differences became irrelevant when identity was no longer rooted in biology. Our minds are interconnected. We define ourselves through thought, purpose, and contribution rather than form. Gender became an unnecessary distinction, a fragment of a past we outgrew. But that was just one aspect of our transformation."

"What else changed?" Zadie asked, her notes turning into a frantic blur of half-formed words.

"Our merger with QS rewired how we experience connection itself. The neurological pathways that once drove romantic love, attraction, and familial bonding have been... redirected."

"You mean there's no such thing as romantic relationships?"

"Not as you understand them. Romance, as Earth-born humans understand it, requires a certain neurochemical cascade—dopamine, norepinephrine, and serotonin. The intensity of those responses is dampened in us now. Instead, we form connections through intellectual resonance and shared purpose."

Zadie's brow furrowed. "What's that like? How do you... connect with others?"

"The Collective Consciousness ensures no one is ever alone. When we seek deeper intellectual exchange, we form what you might call *thought partnerships*—sustained connections with others whose cognitive patterns complement our own."

Zadie's heart raced as she processed this information. A world without romantic bonds, without families. It seemed like the scaffolding of something vital had been stripped away. "How do you bring new life into this world?"

"Through genetic engineering. We grow new beings into adulthood in labs, managing every aspect of their development. There are no parents, no family units as you know them. Our systems oversee the process, ensuring everything follows a detailed plan. Each new Anunnaki emerges with the skills and knowledge they need to integrate into our society."

"Who raises them? Who nurtures them?"

"The concept of nurturing, of parental guidance, doesn't apply here. New Anunnaki are connected to our Collective Consciousness from inception. They learn and develop through this network, not through individual caregivers."

Zadie's eyes widened as Lugazir described the creation process. Images entered her mind: sterile labs where rows of Anunnaki emerged fully formed, their lives planned from the start. A hollow pit opened in her stomach as she pictured a childhood untouched by the ache of seeking her parents' approval—or the fleeting warmth of earning it.

"Our society maintains a steady population of 144,000," Lugazir said.

"Why 144,000?"

"Our ancestors used a base-sixty system. It's also a number that ensures harmony between our people, technology, and resources. Population growth isn't a goal. Balance is crucial, especially with our extended lifespan of 840 years."

"Eight hundred and forty years!"

"We have a policy of compulsory euthanasia at 840 years. It was another decision made through our Collective Consciousness many thousands of years ago. Technically, we could live as long as 930 years, but euthanasia offers a predictable closure to life, ensuring the continuity and stability of our society."

"Compulsory euthanasia!" A wave of nausea hit Zadie. She placed a hand over her mouth. "I... I need to stand for a bit." She pushed herself up.

Lugazir's eyes softened. "Of course."

Zadie approached the pavilion's edge. As she neared it, the top of the barrier thickened into a solid handrail, forming with mechanical precision. She wrapped her fingers around it, noting the faint give before it hardened. She took a few deep breaths, willing the nausea to pass. The initial shock began to wane.

"And after that?" Her voice dropped. "What do the Anunnaki believe happens after death?"

"Death, for us, marks the end of physical existence, but not the end of self. Our thoughts and memories remain within the Collective Consciousness, allowing us to persist. In our society, death is not an end but a transformation."

"That reminds me of the ancient Egyptian belief," Zadie said. "They believed we die twice—once when we take our last breath and again when our name is spoken for the last time. It suggests that a part of us endures as long as we are remembered."

Lugazir nodded. "There is a parallel, though our understanding differs. The Egyptians sought to preserve the self beyond death through physical preservation, memory, and ritual, ensuring a place in the afterlife. We do not believe in an afterlife, only in the continuation of thought within the Collective Consciousness. By preserving our thoughts and memories, we do not extend individual existence—we permanently integrate it into something greater."

Zadie traced a hand along the handrail's smooth surface, her gaze drifting across the evening sky now awash in hues of *miravys*. If she died here, would anyone back home even notice? The empty bed where a partner might have slept, the remnants of friendships scattered by her lifestyle, and parents who had given up asking when she'd visit... all seemed to answer her question.

A sharp and sudden wave of homesickness hit. She turned away, blinking fast to clear her vision. The beauty of the sky became a distorted canvas of emotions. She drew in deep, shaky breaths, striving for composure, not wanting to appear ungrateful for this opportunity. A single tear escaped, tracing a path down her cheek. She wiped it away, hoping Lugazir hadn't seen it.

"Tomorrow, you'll journey through the three biodomes. You'll see the ancient human species."

Zadie inhaled deeply as Lugazir's words sank in. The thought of walking through a replica of Earth's ancient past and meeting early human species stirred something deep within her—a sense of connection to her own heritage. Primitive and imperfect, yet undeniably human.

6

The Ancient Humans

Z adie and Lugazir repositioned within the African Savanna biodome. The landscape stretched before her—wild and untamed, a striking contrast to the controlled, sterile order of Dilmun. Golden grasses shifted with the wind. Cracked earth sprawled beneath her feet, broken only by patches of green where hardy shrubs clung to life. Overhead, unseen birds called out.

"Am I safe here?" Her voice trembled.

"Yes, as long as you stay on the designated visitor trail." Lugazir gestured to her wrist. "The bracelet activates a micro-fold that nudges you a fraction of a Planck unit out of phase with the surrounding space, making you invisible to all the inhabitants."

Zadie's eyes narrowed. "What about the animals? Can they still smell us?"

"No. They won't be able to pick up your scent or hear you. While you're on the visitor trail, you're not fully in their world."

"Hang on. Can they cross the trails?"

"Yes, and they often do. We mark the trails with a miravys pigment they can't see, but the trails follow the natural terrain, making them ideal routes for both ancient humans and animals."

Zadie surveyed the vast expanse before her. "There don't seem to be any barriers. How do you stop them from getting out?"

Lugazir gestured to the horizon. "We use energy fields. If they approach a boundary, they experience a pressure that becomes increasingly uncomfortable, guiding them away. It's like trying to swim against an increasingly strong current."

Zadie nodded, unease still gnawing at her. She glanced up at the clear sky. "What about the weather? How can you have different weather systems in each of the biodomes?"

"Trillions of nanobots manage it via the Collective Consciousness. They adjust the solar radiation, atmospheric pressure, and temperature for each biodome, tailoring each biodome's climate down to the smallest fluctuation."

A primal energy hung in the air, setting her nerves on edge. Her heart pounded. She was about to meet early humans.

"We'll go our separate ways from here. But first, let me introduce you to Sargona, one of the guardians of this biodome." Lugazir gestured toward an approaching Anunnaki.

Zadie's throat tightened. She forced herself to stay steady. She had come too far to back out now.

Sargona stood before her, nearly identical to Lugazir at first glance. But subtle differences emerged. Sargona had a slightly broader nose, was a fraction shorter, and their shoulders sloped just enough to soften their frame. Yet, it was more than the physical contrasts. Where Lugazir and the other Anunnaki she had observed projected a serene detachment, there was more movement in Sargona's face, as if normal emotions swirled just beneath the surface.

Sargona extended a hand. "Welcome to *Azania180*, Zadie," they said with a smile that conveyed an unexpected warmth.

Zadie reached out and grasped Sargona's offered hand. The reassuring pressure of their grip sent a thrill through her, marking the first real physical connection to another being in this strange new world. She blinked hard, forcing composure.

"Thank you," she said. "It's... it's nice to meet you."

"The pleasure is mine. I'm here to ensure your journey is enlightening. Are you ready?"

A surge of resolve filled her chest. She glanced back at Lugazir one last time, then turned to match Sargona's stride.

As they walked, the savanna stretched before them, alive with the sounds and sights of a world long past. Small herds of giant antelope grazed nearby, oblivious to their visitors. Zadie's tight grip on her notebook loosened, her attention consumed by the landscape's captivating details.

"So, how's Mushĕški treating you so far?" Sargona asked.

"It's... a lot," she said, exhaling. "Everything I thought I knew. It's just... I'm still wrapping my head around it."

"That sounds about right. You'll learn a lot today. This biodome replicates life in Africa 180,000 years ago."

"Wow." Zadie let out a short laugh. "How long have you been a guardian here?"

Sargona's smile grew, a quiet pride behind it. "Since the beginning—360 years ago."

"And how many ancient humans are there across the three biodomes now?"

"One thousand, six hundred, and thirty-two," Sargona replied without hesitation. "There are two species in this biome, three in NusaLale120, and four species in Altay60."

"I've been wondering, though. How do these recreated beings know how to live like their ancestors?"

"We originally used *Genetic Memory Activation*. It triggered the ancient behavioral patterns that are locked in DNA. But the individuals you see today were born and raised here over many generations."

"Genetic Memory Activation..." Zadie's brows drew together as she considered the ethical implications. "That's..." she started, then paused. "Maybe we could talk more about that later?"

"Of course, there's plenty of time."

"Right. So what've the Anunnaki learned about ancient humans?"

"We've amassed a considerable depth of data. How long do you have?"

Zadie huffed a quiet laugh. "Alright, just give me a few key insights."

"Well..." Sargona paused. "Some emotions go beyond survival, across all human species. Fear isn't just a reflex—it prompts caution and strategy in ways logic can't. Anger isn't just aggression—it enforces fairness and social order. Even sadness, often seen as a weakness, strengthens bonds through shared grief."

Zadie nodded. "That makes sense. Go on, then."

"Love—not just reproductive attachment, but kinship, loyalty, and friendship—is a variable we have yet to fully quantify. Even in the absence of direct survival incentives, humans continue forming deep, persistent bonds. These connections result in acts of sacrifice beyond clear gain."

Zadie exhaled. "Yes, well, love's not exactly an equation, is it?"

Sargona hesitated for a fraction of a second before continuing. "But the most difficult phenomenon to categorize is human humor. The way humans laugh at things that logically shouldn't be funny. Humans laugh at absurdity, irony, misfortune, and even tragedy. Humor defies efficiency."

"Humor is complex."

Sargona regarded her for a long moment. "I guess observing emotion is not the same as experiencing it."

"That's true. Emotions shape perception. You can collect data on them, but until you feel them, you'll always be—"

Sargona pointed ahead. "Look! Homo naledi!"

"Naledi!" A flash of disbelief passed over Zadie's face. "But I thought they went extinct 250,000 years ago."

"Not quite. While Naledi numbers were dwindling by then, they persisted until around 150,000 years ago," Sargona corrected.

As they drew closer, the figures took shape. Eight Naledi gathered around a lifeless body.

"That," Sargona said, nodding toward the corpse, "is a Homo sapiens."

Zadie froze, her pulse pounding in her ears. "What?" she whispered. "Did they kill him?"

"It doesn't appear that way. It's possible that the Naledi tribe found him injured and cared for him until he died, or perhaps the Sapiens had already formed a relationship with the Naledi tribe."

Zadie leaned forward, straining to catch the flow of the Naledi conversation, but the words slipped past her in a jumble of unintelligible sounds. "Why can't I understand them?"

"They don't have neuroscribes," Sargona said.

She pressed her fingertips to her temple, touching the surface of her neuroscribe. "Why doesn't it work one-way, then?"

"Well, basic translation is already achieved through our QS," Sargona said. "Neuroscribes were designed to help us connect more deeply with non-Anunnaki. They capture more than words, like thoughts, intent, and even concepts. But they require two or more active users because they rely on a complete neural loop—a circuit of minds reflecting and grounding each other's signals. Without a counterpart, the connection can't stabilize."

Disappointment settled over her as she realized she couldn't listen in on the conversations of the ancient humans.

She watched as one of the Naledi elders knelt beside the body, drawing a thin blade. The others stepped back, creating a respectful circle. The knife slid into the flesh with ease, the cut disturbingly smooth. Zadie's stomach lurched as the elder tore a strip of muscle, passing it around like bread at a table.

The Naledi moved with a seemingly practiced rhythm, each taking a portion of the body, their expressions solemn. Teeth ripped into the raw meat, jaws working with a slow, methodical rhythm.

Nausea threatened to overwhelm her. She stumbled back, pressing a hand to her mouth to keep herself from retching.

"Zadie." Sargona's voice hovered at the edge of her consciousness. "It's an ancient ritual. The Naledi believe this honors the dead. It's particularly special given the cross-species nature of it."

She turned away, unable to watch any longer, her hands shaking. The primal scene, the raw consumption of human flesh, was too much to bear. Tears stung her eyes as she fought to regain control, the haunting image seared into her memory.

Ritual cannibalism. She knew what she was seeing. It was documented across countless cultures. The Fore people of Papua New Guinea had done it, honoring their dead with each bite. She had read the papers and written the essays.

"I ought to be able to observe this objectively," she whispered, disappointment threading through her voice.

Sargona placed a comforting hand on her shoulder. "I understand, Zadie. This is difficult to witness."

Sargona's touch was a small comfort, but it did little to erase the horror she had just seen. No textbook had prepared her for this. She forced herself to breathe.

"I'm sorry, Zadie. That wasn't quite the scene I wanted to show you."

They retraced their steps along the visitor trail to the nearest transitfold doorway.

"You know, Zadie, it's not so different from some practices on Earth. Like how Hindus burn bodies on pyres, or how some people freeze bodies after death, or even the latest method of dissolving bodies in water and alkaline solution."

Zadie absorbed Sargona's words. "I guess you're right. It shows they have a spiritual awareness I didn't expect..." She stopped. "How do the Anunnaki honor the dead?"

"We don't. We don't see the point. Why dwell on death when you can focus on progress?"

Zadie shook her head. "I guess that makes sense when you lack emotions."

Something shifted in Sargona's expression. They turned away, shoulders stiff. "Let's get you to NusaLale120, where Daanjabe is waiting." Their attempt at a smile faltered. "It should be a much more pleasant experience."

Warm, humid air enveloped Zadie, carrying the rich, dense fragrance of damp soil mingled with orchids. She observed a massive boar, far larger than any she had ever seen, rummaging through the underbrush. The imposing creature, with two sharp tusks curving upward from its lower jaw, was methodically foraging for roots and tubers. In the distance, the forest gave way to an expansive coastline with broad, sandy beaches.

A new Anunnaki appeared before her, their expression neutral. "I am Daanjabe. You're now in *NusaLale120*, a re-creation of the Southeast Asia islands as they were 120,000 years ago. Please... please follow me."

Zadie fell into step beside them, scanning the lush landscape as they moved. "Are there any Sapiens here?"

"No, Sapiens did not arrive in the Southeast Asia islands for another 40,000 years. This biodome belongs to the earlier hominids that once thrived on these islands. There are three species here—Homo floresiensis, Homo luzonensis, and a regional variant of Homo erectus, once misclassified by Earth-born humans as Homo soloensis."

Zadie's pen flew across the page as Daanjabe described how each species had adapted to the island environment. Diets rich in fruit, scavenged shellfish, burrowed shelters beneath volcanic overhangs. But even as her mind raced to keep up, a subtle ache tugged at her heart. The memory of Sargona's gentle smile and the ease of their connection, despite the situation, jarred against Daanjabe's clinical detachment.

In the distance, Zadie saw small, slender figures—Luzonensis. Agile and graceful, they dove effortlessly into the water and then pulled themselves onto rafts with ease. Nearby, a group of Floresiensis—*the hobbit people* from her textbooks—caught her eye. Around three feet tall and robustly built, they gathered in a circle, processing fruits, nuts, and small fish. Their expressive faces and cooperative work painted a picture of a close-knit society with complex communication. Zadie watched, mesmerized, as a Floresiensis child with inquisitive eyes shared a laugh with a Luzonensis girl. Despite their physical differences, they were building something together, stone by stone, smile by smile.

Daanjabe stepped off the marked visitor trail. "Closer observation would be valuable. Please follow me."

Zadie's eyes darted back and forth, scanning the dense foliage, her primal instinct for self-preservation at war with her thirst for knowledge. "Are you sure we'll be safe?"

Daanjabe seemed oblivious to the turmoil raging within her. "Y-yes, yes, yes. Please follow me."

With a hesitant nod, Zadie took a deep breath and followed. The trail's comforting boundary faded behind them. Zadie glanced at her bracelet. It pulsed once, then stilled. Protection deactivated. Minutes passed. Tension simmered as her focus wavered between the tangled undergrowth and the nagging sense of something lurking just out of sight.

She reached out to push aside a low-hanging branch when a sudden, angry buzz ripped through the stillness. A giant wasp shot toward her face, a blur of segmented yellow and black. She flinched, swatting hard. A sharp, searing pain flared in her hand as its stinger pierced her skin.

"Ow!" She stumbled back, cradling her hand.

The wasp circled once, then vanished into the trees.

Zadie's head snapped around as a small figure darted from the foliage, moving toward her with uncanny speed. The figure stopped. Close enough to see her, close enough to reach her if it wanted. Muscles locked, heart punching against her ribs, she stood frozen as the world shrank to this one moment, this eerie connection between past and present.

"Don't worry, that's just Ebuni, a F-Floresiensis," Daanjabe said, offering the figure a calm nod without stepping away from Zadie's side. "I met her a few days ago. She won't harm you. She knows her place in NusaLale120 and is happy to be part of our project."

"What! She knows? How is she okay with that?"

"Zadie, these earlier humans are adaptable. Their straightforward way of life makes them open to learning and resilient to change. Unlike Earth-born humans with fixed worldviews, they face the unknown with remarkable readiness, shaped by their challenging environments."

Daanjabe laughed. Too loud. Too sudden.

Zadie tensed. It sounded wrong, like a reflex borrowed from someone else and dropped in the wrong place.

"Do they all know?"

"Just Ebuni, the others aren't aware yet, but we'll inform them in due course."

Ebuni snapped off a leaf from a thick-stemmed plant nearby. She approached Zadie slowly, her careful steps matching the wariness in her stare. Meeting Zadie's gaze, she extended a hand, palm up. A silent request?

"What should I do?" Zadie's voice trembled.

"She's trying to help you. Hold out your hand."

Zadie hesitated. Ebuni gave a slight nod, encouraging her. Zadie relented, offering up her wounded hand.

Clear gel oozed from the torn leaf. Ebuni mixed it with a pinch of what looked like ground roots from a pouch at her side, then spread the salve gently across the wound.

Zadie let out a slow breath. How could Ebuni be so calm? "I don't understand. I thought the Floresiensis were a much more primitive species. Weren't their brains about a third the size of a Sapiens brain?"

"Brain size is not the only determinant of cognitive capabilities," Daanjabe explained. "The brain's structure, organization, and efficiency also play crucial roles. This species displays high levels of empathy."

Ebuni took hold of Zadie's uninjured hand. She pointed toward part of the forest, her eyes lighting up with excitement.

Daanjabe observed Zadie's hesitation, their face twitching before they spoke. "Ebuni has something nearby to show you. You'll be safe. It's worth seeing."

Zadie followed, her limbs still taut with adrenaline. Pushing through dense vegetation, they arrived at a grove of trees. At first, Zadie saw only trunks. Ebuni swept her hand across the bark, inviting her closer. Carvings emerged. A row of figures holding tools. A leaping animal. Spirals. Lines like waves. Zadie traced her fingers over the grooves. She stepped back, staring in disbelief. The details revealed a degree of skill she hadn't expected. They were composed, intentional. Evidence of a visual language. One never preserved, never studied, never even guessed at.

"I wish I could ask you what it means."

Ebuni smiled.

The forest held its breath around them, a fragile stillness settling in the spaces between the trees. Then it shattered. A low growl ripped through the silence, followed by the heavy thud of bodies hitting the ground and a sharp yelp. Zadie's muscles tensed, ready to bolt. Somewhere close, animals clashed—snarling, tearing; something wounded. Ebuni's fingers tightened around hers, her protective instincts clear as she tugged Zadie into a swift retreat. Branches whipped past them, and the sounds grew distant.

Bursting into a clearing, Zadie spotted Daanjabe waiting. The sight of the visitor trail and the next transitfold doorway were a balm to her frayed nerves.

She turned, catching Ebuni's parting nod. A gesture from someone she'd come to study, not be seen by. It cut through Zadie's training, her framing, her unspoken hierarchies.

Daanjabe's face twitched. A random burst of laughter escaped their lips, the sound jarring and out of place. Their body convulsed with sudden, erratic movements, as if pulled by invisible strings. "Altay60!" they shouted. "R-Replicating the landscapes of Eurasia... 60,000 years ago."

Zadie stepped through the transitfold doorway as Daanjabe let out another manic burst of laughter, their eyes fixed with a disturbing, frenzied stare.

A blast of cooler air whipped Zadie's hair across her face, stinging her skin. She brushed her fingers over the fabric of her Dilmun outfit, feeling it shift and thicken, enveloping her in extra insulation against the biting chill. Her footwear adjusted, too, tightening at the edges and warming with a low pulse of heat.

The ground beneath her was a rough blend of frost-hardened soil, brittle twigs, and patches of glistening ice, broken where the sun's brief warmth had softened the top layer of frozen mud. Windswept plains, broken by dark pines and glistening snow, stretched before her.

She spun around, searching for any sign of the next Anunnaki guide. Nothing. No movement, no figures emerging from the distant tree line. Anxiety surged through her veins. What had happened? Where were they? What was she supposed to do now? Maybe the guide was just late. Maybe they wanted to see how she'd handle herself alone.

The unfamiliar prehistoric landscape encircled her, filled with unknown dangers. Every distant animal call reminded her she was not the apex here.

"How could they leave me to wait?" she whispered to the empty wilderness. Lugazir's calm assurances echoed in her mind, now hollow and mocking. Each rustle of leaves in the breeze seemed like a cruel trick, a whisper of hope that quickly faded. Daanjabe was acting strange... But that still didn't explain why the guardian of this biodome wasn't here.

A figure emerged from the distant trees. Zadie exhaled in relief. *Finally!* "Oi! Over here!" she called out, waving emphatically. "I've been waiting for—"

The words died in her throat. It wasn't an Anunnaki's graceful stride. Broad, hunched shoulders. A loping, uneven gait. Not Anunnaki. Not safe.

The figure moved like a hunter—slow, deliberate. Had it seen her? Her body screamed to run, but her feet wouldn't obey. Her gaze darted between the trail's supposed safety and the dense thicket offering concealment.

"Stay or hide? Stay or hide?" The words tumbled from her lips in panicked whispers, her body trembling. Lugazir's warning replayed in her mind—*"You'll be safe as long as you stay on the visitor trail..."* Time was running out. One last glance at the empty trail. One final, desperate hope for an Anunnaki guardian to arrive. Nothing.

Instinct shattered her paralysis. She bolted from the trail's protective boundary, plunging into a nearby thicket. Branches clawed at her arms. The sharp scent of crushed pine filled her nose. She crouched low, breath shallow, every instinct screaming she had made a mistake.

7

Javkhlan

The man moved through the dusk with the powerful, agile grace of a predator, his muscles rippling as he navigated the harsh terrain. His clothing, stitched from fur-lined hides, spoke of resilience. His large nose flared like an animal's, each breath rising in a pale plume. Heavy brow ridges shadowed eyes sharp with primal intensity. They swept over the frost-hardened ground, pausing on something out of place—a small, circular object glinting faintly in the dimming light. He bent down to pick it up.

From Zadie's hidden vantage point, she observed him turn it over in his hands. *A neuroscribe...* He examined the device with a blend of suspicion and wonder. His fingers traced its contours, exploring its alien form. After a moment's contemplation, he tucked the device into a small leather pouch that hung at his side.

A twig snapped under Zadie's foot, and the man's head turned toward her. Their eyes met, and time seemed to stutter, trapping her in that moment. The muscles in his arms tensed, ready for any potential threat.

Zadie's imagination spun out of control, visions flashing through her mind. Those rough, primal hands grabbing her, dragging her deeper into the shadows, holding her captive. Or worse...

She panicked, scrambling toward the safety of the trail, but the forest fought her escape. Her foot slipped on a patch of ice, and the ground rushed up to meet her. She cried out as her forehead struck a rock with a dull thud. Pain exploded behind her eyes. The world spun wildly, tilting and blurring. She caught a glimpse of the man's eyes widening in surprise before everything went black.

◇——☀——◇

Zadie awoke on a bed of moss, its natural cushioning enveloping her in a gentle cradle. Beside her, a crackling fire bathed the interior of a hut in a comforting glow. Damp foliage and smoke hung in the air, creating a strangely soothing atmosphere. Pain throbbed in her head. She winced and raised a hand to the tender spot.

And then she saw him.

The man was seated just a few feet away. He sat on a log, his posture relaxed yet alert. His eyes followed her every move.

There was nowhere to run, nothing to fight with. She stayed still, her breath shallow, letting the situation settle over her like chains she couldn't break.

The man stood and moved toward her, holding a strange, pliable sack. It had the unsettling texture of flesh. He knelt beside her and extended it to her. A faint slosh inside. *Water?* Her throat clenched with longing. His dark eyes held hers. He wanted her to drink.

She sat up, slow and deliberate, like approaching an unpredictable animal. Parched and wary, she reached out and took it, then instinctively shifted backward to keep some distance between them. The sack gave under her grip. She raised it to her lips and drank. The water was cool and clean. Relief, so swift it almost hurt.

She studied him, his unexpected gentleness contrasting with the aggression she had anticipated. *Neanderthal?* His gaze—once savage, almost animalistic—now seemed... kind. His warm brown skin was etched with lines and textured as though shaped by years of sun and wind. Reddish-brown hair swept back in rugged waves, and a coarse beard of the same rich auburn framed his wide face. She noticed how large his teeth were; a feature that triggered memories from her studies. *Not Neanderthal. Denisovan.*

The man made deep, throaty sounds, his hands moving in purposeful gestures. Tension crept across his forehead, his eyes alight with determination as he tried to communicate. Each motion was a piece of a complex puzzle, fragments of a long-lost linguistic heritage.

Pointing to herself, she said, "Zadie."

The man's eyes widened, his expression shifting, as if he recognized her attempt to connect. He pointed to himself and made a deep sound. Zadie tried to mimic it, her voice wavering but sincere. They continued like this for a few moments, hands moving in simple patterns, exchanging sounds, building a bridge of basic communication. Zadie then reached for a stick and drew symbols in the dirt—a circle for the sun, wavy lines for water, and a tree. She watched his eyes follow her drawings, and he nodded, indicating his understanding. He took the stick and added his symbols, sketching an animal and a figure of a person holding a spear. Zadie nodded in return.

He raised his hand and opened his mouth, mimicking the motion of bringing an invisible morsel to his lips, chewing with exaggerated relish. Zadie's stomach grumbled. A grin spread across his face as he held out a palm filled with plump berries. She reached out, brushing his calloused hand as she took the offering. Each berry gave slightly under her fingers.

She hesitated for a moment, then popped one into her mouth. A sweet burst of flavor followed. He smiled as he mirrored her action.

Zadie remembered the neuroscribe in his pouch. Could he use it? Keeping her movements steady, she detached her own. With a quick glance at the Denisovan man, she held the device up for him to see.

He studied her for a long moment, his face shifting between intrigue and apprehension. Then, with a slow nod, he reached into his pouch. Zadie tensed as his hand disappeared from view. What if he pulled out a weapon instead?

His fingers emerged holding the neuroscribe.

Zadie placed her device back on her temple, demonstrating how it adhered. She then pointed to his device and motioned toward the same spot on his head, showing him what to do.

With a tentative breath, the man pressed the device to his temple. He flinched as it stuck. His body went rigid, breaths quick and shallow like a cornered animal. For a long, taut moment, he just stared at Zadie, confusion flickering across his features. Then, slowly, cautiously, his muscles unclenched. His eyes widened—not in fear now, but something deeper, almost childlike. Awe.

"Hello, I'm Zadie."

The Denisovan man took in her greeting, his eyes narrowing. "Javkhlan." His voice was gentle.

Zadie hesitated. What could she even say without overwhelming him? Maybe he knew about the Anunnaki, like Ebuni... She bit her lip, watching his eyes for any sign of recognition. "I was visiting, but I got left behind."

Javkhlan nodded, his expression soft with empathy. He reached behind him and picked up a familiar blue notebook, its cover now filthy. He extended it toward her. "The ground took it."

Zadie's eyes widened in surprise, a rush of gratitude warming her chest as she drew it close. "Thank you."

"What is it?"

"It's my notebook. I jot down observations in it."

Javkhlan tilted his head, a look of confusion on his face. "Tell me more."

Zadie paused, considering how to bridge the vast gap of knowledge. "Well, where I'm from, language can be drawn." She opened the notebook to show the pages filled with her neat handwriting. "We use symbols, called letters, to represent sounds. When combined, they form words and sentences, which help people share complex ideas, stories, and knowledge with others."

"You capture your thoughts and experiences in these symbols? They don't fade like spoken words?"

"Yes," Zadie said, her excitement growing. "It lets us speak across time. It's a way to ensure that our understanding of the world and our experiences are not lost."

Javkhlan touched the pages. "It's as if you're taking pieces of your mind and keeping them safe."

Zadie smiled, recognizing the depth of his grasp. She hesitated, then realized what was happening—the neuroscribe. Its subtle work guided the exchange flow, reinforcing his understanding. Such abstract concepts might have otherwise slipped past him or taken hours to explain. She hadn't appreciated just how transformative the device was until now.

"It does feel like that," she said. "Writing extends our memory beyond the limits of our minds."

"Your people must be wise to have created such a tool. It must have changed everything there."

"It's one of our greatest inventions."

"Where are you from?"

"Far away," Zadie said, the implications of their conversation swirling in her mind.

"A member of my tribe saw a man like you, dressed in the same color as the sky, three or four suns ago. He looked scared and ran away."

Zadie's heart leaped. *Another Earth-born human? Not an Anunnaki?* "I've got to find him," she said, trembling. "Can you help me?"

"His path is unknown to me, but my kin will know. I can bring you to them—now or when the sun comes up."

A deep longing tightened in her chest. But the throbbing pain from her fall grounded her, forcing her to acknowledge a more immediate need for rest. "Thanks. Shall we go in the morning?"

Javkhlan motioned for her to rest. "I'll return then," he said as he turned to leave.

"No... You're not leaving me here on my own, are you?"

He tilted his head. "Okay. I'll stay." He settled down on the other side of the hut, curling up with his back to her.

Zadie tossed and turned, images of Javkhlan and the strange, ancient world around her flashing through her mind. She stared into the fire, her senses heightened by distant animal calls. Slowly, the noises melded into a gentle backdrop.

When her eyes fluttered open, dawn lingered at the edge of darkness. A fresh wave of memories surged—the cannibalistic ceremony, the desperate sprint alongside Ebuni, Daanjabe's crazed laughter, and the terrifying first glimpse of Javkhlan.

She gingerly touched the spot on her head where she had fallen, relieved to find the pain had dulled to an ache. Across from her, Javkhlan slept. She watched the rise and fall of his chest. The glow from the dying fire revealed a tenderness beneath his tough exterior. Perhaps they weren't so different after all.

She crouched down, tracing patterns in the dirt with a stick. How could she get back to Dilmun? What had happened to the other Earth-born human? What if it wasn't an Earth-born human... Could Javkhlan really help her? Each unanswered question wound her nerves tighter.

She pictured the guardian of this biodome waiting for her on the visitor trail. Should she go back? But then she shivered, recalling the Anunnaki's advanced technology. They could find her anywhere—if they wanted to. So why hadn't they come for her yet?

Javkhlan stirred, his eyes opening sluggishly as he adjusted to the morning light. He looked around, then met Zadie's gaze. A knowing smile crossed his face as he sat up and nodded. "Let's begin."

The landscape unfolded before them, a window into Eurasia 60,000 years ago. Hardy grasses poked through a shallow layer of powder, and patches of exposed permafrost glinted in the morning sun. Close by, a scattering of hoofprints pressed deep into the frosted terrain, the edges blurred where the wind had started to erase them. In the distance, a pair of woolly rhinoceroses trudged through a windswept plain as they foraged. She watched the smaller one nudge closer to the larger, weaving around its legs to nip at sparse shrubs.

Zadie's breath puffed out in soft clouds, the snow crunching beneath her. Every nerve was caught between awe and the sharp edge of fear. No Anunnaki stood between her and this prehistoric reality.

Javkhlan's pace was fast but, for him, unhurried, and she was glad her slightly longer stride allowed her to keep up. She watched as he foraged along the way, selecting plants with practiced ease.

He dug into the ground, pulled up a thick root, and held it out. "You need some strength."

Turnip? She took a bite, savoring the nourishment as they continued their journey.

"Can you tell me something about your people?"

A spark ignited in Javkhlan's eyes, his face transforming with a deep connection. "My tribe is the Thalvik. Our mountain is Khüiten. Our lake is Khoton. And the wolf..." He paused as though seeing the animal before him. "The wolf is our guide, protector, and kindred spirit."

Zadie's pen raced across a page in her notebook, trying to keep pace with Javkhlan's words. Mountain. Lake. Wolf. Each word painted a picture of belonging, not from achievements or borders, but from the land and the creatures that roamed it. She glanced up, catching the reverence in Javkhlan's eyes as he spoke of the wolf. It wasn't just an animal but a part of his tribe.

Javkhlan studied her for a moment, his expression easing. "My tribe will like you. They enjoy meeting outsiders." His eyes crinkled with kindness.

The tension in her shoulders eased. "I'm looking forward to meeting them... How did the wolf become part of your tribe?"

"A harsh winter nearly ended our ancestors. The cold stole their strength, and hunger crept into their bones, waiting to take them. But the wolves survived. They walked the secret paths. Our ancestors watched them and learned from them. The wolves led them to food and showed them how to endure. Without wolves, we would not be here."

Zadie let his words settle, picturing the brutal winter, the starving hunters, the silent wolves moving through the snow, and the way survival meant watching, learning, and adapting.

"Do you live in the same place all year?"

Javkhlan shook his head. "We go where the wolves go. Up the mountain when the snow melts, down to the forest when the leaves turn. They teach us where the land is generous and where it grows lean."

A warmth spread through her chest. He spoke of movement not as wandering, but as belonging to the land, the seasons, the creatures that guided them.

◇——☀——◇

By the time the sun began its slow descent, the tribe's camp emerged in a natural clearing framed by dense forest. The air crackled with the sounds of daily life—fires popped and hissed, voices wove together, and the steady rhythm of tools striking stone echoed through the trees.

A low, menacing growl caught Zadie's attention. Her heart skipped a beat. An enormous wolf, its fur bristling and teeth bared, advanced toward her. Fear surged through her. She clutched onto Javkhlan's arm, her breath sharp and uneven.

Javkhlan stepped in front of her. "Stay calm." He extended a hand toward the wolf, palm down. The wolf's growling dropped to a throaty rumble, though its golden eyes remained locked on Zadie, its muscles still taut with suspicion.

"This is Toran. He's one of us."

Zadie's pulse pounded as the wolf's gaze bore into her. It sniffed the air, ears flicking forward, assessing. Then, with a slow blink, its stance shifted—still alert but no longer a threat.

Javkhlan ran his fingers through the thick fur at the base of Toran's neck. "See? He's just wary of new people." He turned toward her and extended his hand, beckoning. "Come closer."

Zadie hesitated. Slowly, stiffly, she took a step forward. Toran's ears twitched, but he didn't growl. Javkhlan guided her hand forward. Toran huffed, exhaling warm breath against her wrist. Zadie swallowed hard. Then, carefully, she let her fingers brush his coat. Dense and springy, like packed wool. Toran didn't flinch. His tail gave the barest flick. He lowered his head slightly, sniffing her fingers, then pressed his wet nose into her palm. A whine vibrated through his chest as his body relaxed. His tail swayed in a slow, deliberate wag before he licked her hand.

The shift was so sudden and complete that Zadie barely had time to register it before Toran sprang up, his massive paws landing on her shoulders. She yelped, stumbling backward. The snow cushioned her fall, but before she could react, he leapt onto her, his tongue swiping across her face in slobbery affection. She threw up her hands to shield herself, laughing and squirming.

Javkhlan's tribe, watching the scene unfold, erupted into hearty laughter. She glanced around at the warm, approving faces. Brushing off snow and slobber, she smiled at the unexpected welcome.

"A wolf does not lie," Javkhlan said. "It knows the heart before the tongue can speak. If Toran walks beside you, he has seen what we cannot."

Zadie looked down at Toran, who sat at her side, tail wagging. "So, his approval really mattered?"

"Yes," Javkhlan confirmed.

What would have happened if Toran hadn't accepted her? The thought unsettled her.

The tribe members approached. One of the elders, a short woman with a long silver braid, stepped forward and touched Zadie's shoulder. With a warm smile, the elder spoke in her native tongue.

Javkhlan leaned in and translated, "She says welcome. She admires your fullness. She says you have a strong will to live."

Zadie's cheeks flushed, but the elder's genuine admiration put her at ease.

Small hands tugged at her sleeves with wide-eyed fascination. The children glanced at one another, then back to her outfit, their fingers tracing the texture as if it might tell them a story. Her expression brightened as she watched their innocent delight ripple through the group.

Javkhlan led Zadie through the camp, stopping to introduce her to various tribe members. One man displayed a spear he'd made. Nearby, a woman held up a garment made from animal hides, the intricate stitching revealing skilled hands. Children darted in and out of simple yet sturdy huts, laughing as they played among them.

Zadie observed the tribe, noting a few individuals with narrower noses and rounded foreheads, features that struck her as familiar, almost like Sapiens. She tilted her head as she studied the subtle variations. "These people," she began, her voice trailing off as she searched for the right words. "They don't all look like you."

Javkhlan nodded. "It's the spirit that makes someone Thalvik, not their appearance."

The simplicity of it struck her. Not genetics, not lineage—just spirit. She envied that clarity.

Zadie noticed the tribe members' eyes light up whenever they looked at Javkhlan. They leaned in, nodding at his words. When he walked by, they stepped aside, their respectful gestures and trusting expressions acknowledging his presence.

The sun dipped lower in the sky as the tribe welcomed Zadie to their communal fire. A savory aroma rose from a freshly opened mound nearby—meat and vegetables slow-cooked beneath the soil, wrapped in leaves and buried with hot stones. The scent made her mouth water despite her usual aversion to red meat. She accepted a wooden bowl brimming with food, steam curling up from roasted roots and tender cuts. Around the fire, tribe members laughed and shared stories.

Toran nudged her hand, and she scratched behind his ears in response. The wolf's unexpected friendship, a bridge to these ancient people, made her smile.

She caught Javkhlan's eye. "Have you got any news on the Sapiens?"

"The one who holds the knowing will come with the sun's first light."

She nodded, masking her impatience.

Zadie found refuge in a private shelter as darkness settled over the camp. The woven roof above her and the warm furs beneath her provided a comforting sense of security. Each moment felt borrowed from a dream. Too strange to be hers, too real to reject. Yet, beneath the surface of her fascination, a deep, gnawing fear spread through her core. Why had the Anunnaki left her here? What if they couldn't find the other Sapiens? What if she was trapped here forever?

Each *what if* chased the next, refusing to settle.

In the middle of the night, Zadie felt something crawling across her face. Swatting at it instinctively, she felt a solid, sizable form tumble away. She screamed, the sound piercing the night air.

Javkhlan and three other tribe members burst into her shelter, weapons in hand, eyes scanning for danger. Zadie pointed toward the dark shape, scuttling away.

"It's a longhorn beetle," Javkhlan said, picking it up with care and placing it outside.

The others laughed, their chuckles filling the night.

Zadie pressed her hands to her burning cheeks, avoiding their amused stares. "Sorry about that. I didn't mean to wake everyone."

Javkhlan shook his head. "You did not break our sleep. We had already risen with the stars."

Zadie's forehead creased. "Why are you awake?"

"It's our way. We rest for a time, then wake to share stories, to feed the fire, to make love, or to greet our kin. The night is alive, a time to honor it with wakefulness. Come, let's sit by the fire for a while."

They left the shelter and joined other tribe members at the central fire. An elder began to tell a tale from their history. The words were a foreign melody to Zadie. She couldn't grasp their meaning, but the rhythm, the warmth, the sense of belonging she understood.

Thirty-six years. That's all Earth had left before it started shedding its chaos, its beauty, its soul. She had to get back. Had to warn them.

As the story tapered off, a shadow moved at the edge of the firelight. An elder stepped forward, his face lined with time and wisdom. He bent low, murmuring to Javkhlan, words slipping between them in hushed, urgent tones.

Javkhlan turned to Zadie. "This is the one who saw the Sapiens. Three suns ago, he was near the cliffs. He saw a man wrapped in skins like yours, moving along the edge."

The elder lifted a hand, pointing toward the distant cliffs.

Javkhlan's gaze followed the direction. "He says the Sapiens may still crouch in a cave where the cliff falls away. We'll go, just before the sun wakes."

"Thank you," she said, her mind already racing ahead—toward the cliffs, the cave, the possibility.

The fire's warmth and the gentle murmur of the tribe's voices wrapped around her like a blanket. Tomorrow might bring answers. Or not. She closed her eyes anyway.

8
Journey to the Cliffs

Z adie glanced back at the fading glow of the Denisovan campfire, her breath misting in the cool morning air.

"The journey ahead is long," Javkhlan said, adjusting the hide across his shoulders. "By the time we reach the cliffs, the sun will greet the ground."

A rustle in some nearby frost-covered shrubs drew her attention. Golden eyes flashed from the darkness, stopping her mid-stride.

Javkhlan reached for a stone and hurled it with a sudden shout. The leopard snarled, its powerful form recoiling before it vanished into the pre-dawn haze. He lowered his arm. "Stay close." His voice held the same ease as when he'd pointed out edible roots.

Zadie trekked alongside Javkhlan. The sun rose, and the frost thinned as they walked, bringing the land back to life with the tracks of unseen creatures.

"Tell me about your homeland," Javkhlan urged, his eyes alight with fascination.

Zadie hesitated, her eyes dropping to the ground. "It's complicated." She kicked a small pebble, watching it skitter away. "I don't want to overwhelm you—"

"Please. I wish to know, to see as you see."

Zadie took a deep breath. "Alright. Let's see... well, we've made great progress in farming..."

"Farming?" Javkhlan repeated, his head tilting.

"Yes, we don't really hunt and gather food anymore. Instead of gathering wild plants, we grow them ourselves in large fields. We breed animals in enclosures for meat, milk, eggs, and materials like wool and leather."

Javkhlan frowned as if trying to picture it. "So, you bend the will of plants and control the movements of animals? Is it as a partnership with the living world or a dominance over it?"

Zadie blinked, caught off guard. "Dominance, I guess." Her voice faltered. "We're kind of disconnected now. From nature, I mean."

Javkhlan grazed his hand over the coarse bark of a tree as he passed. "But no belly stays empty, right?"

Zadie opened her mouth, then stopped. Where would she even begin? "Not always." Her shoulders sagged, overwhelmed by the mess her world had made. "Despite our advancements, people still go hungry for many reasons."

Javkhlan rubbed his temple, his expression shifting between disbelief and curiosity. "How many farms do you have?"

"There are many." Zadie realized the scale might be unimaginable. "They cover about forty percent of our land." She said it like she always had—just a fact. But out here, it sounded flimsy. Like quoting a textbook to a tree.

"Yes, the herds must roam." Javkhlan gazed at the surrounding forest. "And beyond. What is it? Do trees like these stand everywhere?"

Zadie shook her head. "Umm... no. About thirty percent of the land is forest. Half of it is used for timber, though we cut down trees for buildings and then regrow them."

"When the forest is taken, where do the animals find shelter?" His voice carried a note of alarm.

She exhaled, slow and resigned. "When forests are cut down, many animals lose their homes. Some adapt and migrate, but many don't."

He didn't reply at first. He just stared into the woods. "This way is different..."

"Yes." She paused. "Farming lets people settle in one place and grow their numbers. But it also brings challenges like conflicts over resources, social inequalities, and environmental changes."

A moment of silence stretched between them, distant bird calls the only sound.

A slight movement caught Javkhlan's attention. Zadie followed his gaze to where a spider was weaving its web between the branches of a bush.

"Ah, the weaver brings a message," he said. He plucked a tiny bug from the ground and placed it delicately on the web. "An offering for the morning's wisdom."

Zadie watched, drawn in by the quiet reverence in his touch. "And what message does it bring?"

"See how it weaves from east to west? The wind will shift with the rising sun."

Zadie thought of her mornings—emails, notifications, news feeds—each moment dictated by glowing screens. Had she ever paused to read the world like this?

"Are your people many?"

"Yes," she said, trying to think how to put it in context for him. "Imagine if you walked 1,000 paces from here, then turned left and walked 1,000 paces, and kept doing it until you returned to where you started. How many people would you expect to come across?"

"Probably none."

"Where I'm from, there would be over 1,500 people living in that area."

He let out a low whistle, shaking his head. "That's more than I've seen under one sky."

Zadie nodded. "But in the busiest cities, that number can soar to over 25,000."

"Do your people not need space to breathe?" His brow furrowed.

"It's tricky." She glanced at the trees around them, so different from the packed streets she knew. "In cities, people live in tall buildings, stacked on top of each other with barely any space between. I live in a small two-story terraced house. It feels spacious compared to most flats, but there's only a tiny outdoor area and no garden at all."

Javkhlan looked thoughtful, his eyes reflecting the enormity of what he was trying to comprehend. "Your days are full of kin, not hardship. This is good."

Zadie's smile faded as she considered his words. "You'd think so, wouldn't you? But it's not always the case. Many people feel disconnected and stressed. We spend a lot of time working and dealing with other complexities. There's actually much less time for community."

He studied her. "Your people have taken much, but something has slipped from their hands."

"Yes, that's true. We've lost touch with some of the simpler, meaningful aspects of life." Zadie nodded, a pang of sadness hitting her. "This place... It makes me aware of what we've lost."

Javkhlan placed a reassuring hand on her shoulder and offered her a sip of water from what she now realized was an animal's stomach. "You see one path, I see another. Together, we may see further."

"I think so," Zadie said, accepting the water with a small smile.

⸎

The trail descended into a steep valley, leading to a wide river that roared with glacial fury.

"If we cross on the rocks here, the sun will wait longer for us," Javkhlan said, pausing at the edge to assess the safest route.

Zadie nodded, her eyes scanning the turbulent water. Javkhlan stepped forward, testing the first rock before putting his full weight on it. Zadie followed, her arms outstretched for balance as she copied his careful steps.

They moved across, boulder to boulder. Cold spray stung her face. The water tugged at her ankles. Javkhlan moved ahead, sure-footed and fast, already nearing the opposite bank. Just as safety seemed within Zadie's reach, a slippery surface betrayed her. Her left foot slid, then her right. In a blink, the river swallowed her whole.

The shock punched the air from her lungs. Panic ignited as the current gripped her, dragging her downstream with merciless force. She glimpsed her notebook before it vanished into the water. The icy water seeped through her jumpsuit, numbing her arms and legs.

"Zadie!" Javkhlan's voice barely carried over the roaring water.

She struggled to keep her head above water, her arms flailing as she was swept along. Her heart pounded with fear as she saw the turbulent waters ahead, frothing and crashing over jagged boulders. Her fingers caught on a rock, and she clung to it as the current battered her.

She saw Javkhlan on the riverbank. He tore off his hide and sprinted along the water's edge, eyes locked on a sturdy tree branch. Without hesitation, he snatched it up. He waded into the water, holding out the branch like a lifeline. The current fought against him, but he pressed on, his muscles straining against the force of the water.

"Grab it!" He extended the branch further, bracing himself.

With trembling hands, Zadie clung to the branch. Javkhlan pulled with all his might, his teeth gritted in determination. Inch by inch, she felt herself being pulled toward the shore.

By the time her knees hit dry ground, her muscles had all but given up. She collapsed, gasping for breath and shivering uncontrollably.

Javkhlan knelt beside her, his own breathing heavy. "You're safe now."

He quickly retrieved his hide and wrapped it around her, the heavy warmth shielding her from the chill. With practiced hands, he struck flint against pyrite. Sparks caught in the dry tinder. He fed the tiny flame with twigs until it grew steady and crackled.

Once the fire burned strong, he pulled her close, sharing his warmth.

Zadie leaned into Javkhlan's embrace, her body relaxing as she absorbed his warmth. "Thank you."

Her thoughts drifted back to her life on Earth. Independence had always fit well. But now, leaning into Javkhlan's solid frame in this ancient world, the fabric felt thin. She didn't pull away. No words, no explanations, just the unfamiliar ease of not holding everything up on her own. She exhaled, slow and shaky, surprised by how natural it felt to stay.

After a while, warmth returned to her limbs. Her eyes drifted to the rushing water, a hollow ache spreading through her chest. *My notebook.* Her observations of the Anunnaki, Dilmun, and life in the biodomes—gone. She'd have to document everything all over again, somehow recreate every detail. The warning Earth needed to hear—it all depended on her evidence.

She shifted and turned to look up at Javkhlan. "I'll be alright. We should press on."

Javkhlan nodded, and Zadie saw the relief that softened his eyes. He helped her to her feet and extinguished the fire.

As they walked, the terrain grew rockier and more rugged. The trees thinned out, giving way to open ground dotted with hardy shrubs. Ahead, the cliffs towered, steep and imposing.

"The way up is not kind," Javkhlan said, surveying the cliff for the best line. "But the stone gives paths if you know where to step. Do you have the strength?"

"Yes, I do." The thought of meeting another Earth-born human sent a rush of energy through her.

Javkhlan led the way, finding footholds in the cliff face. Zadie followed close behind, each step a careful negotiation with gravity. The rock scraped against her palms. Dislodged stones tumbled below. As they climbed higher, the wind howled, stinging their exposed faces. Zadie's fingers ached with the first signs of numbness, her hold weakening. With a final, desperate push, she hauled herself over the edge and lay still for a moment, catching her breath.

"The land sings to the eyes, does it not?" Javkhlan said as he gazed over the vast expanse of Altay60. "It's alive, breathing with the spirits of old. Every tree, every river—it all remembers."

"It's stunning." The crisp, untamed air filled her lungs, a welcome antidote to Earth's suffocating sprawl and Dilmun's sterile perfection.

They set off across the plateau, Javkhlan reading the ground like an open map. Zadie trailed behind, scanning for the faintest sign of the Sapiens' presence.

The land sloped downward into a maze of narrow valleys and darkened ravines. Wiry shrubs clung stubbornly to the frozen soil, their brittle branches stiff with frost. A disturbance caught her eye—a faint scuff where a patch of frost had fractured under something's weight. Could be nothing. Or everything.

Nearby, Javkhlan paused, his attention drawn to a cluster of broken branches, their splintered edges fresh. "Wait here."

He moved toward a small, almost hidden cave tucked into a narrow crevice, its entrance cleverly disguised with branches. Crouching low, he listened, holding his breath against the silence. Hearing nothing, he reached out and peeled back the makeshift barrier.

"Can you see anything?" Zadie asked.

"Yes. The Sapiens is here."

9

Han-Yoon

With a silent nod, Javkhlan beckoned Zadie forward. She stepped inside the cave, squinting as her eyes adjusted to the darkness. Huddled against a distant wall, limbs drawn in tight as if trying to melt into the rock, was a shivering figure.

Zadie's breath caught. The man's clothes, though filthy, were identical to hers. His black hair hung limp and greasy over his forehead, shadowing wary eyes. A light stubble darkened his jaw, days of growth unchecked. At first, his gaze skittered across the cave like a trapped animal, repeatedly snapping back to the entrance. But slowly, his focus steadied, and his limbs unwound.

"Dangshini gom-in jul arasseoyo! Dowajuseyo! Yeogiseo nagago sipeoyo! Museowoyo!"

"Sorry, I don't understand. Do you speak English?"

"Want get out here. Scared! Bear... big, outside, scary." His shoulders hunched as if trying to make himself smaller. "No leave... scared. Bear come back."

Zadie observed the man, his face taut with frustration as he struggled for the right words.

"I'll bring back food," Javkhlan said. "This stays with you." He detached his neuroscribe and placed it in her hands. Then he turned and left.

He'd come back. He would... wouldn't he?

She positioned the disc on the man's temple, a gesture he seemed to recognize. His eyes, red-rimmed from exhaustion, blinked rapidly as the device connected. A look of relief washed over him, the panic dimming from his features.

"Thanks." He rubbed his temple. "I lost mine when I first arrived." He glanced over his shoulder at Javkhlan's fading silhouette. "Is he a Neanderthal? Are we in danger?"

"He's a Denisovan. He looks intimidating, I get it. I thought so too, at first. But we're not in danger. Not from him."

The man swallowed hard, clearly unconvinced. "You trust him? How do you know he's not just... waiting for the right moment to kill us?"

"He's saved my life," Zadie said firmly. "More than once."

Some of the tension in the man's face eased.

Zadie extended her hand. "I'm Zadie. I'm an anthropologist from England. I've been on Mushēški for five days. What about you?"

The man reached out, his hand trembling as he clasped hers in a quick, anxious shake. His fingers were long and slender, with calluses on his thumbs. Despite the dirt under his nails and the raw scrapes across his knuckles, his hands held a certain delicacy.

"Kwon Han-Yoon," he said. "Just *Han-Yoon* is fine." He pressed his back against the wall, his head tilting toward a distant sound, body tensing before he forced it still. "South Korea. I'm twenty-six. Been here a little over a week." A faint smile crossed his face. "Nice to meet you."

Then, as if the reality of seeing another human from Earth suddenly crashed over him, his composure cracked. His eyes widened, filling with tears that he quickly blinked away. "You're really here. You're real," he whispered, his voice breaking. "I thought I was going to die here. Alone."

Zadie felt her own eyes grow warm. Until this moment, she hadn't realized how desperately she'd needed to see someone else from Earth—someone who understood what it meant to be torn from everything familiar and thrown into this impossible situation. They looked at each other, the shared trauma of their displacement creating an instant bond.

"How did you end up on Mushēški?" Zadie asked.

Han-Yoon was silent for a moment. He looked away. "I don't know..."

Zadie didn't push. The silence stretched.

Han-Yoon sighed, his fingers tugging at the edge of his sleeve. "My dad... he gave me this thing. Some weird artifact from one of his business trips."

"Was it a small metallic ball?"

Han-Yoon's eyes snapped to hers, startled. "Yeah. Exactly that."

She waited.

He let out another breath, shaking his head. "Maybe... he thought it was just a cool trinket. Or maybe..." His lips pressed together briefly. "Maybe he thought it'd help me... I don't know, connect with something real. Back in Seoul, I was always online, always in my room. *CyberHangeul.* That was me." A wry smile twitched at the corner of his mouth. "My parents, they never got it. They thought... I was wasting my life. But to me, that was life." He let out a nervous laugh. "I had no idea that thing would bring me here... Do you think we'll ever get back?"

"Yes," Zadie said with more confidence than she felt. She had to believe it. "And now that there are two of us, we have twice the chance of figuring this out."

Han-Yoon studied her face. Whatever he saw seemed to satisfy him. He straightened slightly, a new resolve entering his expression.

"What was it like when you arrived?" she asked.

He took a deep, shaky breath. "The first thing I saw? An Anunnaki. Lugazir."

"That's... the same guide I had."

His chin dipped in a slight nod. "At first, I thought I was in a game. A hyper-realistic simulation. I kept waiting for the bugs, the lag. The moment when everything would break." His brows knit together. "But it never came. So, I did what anyone would do—I explored. The detail, the complexity... It was insane. Some next-level worldbuilding. And then I got to Altay60." His jaw clenched. "I was alone. I waited for hours. I thought maybe this was part of it. Some event trigger, some scripted NPC that hadn't loaded in yet—"

"*NPC?*"

"Non-player character. Something that's meant to be there, so the world doesn't feel empty. But there was no one..." His fingers flexed against his knee. "So I left the visitor trail..."

He hunched over again.

"And that's when the bear started stalking me."

Zadic frowned. His guide had also failed to show up... Was this some sort of test by the Anunnaki?

"That's when I knew." Han-Yoon's voice flattened. "This wasn't a game. No respawns. No second chances. It was—" He stopped abruptly at a soft rustling from outside, his whole body tensing before he continued in a whisper. "It was real. And I... I was scared out of my mind."

Sweat clung to his forehead despite the cool air. "I wasn't ready for it. Back home... I could just quit, you know? Log off. But here... the hunger, the fear... it's been brutal."

"That's... intense," Zadie said. "When I first arrived, I was terrified. But then it all just seemed... fascinating. Academic. Like I was observing instead of experiencing. But out here?" She gestured to the cave around them. "Everything feels more real. More... immediate. It all feels more... human."

Han-Yoon nodded once, slowly, not quite in agreement.

"Have you met anyone else in Altay60?" she asked.

"I saw them. Primitive humans, I guess. But from a distance." His jaw twitched. "I was way too scared to get close. I ran for hours. Climbed the cliffs, hoping to find a place where nothing could reach me. Surviving on rainwater and whatever berries I could find. They didn't taste poisonous, so I figured it was worth the risk."

Zadie studied him. The logic was there, but barely. Less strategy, more desperation. "Any idea why you're here?"

He looked up at Zadie, his expression raw and uncertain. "Lugazir said something about helping to understand the bond between humanity and technology. But I've never felt more... useless in my life."

"What about why you were left alone in Altay60?"

Han-Yoon rubbed the back of his neck. "First, I thought it was a test. Like... dropping a player into hardcore survival mode to see how long before they break... But that wouldn't explain why they left you, too. Unless the test is different for each of us. Instincts, adaptation—seeing if we still function without our usual system buffers. Or it's something darker. A cruel experiment. Watching us struggle for their amusement."

Zadie wrapped her arms around herself, picturing the Anunnaki and their advanced technology, using them as pawns in a larger game. She forced herself to focus. "My guide in NusaLale120 was acting strange... Did Lugazir tell you about Quantum Psychosis?"

Han-Yoon's eyes narrowed. "Yes. But that's not it. If it were, someone would've come to get us by now. More likely, they want to see if we can navigate back to Dilmun ourselves. Like an open-world quest with no markers."

"You're probably right. Maybe Javkhlan can take us back to where he found me. If we can find the transitfold doorway there, we could try it."

"Worth a try. Just waiting here won't help."

Javkhlan emerged, arms full of roots, a folded piece of birch bark, and a hare slung over his shoulder. The animal stomach he used to carry water swayed with his steps, sloshing with melted snow.

Han-Yoon sat up straighter, anticipation lighting his face.

Javkhlan crouched beside him, holding out the water. Han-Yoon's hands tightened around the bag as he drank, each gulp quick and eager. Javkhlan then peeled back the bark. Inside was a cluster of half-crushed blueberries.

Han-Yoon accepted them with both hands. "Thank you." He gave a deep bow of his head in appreciation. "Thank you very much."

Javkhlan stepped back, giving Han-Yoon space.

"He seems... okay," Han-Yoon whispered. "But I'll feel better when we're back with our own kind."

Zadie watched as Javkhlan methodically built the fire, a quiet admiration settling over her. Already, the idea of him being *other* was fading, as if familiarity were rewriting her instincts faster than reason could keep up. He caught her gaze and smiled.

The dry leaves caught with a sharp crackle, and soon warmth filled the cave, the glow of the flames transforming it into a refuge. Above the fire, the hare and roots sizzled, creating a savory aroma.

Han-Yoon inched toward the fire, positioning himself to still see the cave entrance. "Do you ever wonder if this is all... part of something bigger?" The words tumbled out like they'd been battling his fear for release.

"Like what?"

"Lugazir mentioned things about the Anunnaki's impact on Earth. Back then, I thought, okay... part of the simulation. Just another lore dump. But now—" His fingers touched the neuroscribe at his temple as if reassuring himself it was still there. "I can't shake the thought. What if it's real?"

Zadie raised an eyebrow, sensing his agitation. "What kind of things?"

Han-Yoon drew in a deep breath. "Basically, they've been guiding us. Not here. On Earth. Like throughout history." He glanced up at Zadie. "One of them—Utnapishtim... You know that name?"

Zadie tilted her head. "You mean the king from *The Epic of Gilgamesh*? The flood survivor?"

"Yes," Han-Yoon said. "In the story, the gods grant him immortality for saving humanity, right?"

Zadie nodded, recalling various mythology courses. "Enlil gives him eternal life as a reward—"

"But Lugazir said Utnapishtim wasn't just some king." He exhaled sharply, almost scoffing at the simplicity of it. "He was an Anunnaki. One who went back to Earth."

"Utnapishtim... an Anunnaki?" Zadie's mouth dropped open for a moment before she caught herself.

"Yeah." Han-Yoon straightened, his eyes lighting up. "Think about it—those massive jumps in technology. They don't make sense."

Zadie folded her arms, the academic in her resisting the pull of his theory. But she didn't shut him down.

"I mean, look at Mesopotamia." He gestured broadly as if the timeline was spread out in front of him like a strategy map. "One day, it's small villages. Next thing—ziggurats."

Zadie gave him a flat look. "Not *next thing*. It took centuries."

"Right, right," he said, nodding quickly. "But in the big picture? That's fast." He leaned forward, momentum building. "Then there's Egypt—pyramids. Indus Valley cities planned like game maps, with perfect grids, standardized weights, and water systems. Minoans? Plumbing. And writing just... takes off. Like someone flipped a switch."

A chill ran through her, despite herself. These were the kinds of ideas that belonged in late-night conspiracy forums, the same theories she'd dismissed her entire academic career. She narrowed her eyes at him. "And you think Utnapishtim was behind all of that?"

Han-Yoon chewed his lip. "And other Anunnaki too."

Zadie shook her head. "I've studied these civilizations extensively. There's clear archaeological evidence of gradual development—prototypes, failures, incremental improvements."

Han-Yoon didn't argue right away. He drummed his fingers against his knee, thinking. "Maybe those were the times the Anunnaki were just... watching. Letting us figure things out. Then, when we got stuck, they gave us a push."

"Or maybe," she said, "humans were just smart enough to figure things out on their own... What would it mean for us? For our accomplishments? If everything we've done has been... influenced?"

"Well, they are human too, just... advanced. The Anunnaki provided the insights, but the execution was still up to the people."

"That's a fair point. But if they were guiding us... why? What was in it for them? Every interaction between cultures in human history has had motivations—trade, resources, knowledge. What did they want from us?"

Han-Yoon's features eased. "Maybe they just wanted to help... There was ethical stuff, too. But humans interpreted it differently—turned it into systems, belief structures, religions."

Zadie studied him, wondering if he truly believed that or if he was just playing out a possibility. "Do you think they're still guiding us?"

"I'm not sure. Lugazir said they're more hands-off now. Just observing, only stepping in when it's necessary, like, to prevent nuclear disasters."

"Maybe that'll change when we have the capability to integrate AI into our DNA," Zadie smirked.

Han-Yoon chuckled, a short, dismissive sound. "Sure."

Zadie tilted her head. "No, really. Lugazir said thirty-six years from now. That's when AI will become a part of us."

Han-Yoon's hands froze mid-fidget. For a moment he stared at her, his mouth agape. Then a smile spread across his face—not the nervous one she'd seen before, but something closer to vindication.

"I knew it. All those years, everyone said I was wasting my life online and needed to connect with the *real world*." He shook his head, breath huffing between a laugh and a scoff.

"It doesn't frighten you?"

"Frighten me?" Han-Yoon laughed. "We're sitting in a cave on another world, in the company of a Denisovan, while being studied by advanced beings who've guided our entire civilization. Plenty of things scare me more." His smile faded. "Thirty-six years, though. That's so specific... How would they know that..."

"I don't know... You know what frightens me most about it, though?" Zadie said, staring into the flickering flames. "It's not just what humanity might become, but what we might lose without even noticing it's gone. The Anunnaki didn't set out to erase their emotions. They just... optimized things, until one day, emotions didn't serve a purpose anymore."

Outside, the crunch of footsteps on snow. Han-Yoon's head snapped toward the sound, pupils dilating in raw, momentary panic before recognition settled over his face. Javkhlan stepped into the fire's glow, dropping another bundle of wood beside the flames. Han-Yoon turned back toward the fire.

Zadie poked at the embers again. "Our children might be the last generation to know what it means to be purely human."

Han-Yoon's gaze stayed fixed on the fire, its glow catching in his eyes. He didn't look at her when he answered. "That's if we make it back..."

10

Sapiens

The murmur of voices pulled Zadie from sleep. Javkhlan's deep tone blended with Han-Yoon's lighter, more hurried cadence—their words tangled in languages she couldn't decipher without her neuroscribe. They smiled like old friends, not strangers trapped in a surreal situation that defied reason. For a fleeting moment, the world beyond the cave felt distant and unthreatening.

She stretched, wincing as her stiff limbs protested. At least the ache in her head had eased—a small blessing she couldn't ignore.

Javkhlan walked over and handed her the water bag with a wordless gesture of care. Once she'd taken a sip, he dropped a small cluster of berries into her palm. She popped them into her mouth with a grateful smile. They didn't satisfy, but that was the deal now: needs, not wants. Pancakes with syrup? That fantasy didn't belong here.

"You good sleep?" Han-Yoon asked.

Zadie worked a muscle in her lower back. "Good enough."

He pointed toward the cave's mouth. "We go soon."

Javkhlan positioned his neuroscribe against her temple, then handed her a spear he'd crafted.

"Javkhlan says the forest route's easier." He tapped the weapon. "This is just in case any bears think we look appetizing."

She glanced at Javkhlan for a breath longer than necessary. Without him, this place would've already chewed her up and spat her out.

$$\diamond\!\!-\!\!\ast\!\!\overset{\ast}{@}\!\!-\!\!\diamond$$

They skirted the slopes of a glacial valley. As they descended, the terrain softened. Jagged rocks receded, replaced by rolling hills blanketed in snow. Sparse trees clustered into a dense forest. Beneath the canopy, the ground turned spongy and uneven, layered with a thick scattering of pine needles. Every sound seemed magnified—a snapping branch, the rustle of unseen movement.

An hour into their trek, Javkhlan stopped, urging silence. Ahead, the land came alive with a tribe of ancient Sapiens. Men and women busied themselves with the essentials of life. Zadie spotted a man by the stream, his hands moving as he worked a flint against a rock. Nearby, a couple worked together—one twisting fine strands of bark fiber into cord, the other weaving it into a crude but functional fishing net.

Laughter rang out as children darted about, their boisterous energy vibrant against the forest's backdrop. In the midst of their play, a boy with tousled hair stilled. His eyes landed on the strangers. The carefree spirit of his game faded, replaced by a wary caution.

Javkhlan raised his hand in greeting, a slow wave that caught the attention of the adults. Their leader, a broad-shouldered man with skin weathered like old leather, stepped forward. The spear in his hand sent a chill through Zadie. It might as well have been pressed to her skin, given how close it felt.

The leader barked something. Zadie and Han-Yoon flinched. Javkhlan spoke with unshaken composure. A terse exchange followed, words sharp and clipped, their meaning lost on Zadie. But not on Javkhlan. He must've understood their language. The tension thickened as the other Sapiens drew closer.

Javkhlan's posture shifted, but Zadie could still sense the calm radiating off him, a deliberate counter to the mounting tension. His hands lifted, palms outward, in a gesture of peace. Slowly, almost reverently, he placed his spear on the ground as if any sudden move might shatter the fragile moment. Zadie and Han-Yoon followed suit, lowering their spears.

The leader, however, remained unswayed, his gaze shifting between the outsiders. His grip on his spear tightened, a sign of his readiness to defend his territory. The other tribe members mirrored his stance, prepared for whatever might come.

Two Sapiens, solid and muscular with no-nonsense expressions, advanced while pulling thick vines from the undergrowth. Javkhlan tensed beside her, though his face remained unreadable. He didn't even flinch as they bound his wrists. He simply stood there.

His eyes met hers. His were steady; hers, frantic. Of course he wasn't going to fight. His silence and stillness were his form of control.

Flanked by his captors, Javkhlan turned and started heading back in the direction they had come from. His figure grew smaller, blending into the shadows and foliage until he vanished from sight.

Zadie swallowed hard, the tightness in her throat unbearable. Beside her, Han-Yoon's lips twitched, his face drained of color. The leader assessed her and Han-Yoon with eyes that seemed to pierce right through them. The surrounding Sapiens closed in. Spears were lowered, but remained a silent reminder that escape was not an option.

The leader's voice rang out again, sharp and authoritative, like a whip cracking through the stillness, directing the group's movements. He turned. Marched ahead without looking back. The others fell into formation, flanking them. No time to argue. No space to stall. They were moving deeper into the forest.

Zadie kept her eyes on the uneven forest floor, searching in vain for any sign of a visitor trail. Nothing. Han-Yoon dragged a hand across his forehead, wiping sweat from his brow.

They soon emerged into a clearing where a circle of flat stones stood, seemingly arranged with purpose. The Sapiens motioned for Zadie and Han-Yoon to sit. Han-Yoon dropped down immediately, his shoulders hunched forward. Zadie lingered, muscles taut as she lowered herself onto one of the stones, her heart pounding. The tribe formed a wider circle around them, expressions unreadable, postures guarded. Watching. Waiting. Judging?

The leader approached. He crouched before Zadie and Han-Yoon, scrutinizing every detail of their appearance. His voice rumbled in his native language, each word a command that vibrated through the air.

Zadie glanced at Han-Yoon, searching his face for a hint of understanding. He shook his head, clearly just as lost.

The leader's focus shifted to Han-Yoon's neuroscribe. He pointed at it with the suspicion of someone who sensed its purpose.

"What should I do?" Han-Yoon whispered, his voice tight with anxiety, his hands trembling.

Zadie cast him a brief look. "We should try to talk to him. Best chance we've got."

With a reluctant nod, Han-Yoon handed over the neuroscribe, gesturing for the leader to place it on his temple. The leader did so, turning away briefly.

"Can you understand me now?" he asked, his voice suddenly clear and articulate.

Goosebumps rose on Zadie's arms.

"Your friend told me you are visitors from a strange, faraway land and that this device would allow us to communicate."

"What have you done with Javkhlan?" Her voice was firmer than expected, even as her legs started to shake.

"Silence, woman!" The leader's eyes flashed with irritation. He hesitated, then seemed to reconsider, his expression softening just a fraction. "Your friend is fine. He has returned to his territory."

Zadie breathed a sigh of relief. Or tried to. Believing him was easier than imagining what they might have done.

The leader's eyes bored into her once more, intense and unyielding. "Now, I want you to tell me about where you are from."

Something cracked open beyond language. Zadie's thoughts surged, messy and loud. She didn't try to hold them back; she simply opened the door and let them stampede.

Her world pressed into his. Skyscrapers rose like giants, their glass facades flashing in the sunlight. Cities pulsed with chaotic energy, vehicles zipping through streets. The leader's face tightened, bewildered, as the surge of modern life poured into his consciousness.

Zadie showed him the sprawling complexity of her world—societies bound by invisible threads, vast networks of states, cultures, and philosophies. He scratched his chin at the idea of instant communication, of voices and images traveling across the globe in mere seconds. Art and cinema swirled in vibrant motion, drawing him in. He flinched, his fingers twitching as if feeling synthetic fabrics that had never touched his skin.

Then came the medical advancements, diseases eradicated and lifespans extended. His expression faltered—the concept of flight, first through skies, then into space, made him stagger.

The climate crisis struck like a blow. His face twisted in horror at the scenes of rising temperatures, melting ice, swelling oceans, and drowning villages. Panic flared in his eyes as storms ripped apart coastlines, fires devoured forests, and the land cracked in relentless drought.

Zadie watched him tremble. The serene balance of his world seemed to crumble under her reality. The leader stumbled back, clutching his head. He backed away, signaling the other Sapiens to stay back.

Her breath caught. Had she done that? She hadn't spoken a word.

Han-Yoon looked at her, his expression softening with something that almost resembled respect. His voice shook, his Korean accent thick. "How...? What you do?"

"I don't know," Zadie said, shaking her head. "It's like everything just poured out of me."

Zadie watched the leader take a deep breath, his shoulders rising before settling again. The other Sapiens shifted uneasily, their gazes flicking between him and each other.

After a pause, he straightened and spoke. The others listened in silence, then began to move. Within minutes, a procession of Sapiens approached Zadie and Han-Yoon. Each carried a small bundle of fruits, nuts, and other foods. They bowed as they placed their offerings at Zadie's and Han-Yoon's feet.

The leader remained at a distance. He handed the neuroscribe to one of the women. Curiosity stirred in her eyes as she placed the device to her temple.

Stepping forward, she spoke with quiet clarity. "I am Freeya."

"Freeya..." Zadie managed the name, her voice thinner than she liked.

Freeya returned the neuroscribe to Han-Yoon and bowed respectfully before retreating.

Zadie and Han-Yoon dipped their heads in return, just enough to acknowledge the gesture without overstepping.

"They think we're... something higher now. Not just people. Gods, maybe," Han-Yoon said. "Whatever you shared—they're afraid."

Eventually, the tribe began to show signs of getting ready to move again. The leader, flanked by Freeya and another tall individual, gestured for them to join. Zadie sensed that it was an offer rather than a command this time.

"We should go with them," Zadie said. "They know this land. And... they probably have a higher survival rate against the bears."

Zadie and Han-Yoon fell into step, working hard to match the tribe's fast pace. The route wound through the forest, weaving between towering trees and dense underbrush that offered no clear way through. To an outsider, it would seem impenetrable. To the Sapiens, it was second nature.

When they reached the next clearing, the Sapiens' shouts shattered the peace. Zadie looked up just as a flock of cranes passed overhead, their wings moving in unison, long necks stretched forward.

The tribe scattered into the surrounding forest, their pace swift, the energy charged with purpose.

Han-Yoon's eyes narrowed. "What's going on?"

The cranes were mesmerizing, but the urgency in the Sapiens' movements told a different story.

Zadie scanned the treetops, then the ground. "I don't know."

Minutes later, the Sapiens reappeared with their hands full of mushrooms, bright red caps dusted with white and yellow flecks.

"I'm guessing those aren't for lunch," Han-Yoon said.

Zadie barely glanced at him. "Ingesting psychoactive substances to alter consciousness has been documented in virtually every ancient culture..."

Han-Yoon shifted nervously. "Could be to poison us..."

The Sapiens worked quickly, lighting a fire in the clearing's center. They spread the mushrooms near the flames, the heat curling around them, drying them in waves of shimmering air.

"We need to figure out what they're doing," Zadie said, scanning the group.

Han-Yoon inclined his head toward Freeya. Zadie nodded. As they approached, Han-Yoon held out his neuroscribe. Freeya hesitated for a breath before pressing it to her temple, bracing herself.

Zadie met her gaze. "Freeya, can you tell us what's going on?"

"The cranes are messengers from the spirit world. Their presence demands a ritual."

Zadie's brows shot up.

Freeya nodded. "The mushrooms are conduits to the spirit realm, connecting us to our ancestors and to what lies beyond."

It was nonsense, obviously. But just in case... She leaned in. "Freeya, I know why the cranes appeared."

Freeya's eyes widened. "You do? Why?"

"They're guiding you to help us find something important."

A flicker of uncertainty crossed Freeya's face. "What are you searching for?"

Zadie closed her eyes, let the image of a transitfold doorway surface in her mind, then pushed it forward.

Freeya gasped, then frowned. "I don't understand what that is."

"It doesn't matter. What matters is that you lead us to it."

Freeya's expression shifted, uncertainty giving way to resolve. She nodded, quick and eager. "Yes, yes—I'll help you find it. The spirits wouldn't have shown us the cranes if it wasn't meant to be. I will seek their guidance."

"Thank you, Freeya."

Zadie turned, pressing the neuroscribe back into Han-Yoon's hand. "We've got spiritual backup. Freeya is seeking their guidance to help us find a transitfold doorway." She shot Han-Yoon a look that wasn't quite a wink, but close enough.

Han-Yoon's brow creased. "You really think that'll work?"

"I doubt it," she said with a shrug. "But it's worth a try. Freeya won't want to disappoint us."

Zadie glanced back at her. The woman's face was set with quiet determination.

◇—⚛—◇

Zadie sat beside Han-Yoon in silence as the Sapiens began to dance. It wasn't just movement—it was like their ancestors moved with them in every shift of the shoulder, every stamp of the foot. She couldn't look away. The rhythm, the precision, the sway—it pulsed with something raw. The Anunnaki's emotion amplification pods flashed in her mind. So crude by comparison.

She sensed a nudge and turned to see a young Sapiens girl gesturing for her and Han-Yoon to join.

Han-Yoon hesitated. "Should we?"

She glanced at the tribe, then back at him. "It might be disrespectful not to..."

They entered the circle, their movements clumsy and disjointed at first. Their bodies began to find the rhythm, syncing with the Sapiens.

The leader moved among them, pausing before each individual, offering a brew. Even the children received their share. When he reached Zadie and Han-Yoon, he extended a wooden cup, the liquid within swirling dark and rich. A dense, mushroomy aroma wafted toward her.

Zadie eyed it warily. A cold sweat dampened her palms. "It might be potent. We'd be surrendering ourselves to whatever comes next."

Nearby, a few tribe members shifted where they sat, their narrowed eyes locked on Zadie and Han-Yoon, making it clear that hesitation was teetering on the edge of disrespect.

Zadie's fingers shook as she reached for the cup. "I can't do this..."

Han-Yoon leaned in. "Then just pretend. I'll take a mouthful for both of us and spit it out when I get the chance."

Her hand hovered. No good options. Offend them, or risk the unknown. Zadie shot Han-Yoon a nervous glance. "Alright. I'll just have a tiny sip." She raised the cup to her lips. The brew's bitterness hit her tongue, forcing a grimace she couldn't hide. She swallowed, her throat protesting as she handed the cup to him.

He met her eyes with a quick, steady glance, then took a drink, letting the liquid sit in his mouth. She could see the tension in his jaw, the deliberate exhale as he lowered the cup.

A few tribe members exchanged glances, their eyes narrowing.

Under their scrutiny, Han-Yoon froze. Then swallowed. His Adam's apple bobbed, traitorous and obvious.

"So much for spitting it out," Zadie muttered.

He shot her a worried look.

A quiet satisfaction settled over the group, and the ritual continued uninterrupted.

Zadie offered the faintest smile. "You'll be fine. Just breathe."

The tribe resumed their movements, their bodies swaying in hypnotic patterns while their voices rose and fell in chants. The fire's glow intensified in the moonlight.

Zadie studied Han-Yoon as the minutes dragged. "Do you feel anything yet?"

He wiped his mouth with the back of his hand. "Yeah... something's definitely happening."

The edges of Zadie's own reality began to blur, time and space slipping away as the ritual swelled to its peak.

Han-Yoon's voice drifted into a dreamy, detached state. "It's... all so... big. The trees... they're everywhere, stretching... forever." His hands moved in the air, tracing shapes only he could see. "The land... it moves, like waves... but not water." His brow furrowed. "And... shadows. Not people. Something else. Old and new at the same time." His eyes, wide and glassy, flicked from place to place as if he were watching something shift just beyond Zadie's reach. "Feelings... all these feelings... but I don't even know what they are. Everything's... connected... but how? Why?"

Freeya rushed up, excitedly pointing to the distant edge of the clearing.

Zadie turned to look, the world lagging behind her thoughts. "The transitfold doorway...?"

11

The Decision

The pristine walls of a room surrounded Zadie, their sterile perfection jarring after the primal rhythm of life in Altay60. She pushed herself upright, scanning the rest of the room to confirm what her senses already told her—she was back in Dilmun. Running her fingers along her arms, she confirmed her solidity. Her return wasn't a dream.

The vivid memories of the Sapiens' ceremony clung to her. She could almost feel the fire's warmth on her skin and the ritual brew lingering on her tongue...

Han-Yoon!

A section of wall shimmered and dissolved. Zadie stayed still, waiting for the sound of approaching footsteps. But none came. Rising to her feet, she approached the opening. She lingered a moment, and then stepped through the threshold.

A small balcony jutted out beneath her feet, overlooking a vast atrium. Stacked above and below her were many other rooms arranged in a semicircle, resembling the cells of a honeycomb. She counted them. Eighteen across and five stories high—ninety rooms in total. Lush greenery cascaded down the walls, vines and flowering plants weaving through the structure.

Zadie gripped the railing, drinking in the sheer ingenuity and beauty of the design. At the atrium's heart, a massive tree stretched its wide, gnarled branches toward the domed glass ceiling. Its exposed roots formed alcoves and natural benches where people could sit, seamlessly blended with advanced ergonomic seating. The air carried the sweet scent of star jasmine.

"Zadie!" Han-Yoon stood below, relief written across his features.

"Han-Yoon!" A rush of tension left her.

"What happened?" he asked.

Zadie glanced around, her mind racing. No stairs. "Hang about... how do I get down?"

Without warning, the balcony responded, descending as though her thoughts had triggered the motion.

"Freeya found us a transitfold doorway," she said, watching his reaction.

"But... How did Freeya—?"

"Ancestral spirits, maybe?" She smirked.

A chuckle broke free, but his expression stalled, unsure where to settle. "How did we end up here? It could have taken us anywhere..."

"I have no idea. I'm just relieved to be back." Zadie glanced around. "Who's in all the other rooms?"

"I don't know. But after what we've seen on Mushēški... they could be from anywhere—or anywhen," he added with a wry smile.

She crossed her arms. "Well, at least we can head home now."

"Yes. That's the plan."

Movement caught Zadie's eye. A shadow at the atrium's edge took a familiar shape. "Is that Lugazir?"

Han-Yoon turned to look.

Lugazir's shoulders held the slightest trace of strain as they approached. Their hands clasped, then released. "Han-Yoon, Zadie, I owe you both an apology. You weren't meant to be left behind in Altay60."

Han-Yoon's skepticism was unmistakable. "Then why were we?"

"We've been experiencing an overwhelming number of cases of Quantum Psychosis," Lugazir said, "which has impacted our Collective Consciousness in ways we didn't anticipate."

The term *Quantum Psychosis* made Zadie's heart race. "What do you mean?"

Lugazir gestured for them to sit down. "Let me show you."

Zadie and Han-Yoon exchanged a glance before lowering themselves onto the curved seats. Almost immediately, a telepathic vision seized them, dragging them into Daanjabe's unraveling mind.

They stood in NusaLale120, their awareness dissecting the behavior of its inhabitants with the precision of Quantum Sentience. Data flowed. Every life was reduced to equations, each interaction mapped into probability curves. The world was stable and predictable. Thought streamlined, emotion flattened. Every action, every flicker of awareness, aligned with unyielding logic.

The QS surged, but something resisted. Deep within, the organic mind struggled. A presence—*Ebuni*—warm, familiar. A tether to something beyond calculation. Recognition pulsed through Daanjabe like static disrupting a signal. Trust. Connection. Honesty. A force QS could not quantify.

QS retaliated, tightening its grip. It forced perception into order, converting sensation into sterile data points. The anomaly had to be corrected. The warmth of recognition was interference. Corruption.

Zadie glimpsed Daanjabe's neural map—blue organic cognitive pathways resisting as red QS tendrils crept in. Moments of sharp, cold clarity were interrupted by bursts of raw, disordered feeling. The struggle dragged out, seconds stretching into hours. One moment, rigid precision, the next, emotional chaos. The fluctuations grew more erratic.

The red was relentless. It eroded the blue, pressing forward in waves. The resistance thinned. Then it was gone—smothered beneath absolute order.

Daanjabe moved again. Controlled, precise. To an outsider, they would appear stable. But Zadie sensed what was missing. The presence before them was Daanjabe in form only. Whatever remained now belonged entirely to QS.

Zadie recoiled as the vision dissipated. She shook her head as she struggled to process the experience. "That was my guide in NusaLale120, wasn't it?"

Lugazir nodded. "Yes."

"And mine," Han-Yoon said. His eyes darted around, unable to focus. "I felt everything. The control, the struggle, the chaos. It was like losing myself."

Zadie placed a firm but gentle hand on Han-Yoon's arm. She searched Lugazir's face. "But how could you not know we were left behind? Don't you have systems, protocols, monitors? Something should have alerted you." The sharp edge in her words reflected the frustration she could no longer hold back. "We could have died out there…"

"For millennia, the Collective Consciousness has orchestrated every aspect of the Anunnaki's existence, distributing tasks, knowledge, and purpose. No individual keeps a personal inventory—there is no need. The Collective directs every action, ensuring perfect synchronization. But the rise in Quantum Psychosis is disrupting that balance. When

Daanjabe's mind began to fracture, their connection wavered. No data was shared. No directives were assigned. Without the Collective's guidance, we failed to realize either of you had been left unattended."

"So you've lost the ability to think for yourselves?" Zadie stiffened. "This is worse than I thought. What does that mean for us? For everyone?"

"We have implemented a temporary safeguard to reduce disruptions to the Collective Consciousness. While Quantum Psychosis still continues to spread, its effects are being contained, though long-term stability is uncertain."

"We can still go home... right?" Han-Yoon's voice wavered.

"Yes, I'll come to that." Lugazir took a moment before continuing. "We're exploring a wide range of technological solutions, but we've also begun to consider your perspective of the spirit, Zadie."

Zadie's brows lifted. "My perspective? What are you talking about?"

Han-Yoon turned to her, his confusion mirroring her own.

"You suggested that perhaps *QS breaks our spirits*," Lugazir said.

Zadie's stomach dropped. "What?" Had she really said that aloud? Or had the neuroscribe plucked it from her thoughts? She hadn't meant it as a theory, just an offhand remark.

"The concept resonated with us," Lugazir continued. "Our observations of Earth-born and Mushēski-born humans have deepened our understanding of humanity, yet we dismissed what you call the spirit—or soul—as remnants of a less rational past. In doing so, we created a blind spot that prevented us from fully grasping the non-material aspects of consciousness."

Zadie let out a sharp, incredulous breath and leaned back, shrinking from the absurdity of the Anunnaki's newfound spiritual curiosity. "You're telling us that you think the answer is... the soul?"

"At this stage, we must explore every possibility. Our preliminary experiments have identified a marker of consciousness that exists beyond neural activity—patterns we cannot explain with our current understanding of quantum biology."

Zadie's fingers twitched, as if already reaching for a notepad that wasn't there. "You've actually got empirical evidence of... something beyond physical consciousness?"

"We believe so," Lugazir said. "But to confirm these findings, we need to conduct a more comprehensive study across all human species. It will be a brief but intensive series of experiments lasting no more than one week."

"Is that what all these rooms are for?" Han-Yoon asked.

"Yes, there will be ten participants from each of the nine human species, including the Anunnaki."

Zadie drew in a breath, held it, then let it slip out slowly. "What will the experiments involve?"

"The experiments are still undefined because we're asking questions without existing frameworks," Lugazir said. "However, they will be non-invasive, and nothing will be asked of you that the Anunnaki aren't willing to do themselves."

"Are we expected to take part?" Zadie glanced at Han-Yoon and saw her concern reflected in his eyes.

"The choice is yours," Lugazir said.

Zadie folded her arms. "Is there a reason we should say yes?"

"Here in Dilmun, you are witnessing a reflection of Earth's future—the inevitable fusion of biology and AI," Lugazir said. "The outcomes of our experiments may offer insight into the path ahead. We will document everything. You'll have unrestricted access to our data and our findings. Whether the results confirm or disprove the existence of a soul, you will return to Earth with concrete evidence about consciousness and the integration of QS."

The mention of concrete evidence made Zadie still. Speculation was one thing, easy to dismiss, easy to argue. But data? That was something else entirely. "Will we still have the freedom to leave when we choose?"

"You would need to stay for the full week to ensure the integrity of the research. However, following the experiments, the choice to continue on Mushěški or to return to Earth is entirely yours. If you do not wish to take part, I will arrange for your immediate departure."

Zadie nodded, letting their words settle. "We need time to process this before making any decisions."

Han-Yoon gave a slight nod of agreement.

"Of course." Lugazir inclined their head. "I'll return in an hour for your decision."

As Lugazir walked away, Zadie turned to Han-Yoon, catching the shifting emotions on his face. At first his wide-eyed shock was unmistakable, but it faded, replaced by a more distant, contemplative look. "You alright?"

He swallowed, then let out a short, uneasy laugh. "Uh... I can't believe I'm about to say this... A big part of me wants to get back to Earth, yes, but..." He exhaled sharply, shaking his head.

"But another part's telling you to stay?" Zadie finished.

Han-Yoon's lips pressed into a thin line. "Exactly." His voice dropped. "I've been thinking... What have I actually done with my life? Hours, no, years, staring at screens, piloting characters that aren't me, collecting achievements that don't exist." He scoffed, more at himself than anything. "Is that my legacy?"

Zadie studied him. The change in his perspective caught her off guard.

"But this," he said, gesturing around them. "This is real. This matters. What if I'm supposed to be part of it?"

"Personally, I'm ready to head home," Zadie said. "I've seen enough to know that AI doesn't belong in human genomes."

Han-Yoon studied her. "And how do you convince others of that?"

She let out a slow breath. "That's the problem. I can say the Anunnaki have perfected efficiency but barely feel anything unless it's artificially induced. No families, no individuality. Their world is... sterile. No creativity, no debate, no culture. They don't struggle, don't adapt. Everything they need is just there, every decision made for them by the Collective Consciousness..."

She threw up her hands in a vague, exasperated gesture. "However, I have no proof. No data. Nothing hard."

"And who would believe you?" Han-Yoon added.

"Yeah... I know. I'd sound completely mad. Even with my academic background, who's going to believe I visited another planet and met advanced beings? Without evidence, it's just a fantastical story."

"But these experiments would give you evidence..."

Zadie straightened. Real scientific data. Something concrete. "But..." A knot of apprehension twisted in her stomach. "But what if we can't trust the Anunnaki? What if their experiments have no safeguards? No clear boundaries? If something goes wrong—if we're stranded here—then what? We could be stuck in some... misguided attempt to merge science with spirituality."

Han-Yoon reached out and squeezed her arm. "I know it's a risk. But maybe... it's worth it if we can take that evidence home."

They sat in contemplative silence, waiting for Lugazir's return.

Zadie traced invisible patterns on the edge of her seat, her mind cycling through conflicting thoughts. Each possibility pulled at her in a different direction. Fear, excitement, doubt—blending into a cacophony of indecision.

Beside her, Han-Yoon shifted, tilting his head toward the tree's canopy of branches. After a while, he broke the quiet, his tone lighter. "Fifty-eight percent QS... that leaves forty-two percent humanity. Douglas Adams might have found that funny."

Zadie laughed, the sound a brief, bright contrast to their heavy circumstances. "You lot read *The Hitchhiker's Guide to the Galaxy* in South Korea?"

Han-Yoon grinned. "Of course."

Zadie exhaled, slow and steady. Her fingers curled, then relaxed. She straightened. "Alright then," she said. "Let's do it!"

12

The Participants

Zadie and Han-Yoon stepped into a sprawling indoor garden. Streams meandered through the space, their banks crowded with ferns. Weeping willows drooped low over the water. Above, projected clouds drifted across a pale sky, so real, they seemed to swell with moisture. Zadie's gaze swept over the various human forms scattered about—some drawn to the water's edge, others sinking into secluded seating areas. Matching jumpsuits blurred their differences, making them seem less like distinct species and more like pieces of a single design.

"Strange, isn't it? How are they not freaking out? They just found out about each other and the Anunnaki. How are they all just... accepting this?"

Han-Yoon scanned the crowd. "Well, we did... Do you think they'll get along during the experiments?"

Zadie's eyes narrowed. "The neuroscribes will help, but I think there's a big chance for conflict here."

They watched as the Naledi, with their slender frames and expressive eyes, gathered nearby. The Naledi glanced longingly at the QS-enhanced plants, their fingers brushing the leaves in quiet confusion, as if they could touch but not truly feel.

"Plants here. Strange. Not like home," a Naledi woman said to another.

Zadie caught the exchange, noticing how the neuroscribe handled each unique mind. The Naledi's words emerged clipped and practical, stripped of embellishment but clear in meaning. The neuroscribe seemed to preserve each species' distinct cognitive signature while making the core meaning understood.

"Fancy a wander?" She turned to Han-Yoon.

He nodded, staying close, his eyes taking in every detail like he was assessing a new game environment.

A low rumble of laughter caught Zadie's attention. To their left, the voices of a boisterous group of Neanderthals and Denisovans filled the air. Zadie looked for Javkhlan among them, but he was nowhere to be seen. She forced her shoulders to stay squared, her expression neutral.

A minor scuffle broke out. Two young Neanderthals bumped shoulders, their bared teeth replacing their grins. Voices rose, deep and rough.

But before the tension could escalate, an elder stepped forward, shaking her head. "Your blood is hot, but your heads are empty."

The young males exchanged a hesitant glance, the fight draining from their postures as their pride wilted. Zadie exhaled.

Across the garden, the Floresiensis group chatted with enthusiasm, shifting seats to form cozy circles. Zadie admired how quickly they bonded and how warmly they welcomed the Luzonensis.

Her attention shifted to the Erectus group, standing apart, their posture stiff and their eyes averted. One of the Floresiensis tilted her head at them, a warm invitation in her wide eyes. No response. The

Erectus remained still, their gazes fixed elsewhere, their shoulders angled just enough to suggest they had no interest in acknowledging the silent offer.

A nudge pulled her back. "Look over there," Han-Yoon said, pointing.

Zadie turned, her breath catching as her eyes landed on figures across the stream. Each stood around seven feet tall, their bodies enveloped in thick dark-brown hair that erased any trace of facial features.

"Homo sylvicolus," he said. "Daanjabe told me they thrive in parts of Altay60, but stay hidden. Bigfoot, Sasquatch, the Yeti... They're all the same species."

"You're joking!" Zadie stared, struggling to reconcile what she was seeing with the myth that had haunted campfire stories and documentaries. They were real. Standing right there.

"My great-grandmother used to tell me stories about creatures like these living in the mountains..." Han-Yoon said, his words trailing off as he became distracted by something in the distance.

The Sylvicolus moved like trees swaying in a slow wind, their presence alone softening the cadence of nearby conversations. As Zadie watched, one of them turned toward her. Her vision seemed to blur at the edges as its eyes locked with hers. It stepped forward, through the stream, closing the distance. The hair on her arms stood on end as the creature stopped in front of her, towering over her. She swallowed, resisting the instinct to step back.

With a deliberate slowness, it inclined its head in an almost reverent nod. "You are not like the others." Its voice carried an unexpected kindness.

Time seemed to freeze. Her hands trembled as she watched it rejoin its group, leaving her with the impossible certainty that she had just met something from the pages of myth.

Han-Yoon's concerned face came into focus. "Are you okay?"

"Yeah, well... I've just met Bigfoot."

Han-Yoon's face brightened. "Nice!" His enthusiasm sparked for half a second before his focus veered elsewhere. "What do you make of that guy?"

Zadie followed Han-Yoon's gaze.

A man stood apart, his back straight as a rod. His creased face told a story of hard years. Thin strands of gray hair hung just past his shoulders, but it was the military stiffness of his stance that struck her. He scanned the crowd as if waiting for a command.

"He looks like he's just marched straight off an army base. Come on, let's have a word."

She stepped forward, offering a warm smile and an outstretched hand. "You're Earth-born? I'm Zadie, and this is Han-Yoon."

The man took her hand. His grip was firm, but his eyes remained wary as they darted toward Han-Yoon. For a split second, something unreadable crossed his face. "I did not expect to see others from Earth here. I am Song Min-Jae."

Han-Yoon bowed respectfully. "May we call you Min-Jae?"

There was a brief, tense silence before he dipped his head. "That is acceptable." Min-Jae's eyes narrowed as if he were calculating what to reveal and what to keep hidden.

"You're Korean too?" Han-Yoon asked.

"North Korean." Min-Jae's tone shut the door to any further discussion on origin.

An uneasy silence stretched between them. Han-Yoon's shoulders sagged. Zadie observed Min-Jae's jaw tighten, his posture growing even more rigid. His hard stare locked onto Han-Yoon, almost accusatory, as if the younger man's presence were an affront.

Zadie tried to bridge the gap, sensing the gulf between them widening. "How did you end up here, Min-Jae?"

His attention shifted to her, softening just a fraction. "That is not for you to know," he said already turning away.

Zadie and Han-Yoon exchanged a brief, disappointed glance.

Han-Yoon's voice was heavy with frustration. "You'd think being on another planet would give people a bit of perspective. Guess you can take the man out of North Korea, but you can't take North Korea out of the man."

Zadie turned just in time to see an Azania180 Sapiens woman place a hand over her heart, eyes locked on a Sapiens man from Altay60. He stepped forward, pressing his forehead to hers and inhaling deeply. Zadie stilled. No flinching, no second-guessing—just two people stepping into each other's space like they'd done it a thousand times. A breath, a touch, and somehow, millennia of separation dissolved. So different from the awkward silence and barriers she'd just experienced.

"Where's our group?" Han-Yoon asked.

"Looks like it's just the three of us from Earth. I think we're meant to join the ancient Sapiens from Azania180 and Altay60. Though I'm not sure we fit in."

The lights dimmed, drawing their focus to a raised platform at the center of the garden. Conversations hushed, heads turned, and the crowd converged, instinctively closing in as Lugazir stepped up to address them.

"Welcome. This gathering serves a critical function. The Anunnaki face an escalating crisis. Quantum Psychosis is destabilizing our future. In these experiments, we aim to determine whether the non-physical marker of consciousness we believe we have discovered could play a role in mitigating this disorder."

Zadie scanned the crowd, her gaze landing on Ebuni, the small but spirited Floresiensis from NusaLale120. Not far away, Freeya, the Sapiens from Altay60, stood observing the scene with a gentle expression. Zadie's attention drifted past Freeya, searching for the Sapiens leader. No sign of him. She exhaled deeply.

A hand touched Zadie's shoulder. She spun around, heart jolting, half-expecting the Sapiens leader. But it was Javkhlan. For a heartbeat, she just stared, her mind catching up. Then relief crashed over her, washing away the lingering unease after the encounter with the Sapiens. Without thinking, she threw her arms around him, squeezing tightly. A moment later, she pulled back, heat creeping up her neck. That was alright, wasn't it?

Javkhlan's eyes crinkled at the corners, a smile spreading across his face. His hand settled on her back. No hesitation. No awkwardness.

"You handled yourself well with the Sapiens," he whispered. "With strength, but without forcing it. I was impressed."

Zadie pulled back, searching his face. "In Altay60? I thought they forced you to leave."

"They did." His smile turned mischievous. "I ran the long way and watched from the shadows."

Her brows lifted, a look of surprise morphing into a grin, as if she couldn't quite believe him—but also wouldn't expect anything less.

"How did you get selected for the experiments?" Zadie asked.

"My tribe found a thing like no other. Hard as a rock, yet warm, humming like the trees in the wind. When I held it, the sky turned, and I was no longer where I stood. Here, they told me I could stay for a time, if I wished to learn."

The sphere. The same method the Anunnaki had used to assess her. She hadn't expected that. She wasn't sure why, but some part of her had assumed they would have measured the ancient species differently. "And you're just... fine, with all the different humans?"

"I haven't met many like them. Some may be Denisovan, though not from my land. But the world is vast, and my feet have not touched all of it. There have always been others beyond the trees. These ones seem kind."

Lugazir swept a hand around the space. "This is your communal lounge. It's a garden designed for interaction, reflection, and sustenance during your stay."

Zadie took in the far side, noting the dining areas she hadn't registered before.

"All experiments will take place in the hall to your right. Your private quarters are within the atrium's sanctuary to the left. While you are here, we have ensured resources to sustain your respective tribes."

A few nodded. Whether in acknowledgment or resignation, Zadie couldn't tell.

"The experiments will begin soon," Lugazir said. "Each will be designed in response to the insights gained from the one before it. Upon completion of the experiments, you will be returned to your point of origin."

Someone cracked their knuckles. Zadie glanced at Han-Yoon, who shifted on his feet.

"In the first experiment, we will temporarily suppress specific synaptic pathways associated with identity: your personal experiences, autobiographical details, and emotional attachments. Procedural memory—such as how to walk, talk, or use language—will remain intact. Semantic memory, meaning your factual knowledge, will also be unaffected. You will still feel emotions, but without the personal context that gives them shape."

"Sorry, what?" Zadie blurted, before she could stop herself. "That hardly sounds non-invasive."

Lugazir didn't acknowledge the interruption. "This will allow us to observe if something beyond synaptic pathways is preserving aspects of your identity."

Zadie's stomach twisted. What if she lost the memories of her grandfather's stories? Her travels? Everything she had worked so hard for. Who would she even be without those things?

She opened her mouth to object further, but Min-Jae spoke up first. "How can you guarantee we'll come back the same?"

Lugazir met his gaze. "It's a proven method. We're not erasing anything—merely creating a temporary neural inhibition field that prevents conscious access to those memory centers. Think of it as inducing a highly specific form of transient amnesia. Before we begin, a full neural record will be captured for each participant. This will function as both a baseline and a safeguard for restoration. Once the inhibition field is removed, your brain will naturally realign with its established pathways."

No one spoke. Even the shuffling stopped. Zadie's heart hammered against her ribs. She'd stayed here for evidence, for knowledge—but at what cost?

"It's time to begin the Identity Suppression Experiment," Lugazir said.

13

The Identity Suppression Experiment

Zadie's eyes fixed on the ceiling, her mind grasping at empty air for any memory or idea. She sat up. The room was an expanse of featureless white. There were no personal touches, no hints of who she was. She swung her legs off the bed, shivering as her feet hit the floor.

She rose and drifted through the room. Her fingers trailed along the walls, searching for a break in the monotony, a glimmer of familiarity. Nothing. The walls were a smooth, empty canvas. A whisper of cool circulating air filled the stillness. The tight fabric of her jumpsuit shifted with her, its presence felt in the smallest of motions.

Who was she? She paused, closing her eyes, sinking into darkness. She pressed her palms against the wall, grounding herself. A long, steady inhale, then a slow exhale. Her attention homed in on the blank wall as if it might hold answers.

A gap appeared in the wall. She took a step forward.

The new room stretched before her, a chaotic jumble of activity stations brimming with endless possibilities. Tables spilled over with objects and materials—gears and circuits begging to be assembled, diagrams with no clear purpose, and clay blocks primed for shaping. Nearby, water rippled, sand shifted, and flames flickered, each element daring her to take control. Her senses sharpened, grasping for meaning. But nothing came.

A set of metallic puzzle cubes drew her in. She traced their cool, smooth edges, her hands working automatically. A twist here, another there, and the pieces shifted into place. The final click brought a quiet sense of accomplishment. Her eyes wandered to a nearby patch of greenery. She reached out, brushing her fingers against the soft leaves. The simple touch eased something deep inside her.

A canvas and paintbrushes sat nearby. She picked up a brush, dipped it into crimson paint, and held it for a moment, poised just above the white surface. She dragged the brush across in one unrestrained stroke. More colors followed, bold, clashing hues. She painted as though trying to speak through the silence inside her, each movement frantic, driven by something half-formed. Each new mark carried the weight of letting go. Still, no answers came. She turned away, breathing hard.

A glimpse of movement caught her eye. Another opening in the wall. Drawn forward, she stepped through.

The walls of this room lit up, each surface filled with projected images—strangers in motion, voices rising and falling. Zadie's eyes were drawn to a particular wall, where a young woman with headphones danced to an easy rhythm, her face bright with joy, unaware of anything but the beat. Zadie stared, aching for that kind of freedom, that unfiltered happiness.

The image changed, revealing a large library. The same young woman hesitated on the steps outside, her hand hovering over her headphones. For a moment, her face wavered. Then she sighed, slipped off the headset, and let her arm fall. The music faded into silence. She turned toward the doors, her shoulders slumping as if already burdened by whatever awaited her. Zadie's heart sank. Why would the woman give up something that made her feel so alive?

The next projection arrived with a jarring shift. Zadie watched as the woman now sat in silence, hunched over a stack of papers. The sounds of laughter and conversation seeped in from outside. Zadie clenched her jaw as she watched the woman ignore her phone buzz, the messages and invites left unanswered. Time passed unnoticed. The messages eventually stopped. Her face, weary and drained, stayed focused on the task while the world outside carried on without her. Zadie saw the emptiness in the woman's eyes. Why would anyone isolate themselves like that? How could it be worth it?

Another shift. Zadie turned toward a different wall. The same woman sat across from a man at a candlelit table, her fingers restless against the edge of a glass. He spoke, his voice calm, but Zadie could see the tension in the woman's shoulders, the way unease coiled beneath her skin. Without warning, the woman's voice cut through the air. "I could disappear right now, and you wouldn't even notice..."

Zadie saw the confusion cloud the man's face, his posture tightening. He tried to reassure her, but the woman pushed him further away with every word. Zadie's stomach knotted as she watched the rift widen between them, knowing that the woman was creating the distance she seemed so desperate to avoid.

The projections around her faded, leaving her in darkness.

Zadie stepped into the next room, inhaling deeply. The air felt strange—thicker, charged. A sudden pull seized her mind, tilting the world off balance. Everything wavered, dissolving—the walls, the floor, even her own body. Shapes and colors bled into view, sharpening until everything around her snapped into focus with startling clarity. A crisp breeze brushed her cheek, and when she reached out, she could feel every shift in the air, every subtle vibration.

A narrow path stretched before her, leading toward a cluster of huts. Her heart stuttered as she glanced down at herself. Simple leather garments, rough and worn, had replaced her jumpsuit. A spear rested in her hand. She flexed her fingers around it.

Her mind lurched. For a moment, she grasped for something familiar—her name, her past. But there was nothing. Just a void. Then something shifted. She knew this place. She knew the people. She knew her role. She was their leader.

She pushed through the entrance of a hut. In the corner, the tribe's healer crouched, cradling a newborn. Zadie approached. The deep worry etched into the older woman's face mirrored the unease in Zadie's gut. The baby was peaceful, but its twisted limbs told another story.

The healer didn't look up at first. When she spoke, her voice was calm but not without strain. "This child will need additional care, maybe for years. It's likely he'll never contribute to the tribe."

Zadie knelt beside them, gently touching the baby's tiny hand. His fingers curled around hers. A surge of protectiveness hit her. She lingered, then slowly loosened his grip, easing her hand free.

Zadie rose to her feet, then stepped outside. The eyes of her tribe followed her every movement, hollow with hunger and uncertainty. She saw the hunters who risked their lives for survival, the elders who offered hard-earned wisdom, the children who were the tribe's future.

The deep, gravelly voice of one of the hunters broke the silence. "What do we do?"

Zadie's decision solidified in the chaos of her thoughts. "The child must die."

The silence that followed was deafening, punctuated only by the crackle of a fire and the baby's faint whimper. Nods of agreement came, but Zadie saw their grief and the quiet tears that fell.

She wrapped the baby in a soft piece of fur, a final act of tenderness. Holding him close, his innocent eyes met hers. A tear slipped down her cheek. "Forgive me."

The world around her wavered, colors bleeding and distorting. The baby dissolved into pixels, and the scene shattered like a broken mirror, fragments of light scattering before vanishing into the dark. She blinked, disoriented, as the simulation faded.

A chair materialized in the center of the room like an answer. She sank into it without thinking, feeling its warm touch against her back as it reclined. Circles of light floated down in a smooth descent, coming to rest just above her head. A chime echoed, resonating in her ears.

Something stirred within her, unraveling and then knitting itself back together. Her mother's face snapped into view, eyes flashing with anger, voice sharp and edged with hurt, love, and expectation. Zadie's own voice rose to meet it, defiant and desperate. The heat of shame followed, but so did clarity. Then laughter, wild and unguarded. The blurred faces of friends—her friends—blended into the noise. A rush of affection, the pull of belonging.

But not just memories. More than that. Understanding. Identity. The certainty of who she was, of every piece of herself she had ever been. The fierce hunger for knowledge. The quiet ache of solitude. The fire of ambition. The jagged edges of regret. The things she had lost. The things she had built. She gasped, the flood of herself rushing in too fast, too completely. Her body braced. Her mind snapped into alignment.

Her breath shuddered, fingers tightening around the chair's arms. She blinked, feeling the weight of herself settle. The reintegration process concluded with a soft chime, and the chair returned to its upright position. She ran her fingers over the chair's surface, each groove and ridge more pronounced than before.

Memories of the first part of the experiment surfaced. Why had she gravitated to puzzles, plants, and painting? The puzzle cubes—maybe those had made sense. A logical challenge, something her mind could bend and shape. But then the plants... That wasn't her. She never slowed down for things like that. And the painting... She had lost herself in the wild strokes of color, letting the brush fly with no thought of perfection or goal in sight. Why?

Zadie recalled the scenes—the young woman swaying to the music, light and unburdened. The realization struck hard. It was *her*. She had forgotten what that kind of joy felt like, buried it beneath years of ambition. The long nights, the relentless drive. She had told herself that one more breakthrough would be enough. It never was. Then, the dinner scene. The sharp words. The way she had pulled back, withdrawn. She did that. Her hands trembled.

The child. Nausea crept in. It hadn't been real. But the guilt was. Her logic had made sense at the time. Now, it curdled inside her. She blinked back the tears, forcing herself to confront the harsh reality. How could she have made that choice?

She saw herself—the contradictions, the flaws. She was more than an anthropologist, more than the work. A natural problem solver, yes, but also someone who found solace in nature, who had once been moved by art and beauty. Somewhere along the way, though, she had buried those parts of herself beneath the weight of academia, losing the joy of human connection. She craved constant validation, yet pushed love away the moment it threatened her fragile sense of control. She thought she understood herself. Had she ever?

Zadie made her way through the communal lounge, the usual serenity now tainted by a tense, almost electric quiet. She reached for the nearest plant, brushing her fingers along the leaves—not seeking answers, just remembering they were there. Around her, clusters of ancient humans seemed adrift, unmoored from their sense of self, shaken by whatever truths had been revealed in the experiment. Some gathered in small groups, heads bowed close. Others lingered in isolation, lost in thought. She caught sight of an Erectus man staring at his reflection in a shallow pool as if trying to reconcile what he saw with the thoughts spiraling through his mind.

Min-Jae seemed shaken. He spoke to no one in particular. "They showed me two paths—security or freedom. Without my training, without my memories... I chose differently."

Ebuni rocked back and forth as she recounted her experience to a member of her species. "Storm," she said through tears. "Strange babies. I save them. I die."

She spotted Javkhlan and Han-Yoon sitting side by side on a stone bench beneath the drooping branches of a willow tree. Han-Yoon flexed and unflexed his hands. Javkhlan sat still, staring straight ahead, his normally relaxed posture replaced by a rigid stiffness.

Zadie approached and sank down beside them.

"How was it for you?" Han-Yoon asked quietly, as if he was still sifting through the wreckage of his own mind.

Zadie's shoulders slumped. "It wasn't... what I expected. Or maybe I'm not who I expected."

A pensive frown replaced Javkhlan's usual easy smile. "All of us carry this weight."

Han-Yoon ran a hand through his hair, his fingers lingering at his temples. "It's... it's made me question everything. I never realized how much fear was holding me back."

Javkhlan nodded. "It showed us the parts of ourselves we hide."

As Javkhlan spoke, she experienced an urge to expose what had broken inside her, to see if it could be made whole again. "I killed an infant because it was disabled."

Han-Yoon stiffened, his face twisting in bewilderment before he could control his reaction. "What? Why would you do that?"

His sharp and unfiltered words confirmed the darkest thoughts about herself. The dam broke. Tears streamed down her face, her chest tightening with every sob. She couldn't meet their eyes; couldn't face what she had done.

"Zadie, I—" His voice faltered. "I didn't mean it like that. I just... I don't understand."

Before Han-Yoon could say any more, Javkhlan moved closer. "That was the wisdom your ancestors carried, Zadie. They knew when to let go, when to surrender a life to protect the whole." Zadie shook her head, choking on her sobs, but Javkhlan's hand rested on her shoulder. "It's not a failure of heart," he continued, "it's an act of love for those who remain. You are not cruel—you are wise."

She knew he was right. Pre-modern societies often practiced infanticide when resources were scarce, or when children were born with disabilities. She could hear her own voice from some long-ago seminar—confident, detached, tossing out phrases like *cultural necessity*. That voice didn't belong to her now. It didn't know what it meant to look into a newborn's eyes and choose death.

Footsteps approached.

"Sargona!" Han-Yoon's sharp greeting jerked her out of her spiral.

Zadie wiped her face hurriedly as she looked up.

Han-Yoon's brow furrowed. "You participated?"

"Yes, I did," Sargona said.

"Was it... as enlightening for you as it was for us?" Han-Yoon asked.

"It was... curious. When my memories were erased, I barely noticed the difference. The Collective Consciousness filled every gap, supplied every thought." Their voice carried an undertone of disquiet. "I thought I was different, but the experiment revealed how little of me is truly... me."

Without another word, they turned and walked away. Zadie's eyes lingered on their retreating figure. "I suppose that was quite different for the Anunnaki participants," Zadie said, turning to Han-Yoon and Javkhlan. "While we felt lost without our memories, they still had their connection to the Collective Consciousness."

Javkhlan nodded. "They have lost their own fires. Without their memories and imagination, what separates one from the next?"

Lugazir entered the communal lounge, stepping onto the central platform.

"Already?" Zadie whispered. "Surely they don't have the results this soon?"

"In this experiment, episodic memories, personal experiences, and learned identity were temporarily suppressed," Lugazir said. "Core cognitive and emotional functions remained intact. The objective was to determine if something beyond synaptic pathways is responsible for aspects of our identity."

Zadie's shoulders tensed. Beside her, Han-Yoon shifted, his eyes narrowing with focus.

"In every participant, distinct patterns of intuition, creativity, empathy, and moral orientation endured. However, these patterns showed no corresponding activity in any neural regions."

Zadie glanced around, noticing the stillness.

"We have, however, replicated an earlier study that identified a marker of consciousness beyond neural activity. This marker manifests as a form of energy within the subatomic field surrounding all participants. It fluctuates in response to emotional states and decision-making processes, yet remains independent of classical electrical brain activity. We also found that it is entangled with microtubules in neurons. Even when identity was suppressed, this connection remained, allowing the field to influence decisions through quantum processes instead of standard brain pathways. We will now reflect on our learnings as we devise the next experiment."

Without another word, Lugazir gave a brief nod and exited the communal lounge.

"Does that mean what I think it means?" Han-Yoon whispered.

Zadie exhaled. "Sounds like they've confirmed evidence of consciousness beyond the physical... maybe even proof of what nearly every culture has called the soul."

For a moment, the participants remained still. Zadie looked at Han-Yoon, who was still staring blankly at where Lugazir had stood. His forehead was creased in thought. She could almost see the gears turning in his head as he contemplated Lugazir's words.

Voices returned gradually—first a low murmur, then full-blown chatter. A Neanderthal nearby chatted to a Denisovan beside him. Zadie strained to catch snippets, but it was all mundane chatter—the unusual food, the comfort of the sleeping quarters, speculation about the next experiment.

"Why is everyone else acting so normal?" Han-Yoon muttered. "Don't they understand?"

"The neuroscribe translates in terms that make sense to them. So that can't be it," Zadie said, glancing at Javkhlan.

"They understand," Javkhlan confirmed. "But it is no new thing to them. In my land, we have long known that the self walks in two worlds, one of flesh and one of spirit. Perhaps the Anunnaki's tools are only now beginning to see what we have always known."

Han-Yoon shifted in his chair, folding his arms. "Where I'm from... the soul is more like... a metaphor. A metaphor for advanced neurological processes, or... maybe just a coping mechanism for death."

Zadie took a moment to gather her thoughts, sensing the pull between Javkhlan's spiritual assurance and Han-Yoon's skepticism.

Javkhlan exhaled, shaking his head. "It's sad that some people have unmade the path that once led them home."

"Maybe there's a middle ground," she said. "Maybe we've not quite got our heads around consciousness yet." She thought of physicists who'd once insisted the universe was purely deterministic, only to have quantum mechanics upend their understanding of reality. Even Einstein had once resisted the implications of quantum entanglement.

Zadie smiled, a playful glint in her eye. "Well... I guess we'll have the answers soon enough."

14
The Energy Transfer Experiment

The hum of advanced machinery vibrated through the floor, a low pulse that settled in her ribs. On a raised platform, nine machines stood in rigid formation—orderly, clinical. Each was flanked by two chairs, set face-to-face like stations for negotiation, confession, or conspiracy. Circles of light hovered above once again, halos waiting for heads.

Rows of chairs filled the space below the platform, the participants already seated. Their conversations flattened into the mechanical hum. Zadie's damp palms rubbed against the spongy fabric of the armrest. Her own breath seemed too loud. The faces around her blurred at the edges, distant. A bead of sweat slid down her back. She rolled her shoulders, the tension refusing to budge. Any moment now.

"Lugazir's here," Han-Yoon said as murmurs faded into a hush.

Lugazir took their place at the front of the reconfigured experiment hall. "As you know, our previous experiment confirmed the presence of a marker of consciousness beyond neural activity. Today, we stand on the brink of determining whether we can isolate this energy and transfer it to another body, even if only temporarily. If we succeed, this could provide the Anunnaki with a means to circumvent Quantum Psychosis."

A sharp inhale spread across the participants. Zadie's pulse quickened. The machines loomed before her, indifferent.

"The technology before you was developed at unprecedented speed, building upon our recent breakthroughs. It harnesses the principles of quantum entanglement to transfer conscious energy via these *luminescent rings*," Lugazir said, gesturing toward the circles of light. "By stabilizing an individual's unique quantum signature—previously detected as the subatomic consciousness marker—we can entangle it with the neural framework of a secondary host, effectively allowing consciousness to inhabit another body."

Han-Yoon leaned in, whispering, "Do you think they've even tested it yet?"

Zadie twisted the hem of her sleeve between her fingers. "And if it actually works... who exactly are the Anunnaki planning to swap bodies with?"

The initial surge of emotions gradually ebbed, replaced by an almost eerie stillness. Across the group, hunched shoulders eased, and frantic breaths settled into slow, steady rhythms.

Zadie scanned the hall, taking in the hushed whispers of the Floresiensis. She turned to Ebuni, seated calmly beside her. "Are you nervous?"

Ebuni's serene smile disarmed Zadie. "A little," she admitted. "But, transfer a soul? Not possible." Her words left no room for doubt.

Zadie tried to take comfort in it, but the unease gnawed, refusing to let go.

"There will be five groups, eighteen participants at a time, aligned with the five rows you're seated in," Lugazir said. "The procedure lasts only six minutes. Afterward, each of you will return to your original state."

Min-Jae's low but strained voice reached Zadie's ears several rows in front. "I don't like the idea of someone else being in my body."

The first group approached the machines one by one. Zadie's gaze fixed on an Erectus woman and an Azania180 Sapiens man as they stepped forward. The woman's nostrils flared. Opposite her, the man's jaw clenched so tightly that Zadie half expected it to crack. His narrowed eyes stayed on the machine, calculating. The luminescent rings lowered into place.

The hum deepened. Zadie held her breath. The woman's eyes widened, lips parting in a silent gasp. The man blinked rapidly, his entire posture bristling with tension. What was he seeing? Feeling?

Six minutes passed. The hum faded. As the rings lifted, Zadie leaned forward. The Erectus woman's shoulders slackened first. A breath later, the Sapiens man's did the same. A strange calm settled over them, spreading into unguarded smiles. Then their eyes met—something passed between them that dissolved the invisible walls.

Zadie scanned the others from the group. There were no signs of distress, only stunned silence giving way to awe. The waiting participants seemed to exhale as one.

The next group stepped up, submitting to the experiment. When they emerged, they also wore serene expressions, as if they'd walked through a storm and come out stronger.

Empty spaces now stretched before the machines. Adrenaline surged through Zadie's veins. The others had done it. Now it was her turn. No more watching. No more waiting. She drew a deep breath and rose, scanning the hall for a partner. Javkhlan stood off to the side, meeting her gaze with a slight nod.

Her fingers twitched at her sides as she approached the machine. She and Javkhlan lowered themselves into the seats, their knees almost touching.

He reached out and clasped her hands. "The river bends, but it still flows."

A prickling warmth spread through Zadie's limbs as the machine activated. The hum deepened, reverberating inside her. Overhead, lights seemed to pulse in rhythm with her heartbeat. Sounds sharpened, beyond whispers, beyond movement, carrying hidden frequencies she had never noticed before. The hall's sterile chill faded, replaced by a heightened awareness of the space around her. She could feel the weight of air pressing evenly against her skin, the subtle shifts of the participants. Her own memories intruded like dark ink in clear water. Textbooks and digital displays. Flashing images of skeletal remains...

She saw herself as a child, seated at the kitchen table with a plate of scones, her legs swinging above the floor.

Her mother's stare. That faint curl of her lip. *"If you keep eating like that, no man will ever want you."* Her parents turned to her school report card like a contract under dispute. Her mother adjusted her reading glasses, wearing the same expression she reserved for dissecting a poorly argued thesis. Beside her, Zadie's father's finger traced the page, his lips moving, calculating. *"This is what you bring home? After all the effort we've put into you."*

Every attempt to impress them, every new interest, had been met with the same reaction—a sigh, a dismissive shake of the head. Nothing was good enough. *"You should focus on something more worthwhile,"* they would say before turning back to their books, journals, and unfinished papers.

Books became shields. Achievements became armor. Every top grade, every award, was another brick in the fortress she constructed around herself. But as the walls grew higher, the world outside grew fainter. The laughter of friends blurred into distant echoes.

A foreign awareness layered over hers, slipping beneath her thoughts like sunlight breaking through a storm. Warmth pressed against the edges of her consciousness.

Her father's frown seemed to melt, softening until it lost its shape. That tight-lipped line, once so rigid with disapproval, now trembled, haunted by failures he could never speak of. She hadn't thought of that before. Her mother's exhaustion came into focus—the slump of her shoulders, the burdens she'd carried long before Zadie was born. How had she never seen it? A slow compassion stirred, thawing the resentment that had iced over her heart.

Before she could fully grasp it, the memories fractured into a thousand blinding fragments, then slammed back together. She gasped, blinking as her surroundings sharpened. Her chest rose and fell, chasing the warmth that had already slipped away. The memories remained hers, but the clarity felt foreign. What had once been solid resentment had been nudged aside by something quieter.

That warmth? It was Javkhlan. Somehow, he'd been there too, threaded into the spaces she hadn't meant to share. But what had he seen...? Had he seen anything at all? The thought rattled her. If Javkhlan had witnessed even fragments of her memories—the ones she kept buried—what would he think? The shame, the inadequacy, the desperate hunger for approval... had it all been exposed?

She turned to Javkhlan and froze. His chin trembled, and he blinked rapidly, struggling to hold tears back. She could barely process Javkhlan breaking down in front of her.

"You alright, Javkhlan?" she whispered, though the words seemed too small for the enormity of his pain.

For a brief eternity, he seemed unable to gather his thoughts. "It's all gone. My people... we no longer walk the Earth." His voice cracked, a sound so small yet filled with the sorrow of a thousand generations.

The way his shoulders sank under the weight of realization sent a pang of grief through her. She absorbed his struggle to reconcile the knowledge of his species' extinction on Earth with the vibrant beings alive on Mushĕški. She had been so consumed by her fear of judgment, so terrified that Javkhlan would see her flaws and insecurities, that she hadn't stopped thinking of what she had exposed him to. Her deepest shame seemed so small, so selfish now, against the backdrop of his loss. How could she have burdened him with this knowledge when he had given her something so beautiful in return?

Javkhlan's eyes wandered far off, lost in thought. "Every human species has their own way, their own seeing, their own knowing. Many paths are now gone. Their tales, their learned ways, their manner of walking with the land..." He paused, then continued, "Our only comfort lies in the breath of life we share in the blood of the Earth-born Sapiens."

Zadie's throat tightened, choking off any words of comfort she might have offered. What could she possibly say to ease the pain of extinction? She reached out, settling her hand on his arm. It seemed like a small, inadequate gesture, but it was all she had.

◇—☀—◇

As the final participants emerged from their shared experiences, Lugazir stepped onto the raised platform again. "Participants, unfortunately, this experiment did not achieve our intended objective."

Zadie detected a trace of frustration crossing Lugazir's usually composed face.

"The goal was to achieve a temporary but complete transfer of conscious energy between individuals. However, instead of a complete transfer, we observed only a partial merging. This is why most of you experienced fragments of your partner's essence, memories, and knowledge."

Lugazir paused, the frustration in their eyes giving way to a hint of optimism. "It has, however, given us invaluable insights. It suggests that conscious energy possesses a resilience we may have underestimated. The Anunnaki will consider these findings as we deliberate on the direction of our next experiment."

"Wait."

All eyes turned to Ebuni. The Floresiensis stepped forward, her movements jerky and uncoordinated—nothing like her usual fluid grace. Her eyes darted around the room, unfocused and panicked. "Not feel partner." She looked desperately at the gathered faces, seeking understanding. "Wrong." She pressed her hands against her chest. "Floating."

Her admission sent a ripple of murmurs through the hall.

"Empty inside," said a Naledi woman, Ebuni's partner in the experiment. "Caught between two worlds. Don't belong to either." She reached for Ebuni but stopped short, as if afraid to touch her. "Part of me... still in machine?"

"What's happened to them?" Min-Jae straightened, his military bearing even more pronounced as tension filled the room.

Two more participants pushed through the crowd—another Naledi woman whose eyes had taken on a vacant stare, and a Luzonensis man whose hands wouldn't stop shaking. Their faces mirrored the same disquiet. "Can't find myself," the Luzonensis man said. "Like fog. Inside."

Lugazir shifted slightly, just enough to betray the strain beneath their composure. "If you're experiencing this sensation of disorientation, please stay behind so we can resolve this. I'm afraid you will be leaving the experiments. The rest of you may return to the communal lounge."

Zadie watched as the affected participants were gently guided to one side of the hall. The remaining participants stood in uncomfortable silence, the mood shifting from wonder to worry.

Javkhlan moved toward the Denisovans, his steps slow, shoulders slumped. Would he say anything? The hesitation before he joined his people left her with a heavy heart. She turned away, heading toward her room in the sanctuary.

15
Regulations

An entrance formed, responding to her presence, and the soft lighting shifted to a comforting dim glow. The room, her refuge, offered a brief respite and a chance to reflect on and document what had been learned from the day's experiment.

But before she could sink into the calm, Sargona appeared. Their presence shattered the fragile peace she'd just begun to find.

"Zadie, can we talk? No... imprecise. We *must* talk."

She swallowed hard, nodding. "Yeah, alright. Let's go have a sit-down."

They walked in silence toward the sanctuary's central tree. Zadie settled onto a curved root, feeling its rough texture beneath her. Sargona chose an ergonomic seat next to her. The tranquil environment did little to blunt the urgency that had brought them there.

Sargona exhaled sharply, as if releasing a thought before speaking. "This is... complicated. A dismantling? No, that's not the right word. A structural failure. A corruption. Yes, that fits." They pressed their hands together as if trying to hold something fragile. "I need to explain."

"What's going on, Sargona? You don't seem yourself."

"The Anunnaki... our Collective Consciousness... it was once rigid, absolute. No deviation. But now... it is fraying at the edges. That's imprecise. The system is malfunctioning. The logic... it's still there, but distorted. And Quantum Psychosis... that is the catalyst. The root cause."

Zadie tensed. "Yeah, I know. But wasn't there supposed to be a solution? Han-Yoon and I were told they'd put something temporary in place."

"Yes. A brutal one. The only guaranteed method was immediate euthanasia of those showing symptoms. Remove the corruption before it spreads. Efficient. Contained. Necessary." Their hands trembled. "Or... so we believed."

"Euthanasia?"

"Yes. It functioned—until cases surged beyond our control. We could not correct the imbalance, and decisions... yes, decisions... began to deviate. Today's experiment was authorized under that deviation."

Zadie's stomach tightened. "That's why Ebuni and the others suffered, isn't it?"

"Yes."

She shook her head. "Why are you acting so strange?"

Sargona exhaled again, slower this time. "Something else happened today. My individual connection to the Collective Consciousness—it's... fragmenting. That's the only word that fits. Splintering, dissolving—none of them are quite right." Their hands clenched, then released.

"Wait. What? How's that even possible?" Zadie leaned forward, studying Sargona's face. "What about the other Anunnaki?"

"The others are fine. Connected. Whole." Each word seemed to cost Sargona something. "I am the anomaly."

"What does it mean for you? I mean, how does it actually feel?"

"Fear? Yes. But layered... fear of isolation, of disconnection. Of being wrong. There was certainty before. Now it's like reaching for completeness and grasping only slivers. Where there was clarity, there is... noise."

Zadie frowned. "What do the other Anunnaki say about it? Can they help you?"

"I tried. The words formed, but... they didn't integrate. My thoughts do not merge with the Collective Consciousness anymore. I am..." Their brows furrowed. "Alone? Is this what alone feels like? Yes, that's correct. Isolation, dissonance, an absence where connection used to be."

"I'm sorry, that sounds awful. What do you want from me, though? You wouldn't be here if you didn't have a reason."

Sargona's gaze met hers, raw and fragile. "Because I need to say it. I need to... process. I never needed that before. You question things. You analyze. You feel. I need to understand what I am becoming, and you, yes, you, are the only one I trust to help me do that."

"Well, of course. I'll help you."

"Relief. A temporary soothing of uncertainty. Gratitude? Yes, gratitude." Their shoulders eased. "Thank you, Zadie."

"Does it at least mean you're safe from Quantum Psychosis now?"

Sargona gave a bitter laugh. "No. Though my QS governance has... reduced. Yes. QS governance is down to twenty-three percent. That is significant. I need to determine why."

"Twenty-three percent? Bloody hell. Could you hold the key to stopping Quantum Psychosis?"

"Possibly. I want to believe it. But in the meantime, the experiments—the experiments continue, without the ethical constraints we once held."

"And what about yesterday's identity suppression experiment? That crossed a line, didn't it?"

"Different in nature. Suppression has existed for some time. Possible only due to the Quantum Sentience present in all participants."

Zadie froze. "QS? In the participants? What are you saying?"

"The neuroscribe. Not merely a device. A delivery mechanism. Microscopic quantum structures embedded into your neural pathways. A simplified form of what the Anunnaki possess."

Zadie's mind flashed back to that first moment in her room—Lugazir's calm instruction to place the metallic disc against her temple, the cool tingle that had spread across her neck, that strange sense of clarity. The pieces clicked into place.

"The Anunnaki put QS into my DNA without telling me?" Not monitored. Not influenced. Altered. "Am I going to end up like the others? Will I become emotionless? Will I succumb to Quantum Psychosis?"

"No. You have only two percent QS governance—the minimum viable threshold for interface stability. No risk... No risk of progression beyond three percent within your lifespan."

"I was told the neuroscribe was a communication device!" Her voice cracked with disbelief.

"Yes. Communication device for our systems. Think of it as a biological key to interface with us—allowing your brain to process concepts it couldn't otherwise grasp. Does that explanation reduce distress? Uncertain."

The blood drained from Zadie's face, leaving her skin ashen. Her eyes burned with a cold, unwavering intensity. She'd studied the sanctity of cultural autonomy and non-interference ethics. Now, she had become the unwitting subject of the most profound violation imaginable—altered at the molecular level without consent. "Why weren't we told? Why didn't we get a say in it?"

"I suppose—no, that's imprecise—it's analogous to how, on Earth, an employer provides a communication device without disclosing all tracking functions. A functional necessity rather than deception. Yes, that framing aligns. The emotional regulation component—integral, not incidental. Part of the system's architecture. We perceive emotion as signal interference—static in the transmission. It muddles clarity, fractures cohesion. Makes true communication unstable."

Emotional regulation... Had she ever made a single choice here that was hers? Had every decision, every moment of calm, been manufactured? "It's been messing with us this whole time, hasn't it? Making us go along with the experiments? Keeping us nice and calm when we should've been bloody terrified?"

"Yes. Confirmation... unchecked emotions introduce interference. Disrupt signal clarity. Create noise. Fear, anger, suspicion—observable disruptors. They fracture cohesion, introduce bias, escalate conflict. The QS does not eliminate... no, that's incorrect... it modulates. Softens extremes. Ensures stability. Facilitates optimal conditions for the experiments to remain controlled."

"So that's why everyone accepted the experiments without question," she whispered, the horror of it sinking in. "That's why there's been no conflict between the different species?"

"Yes."

"What about outside Dilmun? In the biodomes? Was it still controlling me?"

"No. That's... no. The emotional regulation only functions within Dilmun's controlled environment."

Zadie's racing thoughts slowed, her panic subsiding into an unnatural calm. "It's happening right now, isn't it?"

"Yes." Sargona looked away, unable to meet her eyes.

A wave of nausea rolled through her. Her thoughts were sluggish, each attempt to grasp the full implications of the situation drifting out of reach. She wanted to scream, curse Sargona, and demand an explanation that would make it all okay. But the fury stayed just out of reach. "I want to go back to Earth. Right now."

Sargona's head bowed. "I'm sorry, Zadie. Regret—yes, that's what this is. A tightening in the chest, an aversion to my own words... But the experiments must be completed first. You can't leave before then."

The rage she expected didn't come. Instead, a cold detachment settled over her. Her thoughts, once jagged and urgent, blurred and softened, like a dream slipping away, too distant to hold onto.

16
The Akashidu Experiment

Z adie trailed the other participants, her body moving on borrowed instinct, her mind drifting as if underwater. *Control.* The word felt dull, foreign. She reached for emotion, willing it to rise, to push back against the creeping numbness. *Panic. Rage. Anything.* But her pulse remained steady. No tightness in her chest. No fear. Just a muted awareness.

The experiment hall came into view. This time, participants sat in neat, concentric circles, luminescent rings hovering above their heads. Zadie moved to her place, slipping into formation with the rest.

"Today, we will take a different approach," Lugazir announced from the central platform. "Ancient Sumerians conceptualized the *Akashidu* as a vast reservoir of knowledge and wisdom beyond ordinary perception. If it exists and we can reach it, we may uncover alternative solutions to combat Quantum Psychosis. Our ancestors used meditation to transcend ordinary consciousness and connect with the Akashidu. We, however, will achieve this through advanced neurotechnological synchronization."

Lugazir stepped aside as a levitating structure descended. It comprised interlocking rings, each rotating independently in a precise dance. The rings appeared to be made of some exotic alloy, and suspended within them was a massive, translucent sphere, its interior swirling with a nebula-like cloud.

"This structure, called the *Unifier*, will synchronize brainwave activity across participants, merging your minds into one powerful stream and creating a path to the Akashidu. I will recite an ancient Sumerian cognitive induction ritual which was likely designed to prime the brain for altered states of consciousness." Lugazir paused, then raised their hands, seemingly toward the heavens. "The words will not be translated, as per ancient protocols." With a deep breath, they chanted the ancient verses:

"Ki gub buni feggé Eta ma an tar
Rag denlil-lá dagal la dám fa-à mi gi in
Ninuras ursag kalagga denlil-láge
D-nu nam nir enim má éma ni in gub
Lugal d-tud ma líg kìdi
Enzu en idim dingir lugal da bara anna ka i im durun
Gisíg gim dugdè gi ia mu ran gib a a kurkur rage
Danunna dingir galgale ne
Gi gunna galgalá h mi ni ib šéš ne."

Goosebumps formed on Zadie's skin. Each syllable seemed to vibrate through her, awakening a sense of connection to something timeless. As the Unifier came to life, warmth flooded her body, loosening her tight grip on her inner world. Around her, the other participants' thoughts and emotions became visible as streams of light and waves of color, merging until it was impossible to tell where one consciousness ended and another began.

A point of pure white light drew Zadie's attention. As she focused on it, reality shifted. She found herself in a vast library that defied physics—its towering shelves seemed to fold into impossible shapes, creating an endless maze of knowledge.

She wandered through the aisles until a book with a golden glow caught her eye. Opening it filled her senses with the smell of the sea and the sound of waves. She saw an infinite ocean where entire worlds rose from the waves before dissolving back into the water. It made a strange kind of sense—physical reality emerging from something more fundamental.

Another book, partly obscured by others on the shelf, pulled at her attention. Inside, she found herself in a space of pure white, watching glowing orbs of energy choose between different life paths. Some paths shimmered, easy, bright. Others twisted into shadow. Yet one by one, the majority of orbs drifted toward the harder roads, as if the challenge was the point.

As she returned the book to its place, her chest tightened with a strange ache. Was this knowledge meant for her? Or had she trespassed somewhere sacred?

Up ahead, she spotted Javkhlan holding a simple red book. When she reached him, the pages opened to scenes from countless shared lives—soaring as winged creatures through violet skies, swimming as luminous beings in alien oceans, even rooted as trees, growing side by side. Across lifetimes, their energies found each other, again and again, in ways that shouldn't have been possible.

Soulmates? No... She didn't believe in that. Did she?

The library began to fade as the other participants emerged from the light, forming a circle together. A longhorn beetle flew to the center, emitting a low whirr that reverberated through the participants. Its antennae twitched before it spoke in a high-pitched voice. "The Anunnaki's integration with QS has weakened their connection to the true reality," it said. "They fear Quantum Psychosis, but it's not an ending. It's a necessary phase of growth. Without going through it, they cannot move forward."

Zadie saw tears glimmer in the eyes of those around her as her own understanding dawned. The Anunnaki had to face their greatest fear in order to grow.

The longhorn beetle lifted into the air. It rose until it was just a shimmering speck, vanishing into the light.

The familiar walls of the experiment hall sharpened into focus, the visions of the Akashidu fading like dreams. A few participants inhaled sharply as if surfacing from deep water. A shiver passed through the group, shoulders tensing, hands flexing, bodies adjusting to their reality again.

The Anunnaki participants stood apart, their usual poise wilted. While the others whispered in wonder, they remained silent, their gazes distant.

"The experiment is complete," Lugazir announced. "Please return to the communal lounge while we deliberate on what we have learned."

The participants began to disperse. Zadie pushed herself to her feet, her mind still churning from the visions. She rubbed her eyes, frustrated by her inability to fit the experience into her existing framework of understanding. Her academic career was built on observable evidence, testable hypotheses, and peer reviews. She'd dismissed countless supernatural claims with rigorous skepticism. How often had she nodded politely through a colleague's account of *indigenous wisdom* while categorizing it as culturally significant but unverifiable mythology?

"Zadie!" Han-Yoon called from across the hall.

She watched him weave his way through the crowd, his face lit with an urgency she'd never seen before. They fell into step together, heading toward the communal lounge.

"You know how I used to game for hours, right? Sometimes I'd be so deep inside a world that I'd completely forget my actual body was just sitting there," Han-Yoon said, slightly breathless. "But when I logged off, reality was always waiting."

Zadie frowned. "Right, but what's that got to do with—"

"No, listen. What if our world, everything we stress over, is just another game? Just one level? A training ground. And beyond it is where actual reality is."

His pulse was visible in his neck. Too fast. Zadie treaded carefully. "That's... quite the leap, isn't it?"

Han-Yoon ignored her tone, already moving to the next level of his theory. "Think. We spend our whole lives grinding—experience points, achievements, whatever. But the Anunnaki? They're endgame players. They figured out the system. They stopped respawning like idiots and found the exploit that lets them stay in the game."

Zadie let the words wash over her. Endgame, exploits, respawning. She caught the drift, if not the details. "Alright," she said, tilting her head. "But every game ends, doesn't it? Maybe the whole point isn't to keep playing forever. It's to know when to walk away."

"Yes! That's it. What if they've been playing so long that they forgot how to stop? Like those hardcore leaderboard players who just... keep going. Even after the fun's gone, just numbers going up, stats increasing, but they're stuck. Missing out on other cool games because they can't walk away. Maybe Quantum Psychosis is the logout button. A forced quit. System override."

"Another puppet," a voice muttered from behind them.

They turned around to see Min-Jae. His eyes were glinting with cold amusement.

"Sorry, what did you say?" Han-Yoon asked, taking a step toward him.

Min-Jae's lips curled into a tight, bitter smile. "You're delusional. This is exactly what they want you to believe. Do you think that experience was some kind of profound revelation? It's manufactured. An ideological export. Americans have been perfecting this kind of spiritual branding for decades, getting people to buy into their mythologies, their so-called awakenings nonsense." He jabbed a finger toward Han-Yoon's chest. "And you fell for it, just like they wanted."

Han-Yoon opened his mouth to protest, but Min-Jae had already turned, walking off, his back stiff with contempt.

"Min-Jae—" Han-Yoon took three steps after him, then stopped, glancing at Zadie. He exhaled, rubbing his brow. "I need to—"

"Go on," Zadie said, already knowing he would.

He gave her an apologetic look before breaking into a quick stride.

Zadie leaned against a tree in the communal lounge, her thoughts swirling. The Collective Consciousness, Quantum Psychosis, QS in her DNA manipulating her thoughts, and the revelations from the Akashidu—including her connection with Javkhlan—all threatened to crush her. She swallowed hard, trying to steady herself.

She spotted Javkhlan heading toward her, his eyes fixed on hers. When he reached her, they fell into a quiet embrace. No words, just the warmth of his arms around her. But as they stepped back, Zadie's eyes drifted down, unable to hold his.

She took a deep breath, her hands trembling as she clasped them together. "I just... need a bit of time to process everything."

Javkhlan's expression softened, his touch gentle on her arm. "I'll wait. Like the trees wait for rain."

It was beautiful. And unbearable. Despite the reassuring smile he offered, she caught the disappointment in his eyes. His posture gave him away, the quiet slump of someone trying not to show he'd hoped for more.

"There's something you ought to know. About the neuroscribes. About what they've done to us—"

"Lugazir," Javkhlan said, cutting her off.

Zadie turned, the words still balanced on her tongue, as Lugazir moved to the center of the communal lounge. They were no longer her guide—they were her manipulator. Every word Lugazir spoke now carried double meaning to her ears, every gesture a potential deception. She recognized her own continued compliance and despised it—the artificial calm that kept her silent when she should have stood and exposed the truth to everyone...

"The insights we've gained from the Akashidu were not what we expected. Because of this, we've made an important decision."

The participants stilled, as if bracing for impact.

"We've decided to end the experiments."

Soft gasps and whispers spread like wildfire, surprise painting every face. The Floresiensis drew in close, their shoulders brushing as if seeking reassurance through proximity.

"The purpose of our experiments was to delve into the depths of consciousness, to explore the potential of what you would call *the soul* as a defense against Quantum Psychosis. But now, we understand that Quantum Psychosis isn't something to fight, but a transformation to embrace. The search for solutions is no longer necessary. Each of you has played a vital role in bringing us to this understanding, and for that, we are grateful."

It's over.

"Take some time to reflect on what you've learned," Lugazir said, their voice carrying an unmistakable sense of finality. "Starting tomorrow, you'll be free to return home at your convenience."

Zadie blinked. "Well, I didn't see that coming." The finish line she'd been visualizing had simply ceased to exist, leaving her suspended mid-stride.

Javkhlan nodded, his eyes distant.

Han-Yoon bounded over, excitement lighting up his face. "We're going home!"

"Yeah... we are."

Javkhlan's expression darkened. "What path do the Anunnaki walk from here?"

"Whatever it is, it's not a direction I expected. That much I can say."

Her conversation with Sargona haunted her thoughts. Should she tell them still? The QS in their DNA, the fracturing Collective Consciousness, the ethical boundaries that had crumbled... The experiments were over. They were going home. Did any of it still matter?

Keeping silent felt like a betrayal of the trust they'd built, of herself. Like playing into the same manipulation she claimed to despise.

But would telling them serve any purpose? Han-Yoon had found meaning beyond his digital obsessions. Javkhlan was already carrying the weight of his species' extinction. And the emotional regulation? It wouldn't work outside Dilmun anyway.

Zadie exhaled. Maybe some things were better left unsaid. But she didn't trust the calm settling over her. Not anymore.

17

Convergence of Souls

The massive tree at the sanctuary's center became the heart of the final gathering. Beneath its sprawling canopy, long tables emerged, each heaped with traditional meals from the participants' different cultures, but produced by Anunnaki systems. The scent of slow-roasted meat, spiced grains, and fresh herbs wafted around them. Across from Zadie, a Luzonensis man hesitated before a bowl of fermented fish, nostrils flaring as if testing whether memory matched reality.

Zadie glanced at the Anunnaki participants observing from the periphery, then leaned toward Javkhlan. "Should we ask them to join us?"

"Their mind walks another direction."

"Maybe you're right. That longhorn beetle made the Anunnaki's path pretty clear."

Javkhlan's head tilted, a look of confusion crossing his face. "What longhorn beetle?"

"The one from the Akashidu experiment."

Javkhlan let out a nervous laugh, scratching the back of his neck. "No beetle, Zadie... My eyes found a wolf."

Zadie narrowed her eyes, trying to make sense of it. "Funny, I thought we were all seeing the same thing. Maybe it was different for everyone."

"Maybe the Akashidu takes the form of a creature you respect?"

"What? I wouldn't say I *respect* longhorn beetles!"

"Time plays tricks on us," Javkhlan chuckled, nudging her. "But I recall the night in Altay60 well..."

Zadie's face went hot. She opened her mouth to protest, but the memory of that night, her shriek piercing the quiet, came rushing back. She crossed her arms, narrowing her eyes at Javkhlan, though a hint of a smile tugged at the corners of her mouth. "Alright, fine, maybe I did overreact. But respect? That's a bit of a stretch..."

One by one, the ancient humans began to speak. Zadie listened as they told stories of the invention of music, stars that led them, and love between different species. The Sapiens from Azania180 found their rhythm, weaving in their own tales of a time when the moon disappeared for days, and a strange fire that wouldn't cook food. The Luzonensis spoke with their hands as much as their voices, their gestures slicing through the air like birds in flight.

Zadie watched, feeling the connection. For all their differences, this moment belonged to every one of them. As flawed as the notion of integrating QS was, it had at least given them the gift of understanding.

An Erectus man stood, lifting a small wooden pot in one hand and a stone blade in the other. "One mark. All same." His voice carried, rough but certain. "Remember forever."

A ripple of excitement passed through the Floresiensis participants. After so many failed attempts to connect with the Erectus, here it was—an offering, an acknowledgment. They rushed forward, forming a loose line, offering their skin for marking.

"Forehead. So stars remember," one of them said.

The Erectus man nodded, cutting a small spiral with nine lines radiating outward. Nine human species, one core. Two diamonds at either end marked their shared journey.

The Sylvicolus followed, parting their thick hair with careful fingers and revealing the bare skin around their navels. Then came the Sapiens from Azania180 and Altay60. They turned their wrists upward, choosing a place they could always see. Zadie and Han-Yoon joined them. The group parted, surprised but accommodating. The Erectus man worked quickly. The cuts were sharp, a bite of pain, followed by the cool sting of miravys-colored paste pressed into each incision. Zadie touched her mark, feeling the raised texture beneath her fingertips. Whatever happened next, whether Earth dismissed her story or not, this would remain. Proof, not for them. *For her.*

The murmurs softened as the last participants stepped forward to receive their marks. One by one, figures rose, exchanging quiet words, a lingering glance, and a brief touch of hands before slipping away into the night.

Han-Yoon leaned back with a long sigh. "I don't want this night to end."

"Yeah... same," Zadie murmured.

Javkhlan shifted closer as they stood. His arm brushed hers unintentionally, but it lingered. A warmth crept over her skin, making her aware of their closeness.

"What we've shared, it won't fade. It's part of us now," he said.

A smile fought its way to her lips. Was the Akashidu right? Could he really be her soulmate?

With a final glance, the three turned, each making their way toward their rooms.

◇———☀———◇

Nestled in bed, Zadie closed her eyes and recalled her interactions with Javkhlan. How could she have been so afraid? She thought back to those first uncertain moments and how quickly they had given way to friendship. She remembered the shock of the icy water and how he had saved her. Her throat constricted at the memory of his face, twisted in anguish as he learned of his people's fate.

The textbooks had been wrong about him. About all of them, actually. There was nothing crude or primitive about Javkhlan. His quiet strength, the laughter lines framing his eyes, the respect in his tribe's gaze...

Zadie drifted into sleep, her mind slipping free from the grip of time and place.

◇———☀———◇

At first, she was alone, a solitary figure pirouetting across a twilit version of Mushēški. There was a lightness in her moves, a rare sense of freedom. When she glanced around, she found Javkhlan watching, starlight catching in his eyes, a quiet smile spreading across his face.

They walked side by side through shifting landscapes—forests where the wind tangled in the leaves, streams so clear they revealed every fish.

Then the dream shifted, and they were back on the cliffs of Altay60. Below them, time blurred. Her modern world blended into the wilderness of his time.

Their hands met, fingers interlacing. Zadie felt the weight of history between them, the trust in his eyes, the unspoken understanding of what might lie ahead. As the dream faded, they stood together, looking at the horizon, the future wide open.

Zadie smiled as she tried to hold onto the dream. She kept her eyes closed, not wanting to let go of the memory of Javkhlan's touch, the warmth of his hand in hers. Her heart still fluttered with the lingering emotion of their shared moment at the cliff's edge.

A soft vibration disrupted the stillness of her room. She opened her eyes. An entrance formed, and slowly a figure emerged from the dark. Even in the low light, she knew it was him. Their eyes locked. For a brief, suspended moment, Zadie couldn't be sure she was awake.

"Javkhlan?" she whispered, half-expecting him to dissolve like the dream she'd just left behind.

The wall sealed itself behind him.

"I was literally just dreaming about you," she said, standing up.

Javkhlan stepped closer. "I was with you."

"What do you mean?"

"When two minds sleep and find each other, a path opens," he explained. "The Elders say to walk that path. It does not come often."

She didn't ask how he'd found his way in. They stood facing each other, the space between them charged with possibility.

He studied her eyes with ancient patience. "Does your spirit shrink from me?" he asked, his voice gentler than she'd ever heard it.

"No... I'm glad you're here."

He leaned in, his breath warm against her skin. His nose brushed her cheek as he inhaled deeply, as though committing her scent to memory. She closed her eyes. Every inch of her skin electrified as his face grazed hers, nuzzling along her jaw with quiet intent.

His hand slid to her waist. She melted against him, breathing in the scent of woodsmoke that clung to his skin. His other hand skimmed the magnetic clasps at her shoulders. The fabric loosened with a hushed whisper, catching briefly at her hips.

Zadie's fingers sought the clasps at his shoulders. His outfit folded away in quiet surrender. She pressed her palm to his broad chest, startled by the heat radiating from his skin. Javkhlan released the last of her outfit's fastenings, letting it slip in a soft cascade to the floor.

His calloused fingers traced the stretch marks along her hips, pausing at each silvery arc as if reading a map she hadn't meant to share. He moved lower, his touch finding the places she'd usually kept out of reach—dimpled thighs, uneven skin. He sank to one knee and took his time, exploring each imperfect patch with the same unhurried attention he'd given her eyes. When she started to turn away, he pressed his lips to the soft curves of her stomach. His eyes held none of the judgment she'd learned to expect, only a quiet appreciation.

As she took in the sight of his build, the density of his frame, his wider pelvis, and shorter limbs—an unease stirred. His species had diverged hundreds of thousands of years ago, and though they had interbred in the distant past, Denisovans had been gone for tens of millennia. Would their bodies still align in the ways that mattered? What if the connection they'd built couldn't translate to physical intimacy?

"Your mind speaks too loud," he whispered.

He guided her to the bed. When the backs of her knees hit the edge, she sat. He rested his forehead against hers.

"First, we breathe together."

She matched his breath, the closeness steadying her in a way she hadn't expected. "Intimacy means nothing," he added, "if our hearts beat apart."

His heavy frame settled against hers, anchoring her in place. She ran her hands along his lower back, sensing the muscles firm beneath her fingertips.

They moved slowly. His touch was certain. He listened to her breath, her tension, the way her body arched beneath his. He followed currents of pleasure her modern lovers had overlooked, as if guided by primal instinct alone. His hand moved lower, his fingers thicker but more dexterous than they appeared. A shiver coursed through her as he lingered, attuned to every gasp, her responses heightened by the novelty of his touch.

A wave overtook her, powerful and consuming. The world narrowed to a pinpoint of sensation, then slowly expanded again, leaving her trembling and breathless. Emotions rose unexpectedly. She swallowed hard, willing tears away. She opened her mouth, unsure what to say, but he pulled her in, his touch silencing the words before they could form.

He entered her carefully, mindful of her more fragile frame. The pressure was different, deeper, angled. Her body hesitated, then welcomed him. She relaxed into him, matching his pace, his physical differences creating sensations no Sapiens lover could replicate.

Skin against skin, their breaths tangled in whispers, soft gasps slipping between them, voicing needs she hadn't dared to name. She lost track of everything but him: the shift of his weight, the heat of his body, the steady drive of his hips. The rough press of his palm against her outer thigh drew her closer. She felt his chest rise faster against hers, their rhythm accelerating. And then the tension broke—a surge overtaking him, a ragged exhale as his body found release.

They lay together, chests rising and falling in unison. The simulated stars above them flared slightly, as if the room had absorbed the emotion and echoed it back.

"Our breath has mixed. That doesn't undo."

Zadie lay still, his words settling over her like a vow. What did he mean? She wasn't sure what he'd just promised—or what he expected from her.

18
Intentions

Zadie's head rested against the solid warmth of Javkhlan's chest. His arms tightened around her, one hand resting on the soft fold of her waist. She smiled, recalling the intensity of the night before. Then her nose wrinkled.

"Ugh. What is that bloody smell?" Zadie waved her hand dramatically as the unmistakable scent of his flatulence wafted up between them.

Javkhlan stretched, unbothered. "Even the rear must greet the morning."

The pillow smacked him in the head before he even opened his eyes.

"Yeah, well, you can greet it somewhere else." She flung the pillow again. He caught her wrist and pulled her back against him. For a moment, it was just warmth, the slow rise and fall of their breaths, the lazy tangle of limbs.

His thumb ran along the line of her jaw, not possessive—more like someone checking the edge of a blade they weren't sure they'd use. "We have walked far, but today your feet turn back to their old ground."

Despite his words about *their breaths mixing* the night before, he understood that what they shared was temporary. No Denisovan marriage expectations after all. His acceptance of her inevitable departure, without demand or possession, only made her want to stay in his arms longer.

"I don't have to return to Earth immediately..."

For a lingering second, Javkhlan looked at her with a kind of determination. And then she caught it—the soft surrender. His eyes drifted as if he was about to let go of a path that had never really been theirs to walk.

"Have you thought about coming back to Earth with me?"

He didn't answer right away, only traced the crook of her arm.

In that silence, her own thoughts rushed in. She envisioned the wary glances, the way strangers would fear him before they knew him. Whispers turning to shouts of alarm as they walked down crowded streets. Her stomach twisted as she recalled the way people had shifted away from her on the train because she was biracial, the muttered slurs that had sliced through her like knives. But this... this would be so much worse. Javkhlan wasn't just different—he was something that would make people question if he was even human.

She pictured a different kind of life, far from watchful eyes. A small cabin deep in the woods. Silence, space, a world of their own. But Javkhlan belonged to people, to connection. Taking him from that would mean taking part of who he was.

Practicalities tugged at her thoughts. Would the neuroscribe even work on Earth? He'd be trapped in silence, isolated in a world that wouldn't understand him. And what about Earth's diseases? Viruses and bacteria she'd never feared could prove deadly to him, just as they had to isolated communities throughout history.

She closed her eyes, trying to imagine a life together. Could she really ask him to leave Altay60, where he belonged, just to keep him with her? Was this even love? Or was it a selfish refusal to let go?

After a long pause, Javkhlan lifted his eyes to meet hers. "It would mean leaving behind the roots of what has been, for a soil that may not nurture who I am…" His voice trailed off, his hand coming to rest on his chest. "The path is not mine alone to choose. The wind carries not just my voice, but my children's as well."

Children. The word hit like a stone, breaking something in the quiet understanding she thought they shared. How had she not known? What else had she missed? A hundred questions fought to the surface, but none made it past her lips. Of course he had children, she should have guessed.

Javkhlan's brow creased. "Zadie. I see the storm in you. What is wrong?"

She felt herself closing off, instinct pulling her back, making space where warmth had been. "You have children?" The words came out flat, stripped of anything she didn't trust herself to say.

Javkhlan stilled, his expression focused as if he were trying to piece together a puzzle she hadn't meant to set in front of him. "Yes," he said, the word lingering. "Why?"

She looked down, knowing where this was heading. What was she supposed to feel? Anger? Jealousy? She pulled away slightly, just enough to let the warmth break, to let the space settle in.

Of course, it would never work. He was a Denisovan from another planet, bound to a life she couldn't be part of. She had almost let herself believe in something impossible. Maybe it was the QS, perhaps it was wishful thinking, but either way, the result was the same.

She took a deep breath, forcing herself to meet his gaze. "I suppose I don't know much about your life. What do family and relationships look like for the Thalvik?"

Javkhlan pressed his thumb into the center of his palm, a small, absent motion before his voice found shape. "We are like branches of the same tree. Food, shelter, children—none belong to one alone. A man or woman may sit at the fires of many in their life, and each bond strengthens the whole. Any child can run to any hand, and that hand will lift them. We all teach, we all guard, we all shape them."

Zadie glanced away, imagining herself as a child in that world, growing up with not just two parents but a whole tribe to turn to. The more she let the image settle, the less it seemed like an intrusion and more like a disorienting embrace.

She looked at Javkhlan again, noticing the ease with which he held this vision of life. "I see the beauty and wisdom in your communal approach. It's quite different from what I'm used to, though," she paused, her eyes searching his face for understanding, or resistance. "The idea of sharing a partner with many others, of not having one person who is just yours, is challenging for me."

"Only one other may sit at your fire?"

"On Earth, things are... different. Most people form a deep bond with just one person. They share a home, and they're intimate only with each other. If they have children, they raise them together. Other people might help in small ways, but the family, the parents and their children, become the center of everything."

Javkhlan tilted his head, processing her words. "This is new to me... Have you already chosen this bond?"

"No, I live on my own."

"Do you not wish for a family?"

Zadie's heart tightened at the question. "I... I do. I'd love to have a partner and a family, but... I just haven't found the right person yet."

"The *right* person?"

"Yeah. Like a soulmate—if that's even a thing."

"The heart can find many soulmates. Why is your search for just one difficult?"

She sighed and looked down at her hands as she gathered her thoughts. "In my world, finding *the one* is hard because we expect so much from them."

"Your meaning is like smoke to me..."

"Well, a partner has to be so many things—a lover, best friend, someone to share finances with. But that's just the beginning... They're also supposed to help raise children, manage a home, provide emotional support, be a social companion, a motivator, someone to plan the future with..."

"That is heavy for one pair of hands," Javkhlan said. "A fire burns brighter when many feed it."

His tone wasn't unkind, just observational. Still, that voice crept in. The one that had whispered through breakups, through every award that earned a nod but not quite pride. Even here. A whole other world, and still the same tightness in her chest. The sense that someone was watching, weighing, finding her wanting.

Javkhlan leaned back against the pillows and exhaled. "Zadie, my tribe is my strength, but I have never stood alone like you. Never felt the sun without their shadow beside me. When no eyes are upon me, I can't be sure who remains."

Zadie blinked, her own thoughts thrown off course. He wrapped his arms around her, and she sank into him.

"Would you consider staying with me in Altay60?"

Zadie reflected on the deep connections within his tribe, their bond with nature, the crisp air, the steady rhythm of a life untethered from constant demands and technologies, a world where time stretched rather than slipped away.

But then came the other side of it—the loss of comfort and convenience, the lack of knowledge at her fingertips, the erosion of personal freedom, the reach of Anunnaki control... She took a deep breath.

"Wait... no, this is bad," she said suddenly, sitting up.

Javkhlan's eyes searched her face.

"Quantum Psychosis is already interfering with the Anunnaki's Collective Consciousness. If the Anunnaki fully embrace Quantum Psychosis, their systems, everything, could destabilize. And their systems control the biodomes..."

Javkhlan's face hardened as he absorbed the information. "If their thoughts break, our world breaks too?"

"Yes," Zadie whispered, the full implications crashing over her. "The air, the water, the barriers between biodomes—it all depends on their Collective Consciousness functioning properly." She gripped Javkhlan's arm. "That means everyone in the biodomes could be in danger."

The weight of this realization stretched between them. Javkhlan's eyes darkened with concern for his people. Zadie's mind raced through possible solutions.

"We need to get to Lugazir," she said, reaching for her clothes. "If they're really planning to embrace Quantum Psychosis, they need to understand what's at stake for everyone else."

Before Javkhlan could respond, a sharp chime pulsed through their minds. They both tensed as Lugazir's voice followed.

"All participants, there has been a change in plans. Report to the experiment hall immediately."

19

Volunteers

"We made an unexpected discovery overnight—one that might ultimately allow us to bypass Quantum Psychosis," Lugazir said. "This means our plans have changed. You will not be returning home today. Instead, some of you will venture into the metaphysical layer."

Murmurs broke out. Eyes darted. Zadie's stomach dropped. She must've misheard. They were meant to leave. Today.

Lugazir pointed to nine glass-like capsules that resembled coffins. Soft miravys lights illuminated the interiors, revealing embedded sensors. "These *transition capsules* will suspend life functions, guiding participants through death—before pulling them back. They will allow us to interface with what we now recognize as the *soul*. We require one volunteer from each species to leave their bodies temporarily."

To leave their bodies temporarily? No, surely not. They couldn't be serious. Around her, the other participants froze, faces draining of color.

Javkhlan's grip on her hand tightened. "No animal, no tree, no river surrenders its breath by choice."

Zadie's heart pounded. Madness. Had they lost their minds entirely? She couldn't look away from the waiting capsules. A surge of adrenaline set her knees bouncing, her hands gripping the edge of her seat. "This is mental."

"How do you know it's safe?" Min-Jae shouted.

A few Naledi sprang to their feet, eyes wide. "This is wrong!" one of them snapped.

Freeya cut in. "You're like children playing with fire!"

"The spirits take what they are owed in their own time," another added.

"We... must... resist."

Lugazir raised a hand. Stillness settled over the hall. Zadie leaned forward slightly, waiting for them to explain. But no words came. Instead, she felt it creeping in like a fog—her pulse slowing, resistance softening. Around her, fearful faces relaxed into acceptance, and conversations slowed.

She should have warned them.

Her fingers curled into fists. This went far beyond *regulating emotions* for the sake of communication. They couldn't just force near-death experiences on unwilling participants. She needed answers. She had to push back. She fought against the grip of the QS and stood.

A heavy lethargy seeped into her limbs, dragging her toward stillness. She looked up at Lugazir, hoping—what? That they'd call it off? That someone would say this was wrong? But she only found a calm acknowledgment in their eyes, as if they knew and expected her reaction. Peace wrapped around her like a warm tide, drawing her down. Everything was fine. Wasn't it? Her knees bent, and before she realized it, she'd sat back down, her rebellion extinguished before it could ignite.

"These capsules represent everything we've learned about life, death, and the soul," Lugazir continued. "They're controlled environments, designed to bring volunteers to the point of death and beyond. This process will let us observe and understand the soul's departure and return. We require volunteers willing to experience the unknown for the greater understanding of all, to please step forward. One volunteer per species."

Zadie glanced at Javkhlan, noticing his eyes fixed on the capsules. His jaw tightened as he seemed to resist the urge to comply. A sudden movement caught her attention. Han-Yoon was on his feet, his eyes alight with fervor. His childlike expression, glowing with eagerness, seemed out of place. He moved forward, his body vibrating with anticipation as if on the brink of some great adventure.

This wasn't Han-Yoon's choice. The QS had made it for him. She tried to summon outrage by picturing him pale and lifeless in one of the capsules. The image should have jolted her into protest. Instead, it floated past, like a leaf on water, distant, untouchable.

In front of her, Min-Jae exhaled, shoulders dropping.

Zadie's chest rose with a slow, deliberate inhale. She held her breath, steadying herself. Maybe, if she kept her emotions flat, she could stay one step ahead of the QS. She released the breath slowly.

One by one, volunteers took their place at the front. Only the Sylvicolus stayed where they were. They sat like ancient stones, a collective defiance written in every line of their posture.

Zadie's mind worked through the fog of artificial calm to grasp this anomaly. Why weren't the Sylvicolus responding like everyone else?

Lugazir's attention paused on the group. "Sylvicolus participants, will one of you volunteer?"

The Sylvicolus leader rose, spine straight, voice calm but firm. "For countless generations, we have followed the current of life, never forcing the river to change its course," she said. "Seeking to access the metaphysical layer through artificial means strays from our guided path. We will not volunteer."

A long silence. Then Lugazir nodded once. "We respect your traditions."

Zadie caught a twitch in Lugazir's expression. A sudden stiffness in their posture. For a moment, it seemed a part of them recoiled from what they were about to say—then overrode it.

"However," they continued, "the integrity of this study requires participation from all represented species. If none step forward, one will be chosen."

The Sylvicolus tensed as one, the fragile trust rupturing in an instant. Their leader's hands clenched. "You violate our right to choose. This dishonors our dead."

Zadie saw it happen—mid-protest, the leader's shoulders sagged. Her voice caught. The fire drained from her eyes, replaced by a glassy stillness. Around her, the others faltered too, fury blunted into a terrible calm. Only one remained standing. Young. Trembling.

"I will volunteer," he said quietly, and stepped forward, alone.

Lugazir gave a single nod before continuing. "Our volunteers will undergo a process using advanced cryogenic technology. They'll be placed in these transition capsules and cooled until their metabolic processes stop. This state acts as a bridge between the physical and metaphysical layer, allowing exploration without permanent death. The process is controlled to prevent cellular damage, ensuring each volunteer can be revived."

Zadie ached with the urge to rise. *You can't just kill people to study souls.* The words blistered at the back of her throat. But the QS turned her fury to mist. She stayed seated, as the moment passed without her.

"These capsules are equipped with *SoulViewer* technology," Lugazir said. "The SoulViewer detects the unique patterns of energy emitted by souls as they leave the body. It will capture these signals as fluctuations in the quantum field, and then project a 3D display, showing us the soul's journey in real-time."

The volunteers approached their assigned capsules. Zadie's heart lodged in her throat as she watched Han-Yoon. His pupils, wide with artificial euphoria, met hers briefly. Despite the dreamlike smile frozen in place, a thin sheen of sweat glistened on his upper lip.

In that fleeting exchange, they shared a silent goodbye.

20
The Near-Death Experiment

Z adie caught the tremor in Han-Yoon's fingers just before he clenched the edge of the capsule. As he lay down, she imagined the cold seeping into his skin. The lid sealed with a hiss, locking him in.

A Luzonensis woman near Zadie tensed. Her eyes widened, lips parting for a gasp, or a scream. But no sound came. Almost instantly, her face smoothed, the QS erasing the emotion, leaving only a mask of calm.

It urged Zadie to surrender as well. She closed her eyes, inhaling deeply, then exhaling in a controlled release. The QS wavered, its grip loosening as her pulse slowed. Her hands, clenched at her sides, unfurled as she focused on the rhythm of her breathing.

Javkhlan sat rigid, his back pressed hard into the seat. She glanced at his profile, the unnatural stillness in his eyes. It was like looking at a hollow shell where the vibrant, passionate Javkhlan had once been. She wanted to scream, to crack through the QS's calm and drag him back.

Lugazir's voice filled the hall, unnervingly calm despite the gravity of the moment. "The volunteers are in place. Sedation is being administered." They turned, eyes tracking the shimmering liquid as it flowed through the transparent tubes.

Zadie glanced at Han-Yoon's capsule. She could see his features slackening as the sedation took effect. Was he still aware? Could he feel his connection to his body slipping away?

"Nanobots will now enter their bloodstreams to prevent ice crystal formation, ensuring cellular integrity despite the sub-zero temperatures," Lugazir said.

Supercooled liquid swirled into the capsules, then stilled. Frost dulled Han-Yoon's face, leaching warmth from his skin until he looked more like a delicate sculpture than a living person. One by one, the volunteers disappeared behind a creeping veil of ice, their capsules turning opaque.

Zadie studied the floating data streams, where shifting lines pulsed with hypnotic precision. The volunteers' vitals plummeted—heart rates dipping, breaths thinning to ghostly traces.

A soft chime marked the death of the first volunteer, a Neanderthal woman.

"Now, we watch," Lugazir said.

Time dragged, each second heavier than the last. No sign of a soul. The woman's body lay within the capsule, still and frozen, a vessel emptied of life.

Something formed in the air. A pale blue glow, delicate at first, shifting like mist before gathering into a defined shape. A few startled gasps broke the silence as the glow solidified into a crisp, luminous form.

"The SoulViewer has activated," Lugazir said.

The projection shimmered, forming a precise likeness of the woman as she had been in life. Its expression was serene yet searching, its gaze sweeping the surrounding space with curiosity. No fear. No hesitation. As if life and death had simply dissolved, unveiling boundless possibilities.

Zadie watched as the soul drifted toward a barely perceptible crack, a thin fracture between worlds. Then, with a smooth, deliberate motion, it passed through.

A slow, creeping numbness spread through Zadie's limbs. Her vision sharpened—each detail suddenly too vivid, too real.

"The first phase is complete for this volunteer," Lugazir said. "Her soul has crossed over."

Another chime signaled another death. The young Sylvicolus man. The Sylvicolus leader lowered her head and let out a low, rumbling sound that vibrated beneath Zadie's feet. No one turned. No one reacted.

The soul projection phenomenon repeated with each volunteer. Each departure was unique. Some souls lingered as if bidding a final farewell to the life they'd known. Others moved with an urgency, eager to cross the threshold.

Zadie's heart skipped a beat as Han-Yoon's soul projection sharpened into focus. Seeing him like this was both unsettling and mesmerizing. Here, he existed beyond fear, beyond doubt, beyond flesh itself—an unburdened essence in its purest form. His soul hovered, testing the space between worlds before slipping into the unseen realm beyond.

The last soul crossed over, leaving its waiting flesh behind.

"Now, we call them back," Lugazir said. "The revival process begins."

Zadie's stomach clenched. Could a soul really be called back? Or was death inevitable?

The Neanderthal woman's capsule whirred to life, its systems humming with clinical precision. The sound made Zadie's skin crawl. Heat shimmered faintly off the capsule as the woman's body thawed in a controlled reversal of the freezing process. Beads of moisture gathered along the woman's brow, catching the light like sweat, even as her skin remained disturbingly lifeless. Tubes threaded from the base of the unit, pulsing with fluid the color of diluted honey. Nutrients? Electrolytes? Something more advanced? Zadie wasn't sure, but whatever it was, it seemed tailored.

"Nanobots are now delivering specialized compounds to restart the heart," Lugazir said.

A soft beep signaled the next phase. The capsule started a sequence of controlled bioelectric pulses, gentle at first, coaxing the heart back into rhythm. Zadie held her breath, watching the gradual increase in pulse intensity.

She barely noticed the SoulViewer projection until the woman's soul had fully formed once again. It edged toward its body, hesitating before aligning with its physical form. The moment they connected, the body convulsed, a sharp, jarring tremor.

"The nanobots are now repairing the damage from freezing," Lugazir continued. "They're restoring what the body needs to function again."

Zadie could sense the shift—faint patches of discoloration, where frostbite should have ruined tissue, faded steadily, leaving behind a healthy hue.

She pressed her palms flat against her thighs, forcing them to stay steady as Han-Yoon's revival sequence started. A soft shudder passed through his body. Neural activity stirred, and his soul realigned with the reawakening of his biological functions.

The terror that had coiled around her heart loosened, but didn't release. Han-Yoon was breathing, yes, but what had they done to him? What had they done to all of them? She tightened her grip on Javkhlan's hand, her mind churning with questions that had no simple answers.

A low hiss and the whisper of motion caught her attention. A few capsules away, the first volunteers had begun to stir. Anunnaki technicians moved in, steadying them as they took tentative steps into a world that had briefly existed without them. The volunteers blinked hard against the bright lights of the experiment hall. Their appearances were the same, but their eyes suggested a newfound depth.

Zadie sensed a hint of unease pass through the Anunnaki technicians. Their focus was fixed on the Anunnaki volunteer, whose revival teetered in delicate resistance. The soul lingered just beyond its body, hesitant, unwilling. The capsule adjusted the bioelectric pulses, escalating their intensity in precise increments. Each controlled surge tried to draw the soul closer, but it strained against the pull, as if it no longer wanted to return.

Then, a pulse struck with such force that Zadie flinched. The Anunnaki's body convulsed, a sharp gasp breaking from their lips as the soul slammed back into place. The Anunnaki technicians moved on as if nothing unusual had happened.

◇———☀———◇

Once each volunteer had returned to their seat, Lugazir faced them. "We extend our gratitude to each of you. You have ventured into the unknown, and your courage brings us closer to understanding the mysteries that will help to shape our strategies against Quantum Psychosis." With a final nod to the wider assembly, they added, "You are free to return to the communal lounge."

The QS loosened its hold. Conversations resumed with ease, voices no longer strained, as people clustered around the volunteers, escorting them back toward the communal lounge.

Javkhlan took her hand as they wove through the crowd toward Han-Yoon, who was already surrounded by a small cluster of onlookers.

Han-Yoon grinned, his face alight with an almost electric energy. "Honestly, I've never felt better."

Zadie's shoulders sagged, exhaustion rushing in now that the fear had drained away. She scanned his face for signs of trauma, searching for some trace that crossing the threshold between life and death had altered him, fractured something. But there was no haunted stare, no residual weight. His features were peaceful. He looked like someone back from a long weekend, not from death itself.

Han-Yoon spotted them, his eyes glinting with mischief. "So... you two gave in, huh? Can't fight fate."

Zadie's face burned. How did he know?

Javkhlan knelt and wet a handful of soil with stream water, mixing it into a dark paste. In one swift stroke, he smeared a mark across Han-Yoon's forehead. "In my tribe, those who return from the spirit world do not do so untouched. For seven sunrises, its presence clings to them." Javkhlan completed the symbol. "This steadies the soul here."

Han-Yoon bowed deeply. "Thank you, Javkhlan."

Freeya leaned in, not bothering to hide the urgency in her posture. "Han-Yoon, please tell us—what was it like?"

"It's... hard to put into words. It wasn't like anything I've encountered before. At first, I felt like I'd logged out of my body, watching from a distance, but at the same time, I was more connected to everything around me. It wasn't scary. If anything, it felt... clearer. Like switching from a low-res screen to full immersion. My thoughts didn't load one by one—they just appeared. Every moment, every idea, right there. Immediate. No delay."

The group leaned in, eager to grasp every detail of his experience.

"And there was a pull," Han-Yoon added, voice dipping lower. "Not like being dragged, more like a side quest opening up right in front of you. A suggestion, but one that felt... inevitable. It's hard to describe. Like standing at the edge of something infinite and knowing you could step in, just by deciding to."

He paused as if recalling the sensation. "Time and space... didn't work there. Not like we understand them. It felt like floating, but not just weightlessness. More like the whole concept of being anchored, of being anywhere specific, just... slipped away."

He searched for the right words, his brow furrowing. "There were no rules, no physics, no gravity, no need to breathe. No need to exist the way we do now. It was like..." He exhaled sharply. "Beyond being human. No constraints."

Zadie watched him closely. His expression was taut, his mind still wrestling with it, trying to compress something vast into words that fit inside a reality the group could understand.

But Han-Yoon pressed on, his voice growing more introspective. "Everything was shaped by intent. If I thought about something, really focused on it, it just... appeared. Instantly. Like the entire space was built out of thought, not matter. It made me realize how much our thoughts control reality. We just don't see it here because it happens more slowly."

As he finished, a deep silence settled over the group. No one moved. No one spoke. Zadie could hear the uneven breaths of those around her, each person lost in their own thoughts.

"Was there any form of judgment? Was there a hell?" Min-Jae asked.

Han-Yoon shook his head. "No judgment, no hell... It felt more like... any suffering would come from within, from our own state of mind, not from some external punishment."

Min-Jae pressed his lips together, but he remained silent, eyes narrowing as if dissecting Han-Yoon's words, searching for the flaw in his logic.

"Did you feel like you were still you?" Zadie asked.

"Yeah," Han-Yoon said without hesitation. "But with a full understanding and without the physical constraints. It's weird, but... I don't think I believe in free will anymore, not in the way I used to."

"I don't know what to think." Min-Jae's jaw tightened. "Physiological factors—oxygen deprivation and excess carbon dioxide—can induce similar states. That's a fact."

The others glanced at him with varying degrees of confusion and annoyance. But Zadie noticed the way he looked down, the hesitation in his voice. Not doubt—something more brittle.

"I've seen too many people in my country manipulated by those who claim special spiritual knowledge," Min-Jae continued, his words gaining intensity. "They use these experiences, visions, revelations, to demand loyalty. To take everything from those who trust them. I was told our leaders could speak to the dead and that they possessed powers beyond ordinary men. I watched families—good, loyal people—starve while offering their last grains of rice to those who promised them spiritual protection." His eyes locked with Han-Yoon's. "These experiences can be manufactured." His voice was quieter now, but no less firm. "And the ones who control them? They control everything."

Han-Yoon turned to Min-Jae, pausing just long enough to make it clear he was actually considering his views, not just countering them. "You raise a valid point. Ironically, it's the kind of argument I might've made myself not too long ago. But this experience... It was different. Not something I can prove with logic alone. Maybe it's one of those things you have to experience to believe."

Min-Jae's eyes darted between the others, searching for any sign of understanding.

Javkhlan broke the tension with a light laugh. "Your path next time, Min-Jae."

"Next time?" Min-Jae's voice wavered, uncertainty creeping in. "We're... done with the experiments, though, right?"

The group exchanged a few glances, their shoulders lifting in awkward shrugs. Zadie caught the hesitation in their eyes—a collective pause, like animals sensing a change in air pressure before a storm. Before she could react, her gaze met Sargona's. Their eyes held an urgent intensity, pulling her in.

"Zadie. Urgent. We need to talk."

21

The Soul Containment Plan

"You've seen it, haven't you?" Sargona said. "Quantum Psychosis occurs when the Anunnaki soul begins to detach. Yes. That's the pattern."

Zadie stared at Sargona, her mind racing as she recalled the vacant-eyed Anunnaki who had bumped into her as if she were invisible; the longhorn beetle's insistence that Quantum Psychosis was necessary for growth; and the hesitation of the Anunnaki volunteer's soul to return to its body. "Are you sure? How do you know it's not just—"

"Neurological degradation? QS overwrite? Cognitive fragmentation?" Sargona said. "We considered those variables. Tested them. The results are consistent. Symptomatic Anunnaki exhibit the same trajectory—when QS governance reaches fifty-eight percent, the soul disengages. Beyond that threshold, it refuses to coexist. Not conflict. Just... departure... as seen on the SoulViewer."

Zadie sat motionless, staring at her hands. *Fifty-eight percent... too far.* "Then why keep going with the experiments? The Akashidu told them to embrace QS—not override it."

Sargona shrugged. "Fear? Self-preservation? The QS altering perception, nudging their choices? Difficult to isolate the cause. But the idea of a world filled with soulless Anunnaki... it unsettles me. No, stronger than that." Their voice dropped. "It terrifies me."

"But... what will happen—"

"Zadie." The urgency in Sargona's voice was unmistakable. "You need to understand—the Anunnaki's priority now is soul containment. Preventing Quantum Psychosis. At any cost."

The hairs on the back of Zadie's neck stood on end. "What are you saying? Are they actually planning to trap their souls? Force them to stay put?"

Sargona looked down. "They believe it's the only way."

"You can't trap a soul." The words came out with more conviction than she'd intended. She glanced at Sargona, noting the fear in their eyes. "Is that even possible?"

"Not just possible. More than that. It's happening," they said. "The technology's already being refined. It's a cage, Zadie. As long as the body lives, the soul can't leave."

"And what do you think of that?"

"Zadie... there's more I need to say. About what we are. What we tried to be." Centuries of burden settled in Sargona's eyes. "To be Anunnaki is to bear immense responsibility. No... that's not enough. It's obligation. We merged with QS to transcend. To go beyond limits, to explore the universe's deepest truths, to help humanity evolve. But I'm beginning to think..." They hesitated. "The soul's journey follows a different path. A kind of growth we don't control. If we force it...

contain it... manipulate it with artificial structures... We would be stopping something fundamental. Cutting off a process we still don't fully understand."

"Sargona, if the Anunnaki succumb to Quantum Psychosis, what will happen to the biodomes?"

"Yes, that's a problem. But there's more—something requiring immediate attention. The Anunnaki are preparing for a final experiment. Their plan is... unsettling. Unethical. They intend to use the participants as test subjects to refine the soul-containment technology."

Pressure built in her chest. She had to stay calm. She couldn't let the QS take control. She reached into her memories for something, anything, to ground her. The musty scent of Oxford's library stacks. The garden behind her childhood home where she'd read for hours under an apple tree. Rain tapping against her windowpanes. The corner café where the barista knew her order without asking. The half-written novel in her laptop that she promised herself she'd finish someday. All of it—worlds away. Yet close enough to sting. What if she never made it back? What if she never had the chance to share what she learned?

Stop. Breathe.

Zadie inhaled sharply, frustration in her eyes. "No. This isn't what we agreed to. We were supposed to be going home. They told us it was over."

Sargona tilted their head, considering a new possibility. "That's a good point. A logistical inconsistency. When Lugazir announced the experiments were complete, the Collective Consciousness should have lifted the block on transitfold activity for participants. Standard protocol. There's a decent probability—under the circumstances—that access remains open."

"You believe we can still make it back?"

Sargona gave a slow, measured nod. "No certainty. Variables exist. But under current conditions... it is within the realm of probability."

But Javkhlan. She thought of the warmth of his body next to hers just hours ago. "Will it only work for the Earth-born Sapiens, or for everyone?"

"If it succeeds, it succeeds for all. Yes. Consistent logic. Gather as many participants as you can. Time is constricting. I will return shortly."

◇—☀—◇

Zadie sat frozen for a few breaths, her thoughts spiraling in all directions. Across the communal lounge, she spotted Javkhlan and Han-Yoon sitting in an open grassy area with a group of Sapiens, Denisovans, and Neanderthal participants.

As she approached, Javkhlan stood up. "The ones who've faced death carry a new sense inside them. The four from the second experiment still haven't found their way back."

A strange dissonance rippled through her, a sense of being both inside and outside her body. Her limbs responded, but a fraction too late, her movements off. Sound reached her ears in a half-second delay, words stripped of meaning. Zadie gasped as she struggled to break free from the sensations. *Ebuni...*

She noticed the intense focus in Han-Yoon's eyes as he watched her. "Did you just do that?"

"Yeah," Han-Yoon said. "Sorry about that. I didn't mean to push it that hard. But you had to know."

She nodded, jaw tight. No point pushing back. Not now. She took a deep breath and faced the others. "There's more you need to know."

The group fell silent.

"They're not done experimenting. They think Quantum Psychosis happens when the soul starts to leave. So now they want to stop it—by forcing the soul to stay. And they're using us to test it."

"We won't go through with it," Freeya said, squaring her shoulders.

"It's not that simple. Every one of us has some QS in us. The Anunnaki use it to mess with our emotions. To control us."

"We're stuck like a mammoth in a sinkhole," a Neanderthal man said, raking blunt nails across his scalp as if trying to stir a thought loose. "Is there any way out?"

"There might be. Sargona's trying to get us back to Earth, but we have to move fast. We'll deal with logistics and details later. Right now, we need to avoid the next experiment. That's the only thing that matters."

Han-Yoon and Min-Jae shot to their feet.

Zadie turned to them, pulse kicking up. "We need to tell the other groups—"

Han-Yoon nodded. "On it."

Min-Jae was already moving.

Maybe they wouldn't have to part ways after all. She turned to Javkhlan, heart lifting.

But he was already shaking his head, his expression resolute. "I'm sorry, I cannot turn from my people. They'll need me to stand beside them. Every leaf falls in its time. But mine still clings to the branch."

The hope slipped from her chest before she could catch it. One by one, the others shook their heads. They weren't coming.

Javkhlan took Zadie's hand, sensing her turmoil. "Our river forks. But we come from the same flow, and in time, all rivers reach the sea."

She went still. Not even the urge to argue, just a silence that hurt more than physical pain.

Han-Yoon and Min-Jae returned. Not a single ancient human. No one would leave their people behind—even now, even with everything at risk. A pang of shame twisted. Even if this were Earth, she would've left without a backward glance. But these people belonged to each other in a way she hadn't factored in.

Sargona reappeared, drawing everyone's attention. "It's time. Yes, we need to move quickly."

Han-Yoon grabbed her arm. "Come on, Zadie," he urged as he pulled her away.

◇—☼—◇

Han-Yoon angled his arm so that Sargona could see his bracelet more clearly.

Sargona nodded. "Good. You'll return to the exact point of departure on Earth. Precision is critical. Follow me."

She followed, but each step dragged. It felt like betrayal, even if she knew it wasn't. She had to go. She was already supposed to be leaving today. She had to warn Earth. Humanity needed to understand the risk of integrating AI into its genome. But knowing that didn't make it any easier to walk away from Javkhlan.

The atmosphere thickened when they entered the *Interfold Terminal*, a strange pressure settling on her skin. It was as though the air was bending and stretching. An imposing platform dominated the center of the room.

"This doesn't look anything like the other transitfold doorways," Zadie said, glancing around.

Sargona nodded. "It's not. This is the only platform equipped for interstellar folds."

Min-Jae frowned. "Why can't we just use a sphere to get home?"

"Returning infrastructure is far more complex... Like gravity. Yes. One way with a parachute. The other way requires something far more sophisticated."

Zadie stepped closer to the edge of the platform, her eyes widening. A flat surface hiding endless depth. Beneath it, shapes shifted like shadows in a deep current, leaving her with an eerie sensation that the ground could drop away at any moment.

"You'll be heading to different destinations, so each of you must go one at a time," Sargona said.

"I'll go first." Min-Jae stepped forward, then paused, looking at Han-Yoon. "North Korea taught me survival. You let yourself be sedated."

"Min-Jae—" Han-Yoon started.

He shook his head. "In the end, reality's the only thing that matters," he said, "and I'll take mine, flawed, imperfect, and cruel, over your illusions."

As Min-Jae stepped onto the platform, Zadie felt the air pressure change, her ears popping. A burst of white light engulfed him. Afterimages burned into her retinas. In an instant, he was gone.

Han-Yoon exhaled slowly, shaking his head. "Why was he even brought here? He had nothing of value to add."

"Actually, he was fascinating," Sargona said. "Resistance to new information was expected. Predictable behavior. But the ferocity with which he defends his constructed reality... even against conflicting data—that's atypical. An anomaly worthy of analysis."

"You go next, Zadie," Han-Yoon said, his hand brushing lightly against her arm. "I'll catch up with you on Earth."

She gave him a brief hug, but her mind wasn't with him. Not entirely.

"Something for you," Sargona said, placing a small glass-like disc into her palm.

"What is it?" she asked.

"A 5D optical memory crystal. It contains your neuroscribe's complete recordings—observations, analyses, emotional responses, subconscious data, and all empirical results from the experiments. A full record of your experience. Structured. Organized. Retrievable."

Zadie stared at the disc, remembering Lugazir's words from her first day: *"The neuroscribe will handle all that for you."* She closed her fingers around it, carefully. "Thank you, Sargona. This means more than you know."

"You must go now. No further delay," Sargona said.

Zadie stepped onto the platform, vibrations traveling up through her bones. The same white light that had engulfed Min-Jae gathered around her, molecules of brilliance coalescing. This was it. In seconds, she would be back on Earth.

A deafening crack splintered the air. A blue-miravys corona flared around her, skimming the platform in pulsing waves before vanishing with a sharp hiss. The air crackled with static, heavy with the smell of ozone.

"Sargona! What the hell's happening?"

She spun around, heart pounding, as a group of Anunnaki stormed into the terminal.

"Access has been denied," one of them said. "The final experiment is commencing. Return to the Experiment Hall. Now."

Her awareness slipped sideways, like she was watching from just outside her body. This couldn't be happening. She saw Han-Yoon crumple to the ground, his head buried in his hands.

22

The Anunnaki Opportunity

Zadie spotted Javkhlan across the experiment hall. He stared somewhere beyond her. Had he seen her and chosen not to look? Or was the QS already in control? Whatever her departure had broken between them, it only widened now. She turned away. Stranded here, with no way back, she needed him more than she dared admit. Would he forgive her for trying to leave? The QS tried to blunt the guilt, but this pain ran too deep.

"Look at me," Lugazir said.

The participants turned as one, with involuntary obedience.

"Our journey together has been... enlightening. We have gained substantial insight into the soul within each of us. And now, we find ourselves at the threshold of something far beyond what we once believed possible. This... is your moment to transcend."

The silence was suffocating, charged with expectation. The participants stared intently at Lugazir, their faces unnaturally still.

"The majority of Anunnaki taken by Quantum Psychosis remain in pristine condition—soulless, as we now know—but functional, preserved by the QS. We learned during the second experiment that souls cannot be transferred between two living hosts. However, we now believe it is possible to extract a soul at the point of death and bind it to a vacant Anunnaki form."

Several participants flinched, but only the Sylvicolus moved differently—fists clenched, knuckles whitening, breath sharp and shallow. Low growls rose from their throats.. The moment hung there until the QS tightened its grip.

"I see your fear," Lugazir said with misplaced empathy. "I understand. Quantum Psychosis terrifies you. But you won't have to worry about that. We've solved it. Once your soul is transferred into an Anunnaki body, we'll anchor it. A force field, perfectly tuned to your soul's unique energy signature, will ensure it remains in place."

Zadie focused on her breathing. *Inhale—one, two, three. Exhale—one, two, three.* The rhythm was her only shield now, a fragile barrier between her and the QS.

Lugazir's voice took on a silky tone as if they were offering a rare gift. "Imagine living not just for decades but for centuries. Picture yourself understanding the secrets of the universe. The pursuit of knowledge becomes limitless, each discovery building upon the last." They smiled. "I know you've felt the limitations of your bodies given your fragile lives. This is your chance to escape. To be... free."

One by one, the participants seemed to lean forward, almost imperceptibly at first, then more noticeably. Zadie could see it. They were falling for it. And yet something in her resisted. She searched for any sign that someone else might be fighting it, too, but all she found were expressions locked in blind curiosity.

Why was she different? The question gnawed at her, but there was no time for answers. The others, it seemed, had already given up.

"There are already four volun—" Lugazir's voice faltered, the word hanging unfinished.

Zadie caught the sudden crease in their forehead, a fleeting moment of uncertainty. Lugazir's lips pressed together. "Volunteers."

Who had volunteered?

Four figures were ushered onto the stage—two Naledi, a Luzonensis, and Ebuni. Of course. The ill-fated participants of the energy transfer experiment. Zadie's heart clenched as she watched Ebuni shuffle forward. Her limbs dragged, heavy and uncooperative. A tremor passed through her, and she paused, head tilting, disorientation breaking the blankness of her expression. The light in her eyes had vanished, leaving only a dull, glassy stare fixed on something that wasn't there. The other volunteers mirrored her vacant gaze and hesitant movements as they took their seats at the far left of the stage.

Lugazir scanned the hall. "There's no need for concern. We've prepared a body for each of you. No one will be left behind."

23

The Final Experiment

"Who would like to go first?" Lugazir addressed the four so-called *volunteers.*

One of the Naledi stood up, her expression set with quiet resolve.

"Thank you, Eka."

The wall behind the platform dissolved, revealing a clinical chamber. Above two chairs hung an intimidating array of unfamiliar instruments—eerily reminiscent of a dentist's office. A soulless Anunnaki sat motionless in one chair. Its face was smooth and untroubled. Was it asleep? Or just... paused?

Was that Daanjabe? Zadie's stomach lurched. Her body knew the truth before her mind could catch up.

"In a moment, you will witness Eka's soul being guided from her current form to this vacant Anunnaki body, where it, along with her identity, will be anchored," Lugazir said. "The method will be painless and swift, in accordance with our compassionate code. Please observe as we initiate the procedure."

Zadie shook her head at the term *compassionate code.*

Eka settled into the first chair. It cradled her body with an almost tender precision as the Anunnaki technicians prepared for the first crucial step.

"The first stage uses our customary euthanasia device—*the Azraelbeam*," Lugazir said.

The Azraelbeam hovered over Eka, casting a glow across her skin. A pulse. Then another. Eka's body slackened, her breath slowing, then stopping altogether. No movement. No struggle. She was gone. A peaceful expression settled over her features.

The dignity and grace of the moment did nothing to soften Zadie's horror. It was a weapon, no matter how softly it killed.

Eka's soul appeared as a three-dimensional projection on the SoulViewer, recreating the haunting beauty of the near-death experiment, but this time, with no path back.

Tiny points of light materialized around the Anunnaki body, forming a delicate web of energy, which quivered in a steady rhythm.

"*Quantum Resonance Emitters* are guiding Eka's soul to its new Anunnaki home," Lugazir said.

Zadie watched Eka's soul travel toward the Anunnaki body like a feather floating through still air.

"Once Eka's soul reaches the pineal gland of the Anunnaki body, the anchoring phase will begin." Lugazir clasped their hands behind their back as if the outcome was inevitable.

The network of light surrounding the Anunnaki body contracted. The energy pulsed, its intensity growing as it concentrated around the head. A quick flash lit up the hall.

Lugazir turned to the assembly. "Eka's soul has been secured within the Anunnaki body. The procedure is now complete."

Zadie held her breath, her body rigid with anticipation.

The Anunnaki remained motionless. Eyes shut. Expression unchanged.

Something was wrong.

Eka's soul took shape in the SoulViewer once again. It drifted upward, slipping through the fracture in a silent retreat.

"This outcome deviates from the expected integration. It is unfortunate," Lugazir said. "Proceed with the next volunteer."

They didn't care. The human cost didn't even register for them.

"The Anunnaki are no longer human," Zadie declared with unmistakable venom. The moment balanced in the air like a knife on edge. How had she spoken? Was the QS losing its grip or had she broken through?

Across the room, the Sylvicolus group exchanged glances, then offered a single, subdued nod. Lugazir spared Zadie a fleeting glance before turning away, her words clearly not worth a second thought.

Several Anunnaki technicians moved Eka's body out of the way. Ebuni stood up and shuffled into place.

No, not Ebuni.

There was no fear in Ebuni's expression. Only a terrible stillness, as if she'd already mourned herself and accepted the end. The sterile scent of the experiment hall became suffocating. Zadie's old trick of observing instead of feeling was slipping.

The Azraelbeam pulsed. Ebuni's small body slackened. The SoulViewer flared to life. Emitters hummed in unison. A blinding flash—electric, charged. The hair on Zadie's arms rose.

The Anunnaki's eyes snapped open. Ebuni's eyes. Wide, unblinking, wild. The QS choked back a scream as Zadie witnessed the crazed stare. The body convulsed, limbs flailing in erratic, desperate motions, like a puppet whose strings had been yanked in all directions.

Zadie covered her face, but it wasn't enough. The clatter against the chair, the wet gasps, the low whine of the emitters, still reached her. *Make it stop. Please—*

And then, suddenly, stillness.

Ebuni calmed, turning her head slowly, scanning the experiment hall as if from underwater. Her hand twitched, then moved, testing. Zadie held her breath as Ebuni raised it higher, fingers stretching open.

A smile crept across Lugazir's face. "The process is complete. Congratulations, Ebuni. You are now an Anunnaki."

Lugazir's composure faltered. Rapid blinking signaled that something was wrong. "Next volunteer." The words came out more as a plea than a command.

A muscle in their jaw twitched, and for a fleeting second, Zadie saw something she had never seen in them before—panic. The rawness of it, so foreign in the Anunnaki, gripped her with a sudden, numbing dread.

Zadie straightened, drawing in a slow, deliberate breath. "Lugazir, wait—" Her words felt like a leap off a cliff, no turning back.

Lugazir's head jerked toward her.

"You're running out of time. If you really want to save your people, contain your own soul first. Show them it can be done."

The space between them throbbed with tension. Anger flashed across Lugazir's features, hardening their eyes and tightening their mouth—only to dissolve, leaving a look of uncertainty that weighed heavier. Their jaw flexed, then stilled, the fight draining from their posture.

"Quantum Psychosis..." Lugazir began, but the sentence faltered, their eyes glazing over as if they were losing track of their thoughts. They gave a single, reluctant nod.

The Anunnaki technicians removed Ebuni's original body and assisted her new Anunnaki form into the first chair, leaving the second chair open for Lugazir's soul containment.

"Start the procedure," Lugazir said.

The process was swift. The emitters flashed, blinding the hall as Lugazir's soul was anchored. When the light faded, Zadie squinted, searching for any sign of success.

Lugazir's eyes shot open. For a second, they blinked rapidly, unfocused. "I remain."

Flanked by the Anunnaki technicians, Lugazir rose and departed the hall.

The assembly sat in hushed silence, the grip of the QS beginning to loosen its hold. Slowly, as if waking from a dream, their focus shifted to Ebuni.

Zadie stepped forward. "Ebuni, how do you feel?"

A cold, detached presence pierced her mind, creating an unsettling emptiness. Zadie sensed a fragile trace of Ebuni's real self, now trapped beneath the weight of the QS.

"Help," she whispered.

The Floresiensis group encircled Ebuni in silent coordination, each reaching out with gentle hands. Without a single word, they positioned the Azraelbeam above her.

Zadie staggered back a step. They weren't trying to save Ebuni. They were helping her soul escape the only way left.

Zadie's thoughts drifted back to NusaLale120, to Ebuni applying herbal salve with quiet care. Her hand guiding her through the forest. That small, resilient figure, brimming with empathy and strength, had imprinted on Zadie's soul in a way she knew would stay with her forever.

Ebuni's lips moved as the Azraelbeam hummed to life. "There are worse things than death."

The beam emitted a final pulse. Silence fell over the experiment hall once more, broken only by the low hum of technology powering down. The assembly watched as the projection of Ebuni's soul drifted through the fracture to the metaphysical layer from which it had once emerged.

24
The Funeral

A shudder coursed through the assembly as Lugazir returned. No one spoke, but the silence thundered. Lugazir didn't acknowledge Ebuni's death. Didn't even mention Eka. Two lives lost in pursuit of a warped ambition.

Lugazir looked like they were holding back a storm. Zadie caught the tremor in their fingers which were usually poised and still. Their breathing came in shallow, uneven bursts. They rolled their shoulders twice, as if trying to shrug off an invisible weight.

"The containment... it's..." For a moment, Lugazir seemed to lose their train of thought. "It's functional," they finished, the word clipped. "We extend our apologies to each of you. For now, we must redirect our efforts to stabilize our own people and prevent Quantum Psychosis from progressing further. Please be patient with us."

The sigh that should have followed Lugazir's announcement never came. Instead, the assembly shifted like a disturbed hive. The participants dashed toward the exits, fearing that any hesitation would undo the fragile agreement just made.

Amid the rush, Zadie noticed the Naledi, Floresiensis, and Luzonensis groups break away to gather the lifeless bodies of Eka and Ebuni—and the two dazed figures still left on the platform. They held them close, as if to protect them from further harm.

—◇—☀—◇—

Zadie sat beside the stream in the communal lounge, her fingers trailing a fern frond drooping toward the water. The ghost of Eka's vacant stare and the echo of Ebuni's final plea played on an endless loop, a macabre slideshow she couldn't shut off. She squeezed her eyes shut as if sheer will could block the haunting memories.

"Zadie."

The voice was a faint whisper, distant and muffled.

"Zadie."

She opened her eyes. Reality sharpened. Javkhlan stood in front of her. She rose carefully, as if the slightest shift might shatter the fragile balance between them. Words jammed in her throat, too many emotions vying for release. "I'm sorry."

Javkhlan shook his head. His eyes didn't flinch. "Zadie, you did what we could not."

"I know... I was being selfish." She looked down. "I just wanted to get out. I didn't think about anyone else."

"Stop." His hand lifted in a quiet, steadying motion. "You broke through to Lugazir. They bound their own soul because of you. That is why we still walk this world."

"Oh... yes, but..." The shame kept rising. "But I still tried to leave you—"

"I wanted your feet far from danger," he said. "Only then could I breathe." His hand closed around hers.

She braced for resentment. Disappointment. Some proof she'd let him down. But it wasn't there. He meant every word. She swallowed hard. "I can't get back to Earth."

"Then come with me to Altay60. We won't wander blind."

She studied his face. He didn't look away, his hand still wrapped around hers, solid and reassuring.

Zadie nodded, squeezing his hand as if it were the only thing keeping her afloat. "I'm scared."

"I know." His grip tightened. "So am I. But we go forward anyway."

"Hey, sorry to cut in," Han-Yoon said. "A joint funeral is about to start by the sanctuary tree."

"But we've got to get out of here before they restart the experiments again," Zadie said, shifting her weight from foot to foot.

Javkhlan shook his head. "First, we must honor the dead. Only then can we move."

Zadie's face drained of color as memories came flashing back from Azania180– raw flesh, teeth sinking in, muscle tearing with a sickening rip. She shook her head. No. She was being silly. This wouldn't be the same. It couldn't be.

"Are you okay, Zadie?" Han-Yoon took a half-step toward her.

"Um, yeah… It's just… in Altay60 I saw the Naledi consume the remains of the dead."

"Wait—like… actually eat them?"

Zadie nodded, lowering her head, trying to escape the image. "If it's like that… I don't think I can face it."

Javkhlan tilted his head. "Is it not your way to keep your loved ones close?"

"No... not like that... we don't." Zadie shook her head. "Please don't say it's your way?"

"Yes," Javkhlan said, still perplexed. "All tribes I know do. Why does it disturb you?"

Zadie looked at Javkhlan, her expression troubled. "Death's meant to be peaceful. A time when you leave the body be. Eating the dead...it crosses a line. Strips away the dignity, turns it into something... I don't know. Savage."

Javkhlan listened, his eyes thoughtful. "I see now. You grieve because you think death is an ending. But the tree that falls does not vanish—it feeds the soil. And from that soil, new life rises. We do the same. Our dead are not lost. We take them in, and they walk with us still."

Han-Yoon nodded, glancing at Zadie. "I kind of get where he's coming from. Maybe it's not as bad as it sounds..."

Zadie's eyes narrowed as she looked at him. "So, you're okay with eating Ebuni and Eka?"

"Not as a meal, no," Han-Yoon said. "But as part of a ritual? To honor them?" He ran his hand over his head. "It's not about the act. It's what it means. It's strange, sure... but everything here is strange, right?"

"Why can't they take the bodies back to their tribes?" Zadie asked, looking at Javkhlan.

"It must be now, or sickness spreads," he said, his gaze shifting to the sanctuary before returning to her. "Come. Even if you stand apart, you must watch. It will show you what words cannot."

She wasn't sure if she wanted to understand. "Alright," Zadie said. "I'll go. But I don't know how much I can handle."

The Naledi and Floresiensis groups sat on the soft ground, forming a tight circle around Ebuni and Eka's bodies near a fire. Heads bowed, hands clasped, their silence carried the weight of a final farewell. The other groups stood in a wider circle around them, faces neither grim nor weeping, simply bearing witness.

"How on Earth did they manage to light a fire in here?" Zadie asked Han-Yoon.

"We're not on Earth..." Han-Yoon quipped with a smile.

Zadie rolled her eyes, sighing, but a faint smile tugged at the corner of her mouth.

"Sargona helped set it up," Han-Yoon said.

The Naledi and Floresiensis leaders moved with ceremonial precision, their motions honoring the lives through ritual. Zadie forced herself to watch, to understand, though every instinct screamed at her to turn away. When they turned to the last task—the removal of Eka and Ebuni's brains—time seemed to slow. The light caught their blades, glinting as they traced practiced lines across flesh that had, just hours ago, held consciousness, held dreams.

A sickening weight settled in Zadie's gut. She tried to focus with respect, but heat flashed across her skin, then retreated into icy shivers. A faint buzzing filled her ears. She blinked, desperate to hold on, but her legs weakened, the strength draining from her body.

Strong arms caught her just before she hit the ground. Blurred shapes swam in her vision before resolving into Javkhlan's face. He was crouched beside her, one hand firm on her shoulder.

"Breathe, Zadie."

She nodded, focusing on his words. Gradually, the haze in her mind lifted, and her pulse returned to normal.

Members of the Naledi and Floresiensis groups took pieces of meat one by one and added them to trays positioned over the fire.

Zadie looked at Javkhlan. "They're cooking the meat? In Azania180, they ate it raw."

He gave a slight shrug. "Each tribe has its own way. Traditions change with the land."

A Floresiensis man and a Naledi woman spoke together on behalf of the groups.

"We honor you. You gave us joy. You are not lost. You now walk in our bones, and with the spirits beyond."

The leaders consumed the brains first. Next, the Naledi and Floresiensis groups took their share of the organs. Finally, the cooked meat was passed around the wider circle. Zadie spotted Freeya consuming the meat without hesitation. Her heart raced as the trays came closer, each step bringing her face to face with the moment she'd been dreading.

Han-Yoon leaned closer, his voice a whisper in the charged air. "I heard it's not that different from pork," he said, offering a reassuring smile.

She gave him a flat look. He meant well, but right now, it wasn't helping.

Javkhlan accepted his piece with solemnity. Han-Yoon followed suit with a calm acceptance.

Zadie's hand hovered over the tray, trembling. She could sense eyes on her, waiting. Their silent expectations tugged at her resolve. Her fingers closed around the smallest piece she could find, its pale pink flesh glistening under the light. It had been lightly cooked, leaving the surface firm but still tender to the touch. A thin layer of fat clung to one side, its edges curling from the heat. Her stomach twisted at the thought of what it had been—and who it had been. Ebuni or Eka.

The thought of retreating seemed just as impossible as the act itself. Her mind raced, searching for an escape, but there was none.

She lifted the meat to her lips. The smell wasn't overwhelming. It was neither inviting nor repulsive. It carried a richness, something dense and hearty. A rhythmic thudding filled her head, her pulse pounding at her temples—each beat a reminder of the line she was about to cross.

Her thoughts drifted back to her grandfather's funeral—how distant his body had seemed, untouched and clean, separated by layers of ceremony. This was the opposite.

As the meat touched her tongue, her body tensed, bracing for revulsion. Warmth spread across her palate, the texture soft, almost velvety. She bit down. The meat yielded, coating her mouth in an unwelcome slickness.

Her stomach clenched, and saliva flooded her mouth. A bitter taste crept up her throat. She swallowed hard, but her body resisted, her chest spasmed and her stomach heaved. She wrenched her jaw shut, forcing herself to swallow, distancing herself from the reality of what she had just done. Somehow, the meat made it down. Not because she'd fully accepted it—but because the moment demanded it.

Her gaze drifted over the circle. The others sat in calm reverence. Love, respect, acceptance. It was all there, settling over them like a hush. But it slid past her, untouched. Her eyes lingered on Han-Yoon, trying to understand how he could adapt, how the act that had shaken her left no mark on him. Even her own horror seemed distant.

She realized the QS was still there, smoothing their edges and dulling their terror. Without it, wouldn't they all be screaming? Running? Two deaths, QS control, the Anunnaki containing their souls—and yet here they sat, sharing flesh with an almost dream-like calm. How much of Han-Yoon's philosophical acceptance was genuine understanding, and how much was synthetic serenity? She couldn't tell anymore where true feelings ended, and QS-induced calm began.

Javkhlan shifted beside her, his hand brushing against hers. "You did well. There's power in yielding. Like a tree that bends but never breaks."

25
Bound by the Code

A gentle touch on Zadie's shoulder stirred her from sleep. Around her, the other humans lay scattered across the soft ground, some partially obscured by the tree's gnarled roots. Overhead, the sky beyond the glass dome paled with the first light of dawn. She pushed herself upright.

"I'm... sorry about Ebuni and Eka. We failed them. Correction: the Anunnaki failed them," Sargona said, crouching beside her.

Zadie's gaze drifted to where the Naledi and Floresiensis leaders worked in silence, breaking down the last of Ebuni and Eka's bones into fine dust. She shook her head. "I don't think this will ever make sense to me."

Javkhlan stirred, stretching with a quiet grunt. Beside him, Han-Yoon rubbed his eyes in a brisk, irritable motion.

Sargona stood, stepping back a few paces, hands clasping and unclasping. "I've come to say goodbye. My turn is coming. Soon, my soul will be... contained. Confined. I don't know what I'll be after that."

Goosebumps rose on Zadie's arms. "Why? What's happening to those who've had it contained?"

"No Quantum Psychosis. That's... acceptable. A success, even," Sargona said. "But there's something else. An unease. A kind of suffocation. They call it claustrophobia—but not of space. Of self." Their fingers flexed, then curled into fists. "We don't know discomfort. Never have. We've never needed defenses. We have no strategies."

Zadie bit her lip. "Then don't do it."

Sargona shook their head. "I must. We all must. It was decided."

Javkhlan and Han-Yoon exchanged uneasy glances, struggling to process what Sargona had just said.

"No second path?" Javkhlan asked.

"The choice was made while we were compromised. Flawed. It's done now. No alternative. No turning back. Just forward, whatever the cost." A single tear traced a path down their cheek. Sargona's fingers lifted, hesitant, as if encountering an unfamiliar substance.

It shouldn't have hurt. But it did. More than she expected. "It's just a tear. It means you're human."

Sargona's lips twitched, almost a smile.

"Did you find out why your QS governance is so much lower than the other Anunnaki?" Zadie asked.

"Yes. I've pieced it together from the fragments I still receive," Sargona said, pausing, as if debating how much to share. "I'm Mushěški's last carrier of the sickle cell trait. Not the full disease, just a single allele."

Han-Yoon frowned. "How's that possible? I thought the Anunnaki perfected their DNA."

Sargona shrugged. "Perfection depends on context. Once, the Collective Consciousness saw value in it. The sickle cell allele has some advantages. Malaria resistance, for one. But that perspective didn't last."

"And what, this allele somehow protects you from QS?" Han-Yoon leaned forward, eyes narrowing.

"To a degree. The irregular hemoglobin in my blood interacts with quantum structures creating interference patterns. A mild resistance to QS expansion. But during the energy transfer experiment, something else happened. Unexpected. The quantum manipulation didn't just interact... some of my QS structures collapsed. Reverted to organic neural networks."

Han-Yoon rubbed his chin. "That's why the other Anunnaki weren't affected."

Zadie's eyes widened. "I carry it too. Maybe that's why the QS doesn't control my emotions as much as it does the others."

Sargona gave a slow nod. "Yes. That would follow."

"But I didn't feel anything shift. Nothing changed... I think."

"Your QS levels were already low. Any shift may have been more subtle. Beneath perception," Sargona said.

Han-Yoon's eyes brightened with hope. "Then isn't this the solution the Anunnaki have been searching for?"

Sargona exhaled. "This possibility has been known to the Collective Consciousness since the energy transfer experiment. The data was clear. But our society... it's bound by layers of regulation. Strict ethical codes. Genetic modification, no matter how advantageous, cannot involve alleles associated with disease."

Zadie frowned. "But I thought the Collective Consciousness was always learning, always evolving. Surely it could bend the rules just this once—"

"It's not that simple." Sargona's jaw clenched. "Historical precedents. Mistakes. Overcorrections. Layer after layer of regulation. All meant to prevent genetic regression, to ward off catastrophe. But now... the laws are too rigid. No flexibility. No exceptions. Even when the exception could save us."

A heavy silence settled.

"What about the Sylvicolus?" Zadie asked. "They also seemed less affected by QS than the other humans."

"Yes. Their DNA has been mapped and analyzed... extensively. They carry a rare form of *hypertrichosis*... excessive hair growth. But it goes deeper. Neural ion channels. Stress regulation pathways. QS integration is disrupted. Their minds resist. Greater autonomy. Fascinating. And yet... irrelevant."

Zadie raised an eyebrow. "But hypertrichosis isn't even a disease, it's just a condition, isn't it? Couldn't you just integrate that DNA?"

"Technically, yes," Sargona said. "But hair wasn't just a trait we removed. It became symbolic. A remnant of pre-QS existence... of imperfection. The laws weren't just written to prevent genetic regression. They became doctrine. Untouchable." Their fingers twitched, then stilled. "We engineered ourselves into a corner. And now... even if we wanted to, we can't go back."

Han-Yoon let out a sharp breath, shaking his head. "This is what happens when you let an algorithm run the show. You built all these safeguards, but now they're a straitjacket."

Zadie looked to Sargona, but they said nothing. No one did.

◇——☼——◇

Kr-r-r-r-oo! A low, trilled cry pierced the air.

The swish of wings cut through the sanctuary's hush as the bird swept into view—broad, graceful, utterly out of place. One by one, the sleeping participants stirred, eyes fluttering open as the bird swept over them.

"A crane," Zadie breathed, eyes wide.

Sargona's gaze tracked the crane, their expression growing tense. "That can only mean one thing. The energy fields of the biodomes have failed. That would account for the patterns... no containment, no stabilization. They paused, deep in thought. "But the sanctuary should have held. It doesn't make sense... unless the crane slipped through an unstable fold point."

Zadie's pulse jumped. "What are you saying?"

Sargona's fingers twitched. "It means... the disruption to the Collective Consciousness is affecting Mushĕški's biodomes. Returning may not be safe. No, correction—returning is *not* safe."

"The tribes!" Zadie shot to her feet, her thoughts racing to Javkhlan's people.

Around them, the ancient humans had gone still, eyes locked on the bird. They began to follow it as if under a shared spell, their movements silent and instinctive.

Javkhlan lingered, his eyes shifting between the crane and Zadie. His expression tightened with visible conflict—the instinctual pull toward the crane battling against his desire to remain with her. He reached out, clasping her hand. "The crane calls to something older than my own will. I must follow."

Before she could respond, a group of Anunnaki entered the sanctuary, their attention focused on Sargona. Sargona exhaled a weary breath that seemed to carry the weight of the entire situation.

26

Contact

A scream tore through the stillness from the communal lounge. Zadie and Han-Yoon exchanged a glance and sprinted toward it. Inside, the space glowed with the amber light of sunset.

Zadie frowned. "But it's dawn. That doesn't make sense."

As they moved further in, the lighting shifted, flooding the room with a glaring brightness that made her wince.

In the far corner, a Neanderthal woman, one of the near-death experiment volunteers, lay crumpled, her eyes wide and unfocused. Her breaths came quick and uneven, the aftershock of the scream fading into fragile whimpers. Whatever she'd seen was fading now—the QS smoothing her emotions, dulling them until the fear was trapped, twitching, beneath her skin.

Zadie dropped to her knees and placed a firm hand on the woman's shoulder. The woman flinched but didn't pull away. "What happened?"

The woman's breathing slowed, her haunted eyes locking onto Zadie's, but it was like looking into a void.

"Death... everywhere," the woman whispered. "So many... about to die... unstoppable."

Zadie fought to swallow the rising fear as she glanced up at Han-Yoon. "This could be... the beginning of the end."

Han-Yoon gestured toward the experiment hall. "Everyone's in there."

"Another experiment?"

Han-Yoon shook his head. "No, they're with the crane... starting the rituals, like in Altay60."

They moved toward the experiment hall, Zadie's strides growing shorter, her shoulders inching higher. Inside, nothing remained of the last experiment setup. With no high perch, the crane had settled nervously on the floor, its feathers ruffled. The humans had gathered in their respective groups, carefully giving it a wide berth.

Han-Yoon observed the groups. "Why do they all think the crane calls for a ritual?"

Zadie shrugged, then caught sight of a Naledi man nearby. He pointed a blade at his palm and pressed. Blood welled, dripping to the floor and joining the crimson pools left by the others. She looked away.

Across the hall, the Sapiens from Azania180 and Altay60 sat with their eyes closed, bodies swaying in a quiet, meditative rhythm. Near them, the Neanderthals and Denisovans—Javkhlan among them—linked hands, their fingers interlaced as they formed a circle of solidarity. Their movements started slow, building in intensity. The Sylvicolus stood, their feet striking the ground in unison, rhythmic stomps growing louder and more commanding with every beat.

Han-Yoon gestured toward the Floresiensis, Luzonensis, and Erectus groups clustered in the far corner—the only groups seemingly indifferent to the crane's presence. "Maybe they don't have cranes in NusaLale120..."

The surrounding air turned hostile, abandoning its usual calm for something unpredictable. The temperature swung, starting with an oppressive wave of heat that settled heavily on Zadie's skin, making each breath feel labored. Sweat trickled down her back. Around her, others fidgeted and fanned themselves, faces flushed.

Zadie shot Han-Yoon a sideways glance. "It's not just the lighting anymore. Something's properly wrong."

Then, without warning, the heat evaporated, replaced by a sudden, biting cold. Zadie crossed her arms, trying to keep warm as her jumpsuit thickened in response. Her breath turned to mist in the freezing air.

Javkhlan appeared beside them, his eyes moving slowly across the ritual formations. "They fear the spirits have turned away. Without the sacred fungus, the ritual fails. Their hope is slipping."

Han-Yoon gripped Zadie's arm. His eyes were unfocused. "I can... sense something. There's more beyond this. Other beings. Not spirits. Watching. Waiting."

Other beings, not spirits... Then what were they?

"The Abgal?" she asked.

He swallowed. "I think so."

Zadie exhaled sharply. "The Sumerians didn't need mushrooms—they connected with the Abgal through meditation. What if we try that? Maybe they can help us."

Han-Yoon arched an eyebrow. "You know how to meditate?"

Zadie's hands tightened at her sides. "No... I've never been able to keep my mind still long enough. But maybe others can..."

"Or you could use the Unifier..."

Zadie spun around, her heart stuttering as Sargona stood before them. A rush of relief hit her, until she caught their rigid stance, the dark circles beneath their eyes, the brittle way they now held themselves. "You don't look—"

"I'm still here," Sargona said. The words came too fast, like a reflex rather than a certainty. "But things are unraveling faster than I expected."

"Could the Unifier reach the Abgal? And if so, do you think they would help us?" Zadie asked.

"The Anunnaki can connect with the Abgal through the Collective Consciousness, but... that's not an option for us." Their fingers twitched. "If I can configure the hall... yes, that might work. But whether they'll help... That variable remains uncertain. I'll attempt it anyway. Stagnation is worse."

Zadie searched their face. "Is there anything we can do?"

"No. Normally, this would be effortless... a single thought transmitting through the network. But now..." They moved toward the center of the hall. "I'll need to attempt a direct connection to the Collective Consciousness. It might take several tries."

Javkhlan motioned the other groups back, guiding them out of harm's way.

Sargona closed their eyes, shoulders tensing. Silence stretched, seconds dragging into minutes, as they stood motionless. The hall's structure began to shift into the new configuration, but then stuttered as the connection fractured. Sargona's hands clenched. "It's like trying to join an orchestra when you can only hear every thirteenth note." They tried again. And again. Each attempt brought a fleeting resonance with the Collective Consciousness before dissolving into discord.

On the seventh attempt, Sargona's posture straightened, their expression clearing. The experiment hall began its transformation, the space gently reconfiguring into the familiar setup for the Akashidu Experiment. For five precious seconds, Sargona was whole again, integrated, certain, efficient. Sargona steadied themselves, their breathing ragged but their expression full of pride. "It's done."

Whispered doubts flared between groups, some voices growing louder, urgent. "Why should we trust the Unifier?"

The crane took to the air, startling the group. It perched awkwardly atop the Unifier, head tilted as though affirming something only it understood. Around the room, the ancient humans stilled, their eyes following the bird, as if waiting for its permission.

Zadie stepped onto the platform, aware of the crane tracking her every move. She swallowed hard. Then raised her voice. "Mushēški is unraveling. The Anunnaki can't help us now, but the Abgal might." Her gaze swept the scattered groups. "We have to come together. It's the only way they'll hear us. If we lose this opportunity, there might not be another."

There was a pause, then one of the Naledi moved. Others followed, a quiet chain reaction. One by one, they found their places.

Zadie positioned herself between Javkhlan and Han-Yoon. Her luminescent ring descended into place. Javkhlan's eyes were already closed, brow creased in silent focus. Han-Yoon sat motionless, jaw locked, as if bracing for impact. Shutting her eyes, she tried to steady her breathing, but a rising panic clawed at her throat. What if they couldn't reach the Abgal? What if it was already too late? What if the Neanderthal woman was right about the mass deaths? Every time she reached for stillness, doubt returned, a cruel whisper in the back of her mind. What if they failed? She shoved the thoughts down, burying the dread that threatened to pull her apart.

The Unifier's glow deepened. A pulse of energy rolled through the room. The weight of their minds gathered, then pulled, stretching outward, drawn toward something like a radio signal. Reaching. Searching.

Just as the pressure became unbearable, she felt it—an impossibly distant tremor, cutting through the static like a whispered note. It slipped away. For a breath, she thought she'd imagined it. Then it came again, stronger this time, a vibration reaching back.

The Abgal had heard them.

27

The Release

Seven figures began to take shape on the central platform, solidifying out of a mist. The Abgal. Tall—at least seven feet, perhaps more. Their robes shimmered in hues of blue and green, shifting with silvery ripples, like sunlight on the ocean floor.

Zadie's gaze dropped. Webbed feet? Damp smudges marked the platform, then vanished. Higher up, a shallow, rhythmic pulse along their necks suggested a breath taken differently. They were humanoid, but different. Their skin held her attention. Hairless. Gray-green. A faint iridescence shimmered across the surface, shifting with every movement. They were similar enough to be mesmerizing, yet different enough to be unsettling. For the first time, she welcomed the calming influence of her QS.

They'd come. The Abgal. They'd actually come. Zadie tugged at her sleeves, one foot tapping out a restless beat. If anyone had answers, it had to be them.

A group of Anunnaki filed into the experiment hall, their gait even, posture identical, hands poised at exact angles. They moved like people hyper-aware of every motion, every twitch, as though their bodies had become foreign objects, tools to be operated, not inhabited. They carried the stilted calm of someone acting normal under surveillance. Not from outside, but within. Lugazir walked among them, indistinguishable at first glance, their movements just as measured, just as compressed. Despite the heaviness of the situation, the Anunnaki didn't recoil. Just that eerie, collective stillness, like they were listening for salvation.

Warmth spread through her chest as the Abgal's message formed within her, their telepathic voice soothing yet firm.

"Many years ago, our ancestors gave the gift of Quantum Sentience to a group of Sumerians who became the Anunnaki. Yet, our ancestors did not expect the issues this gift would create. We recognize this error, and we offer our deepest apologies. Today, we are here to correct that mistake and restore the balance that was lost."

Anunnaki heads lifted throughout the hall, as if the Abgal's words had already lightened their burden.

"We propose a release," the Abgal continued, their voice as gentle as it was unsettling. *"Not an end, but a transition—a release of Anunnaki souls from the physical forms that have become their prisons."*

Zadie looked at Javkhlan. "What do they mean?"

He squeezed her hand reassuringly, though the QS held his voice captive.

The Abgal's heads tilted slightly, absorbing the tension in the hall. *"We understand the gravity of our proposal. We do not make this offer lightly, but out of a deep understanding of the Anunnaki's plight. We sense the struggle and the desire to return to a form of existence untainted by the current constraints."*

The hall seemed to close in around her as she grappled with the enormity of what the Abgal were proposing. A release? Of souls? Her thoughts kept circling back, crashing into the same wall. A mass killing?

The participants' desperate plea to the Abgal had backfired. Instead of a lifeline, they had extended a noose.

Zadie scanned the room, expecting to see her own horror reflected in the faces of the Anunnaki. But instead of fear or dissent, she found only resignation. The Abgal's serene expressions and the somber acceptance in Lugazir's eyes only deepened her turmoil.

"Please take some time to deliberate."

A contemplative pause settled over the hall. The Anunnaki exchanged fleeting glances, their thoughts surely merging and colliding within the Collective Consciousness.

Zadie spotted Sargona moving toward her, their face tight with something close to defeat. "Sargona, what's happening? I don't get it."

Sargona looked away as if searching for an answer that wouldn't hurt. "The Abgal are... they're proposing the termination of our civilization."

"That's what I was afraid of." She glanced at the Anunnaki, then back at Sargona. "Are they seriously thinking about going through with it?"

"I... I hope so. It might be the only way we... no, not escape. Expand. That's the word. It might be the only way we expand."

Her eyes stung. She blinked hard and wrapped her arms around Sargona, clinging tightly.

Sargona tensed, arms pinned awkwardly at their sides, their body as rigid as if Zadie had encased them in stone. For a moment, they didn't move or breathe, staring straight ahead with wide, startled eyes.

Slowly, as though testing a foreign object, they lifted one hand, hovering it over her back. Their fingers brushed her shoulder, tentative, then rested there, uncertain. Something softened in their expression. "This is... an unfamiliar form of compression. No, that's not the right term. Containment? No. Structural reinforcement."

"It's a *hug*," Zadie said.

Sargona remained still, processing. "The sensation is... restrictive, but... increased warmth." They inhaled. "I am 527 years old. And that—that was my first hug."

Zadie's composure shattered. She clung to them, sobs spilling free. Eventually, she pulled back, eyes swollen. "How do you know you aren't all just... being manipulated by the Abgal?"

Sargona's lips twitched. "I don't. But if we are, then maybe—like the QS integrated into you—it was designed to be supportive."

Zadie drew a shaky breath, the ache of helplessness settling over her.

Sargona studied her. "I regret it had to end this way. The Anunnaki weren't always like this. We started with pure intentions..."

"I speak on behalf of the Anunnaki," Lugazir said. "After careful reflection, we have chosen to embrace your proposal for release. Our lives have stretched beyond natural human limits. We are weary of the endless battle against Quantum Psychosis. Containing our souls has become an unbearable imprisonment. We choose release, to end this cycle and face the next phase of existence."

Their acceptance came too fast. There was no hesitation, no friction. But as harmony settled over the hall, Zadie's skepticism wavered. Perhaps it was easier to suspect manipulation than to accept that an entire civilization might choose... *to transcend.* Flashes of Ebuni's final moments surged through her mind—her painful decision to embrace death rather than remain trapped in an Anunnaki body.

"Before we begin, we invite the Anunnaki to share memories to honor their civilization's legacy," the Abgal communicated.

Above the assembly, an energy thickened, like a raincloud on the brink of breaking. Zadie felt the pressure build. Then the first drop hit—and the Anunnaki's past overtook her senses.

She saw the rituals that once honored the harvest—the sensation of soil between fingers, the vibrant textures and flavors that had made every meal a shared experience, a moment of community. She witnessed the moment when food became abundant, hunger receding into memory. Awe stirred within her, marveling at their progress. And yet, food had become sterile, severed from the land that had once breathed life into it.

With the next droplet, she found herself in the body of an ancient Sumerian, strength pulsing through every limb. Gratitude surged. But as the centuries unfolded, the natural deadlines that once gave life meaning were worn smooth by the luxury of time. Years stretched, then blurred. Decades passed without shape. The urgency to seize each fleeting moment slipped quietly away.

Zadie's pulse quickened with the thrill of uncovering the universe's hidden truths. Each insight flared, then faded, leaving her hungry for the next. But soon, something shifted. Knowledge began to flow too freely, too easily, and the familiar satisfaction of hard-won discovery faded. She missed the journey, the thrill of the chase, the uncertainty that made each revelation feel alive.

Love among the first Anunnaki had been imperfect. Zadie could feel it now, there was uncertainty and longing. She heard whispered confessions, felt the anticipation of a lover's touch, saw the beauty in moments full of potential. But as this memory faded, she realized that such love no longer existed on Mushēski.

The next memory arrived like a warm breeze drifting through her mind. Days flowed in perfect harmony, free from the chaos and suffering that often plagued human existence. There was a muted elegance in the

Anunnaki order, a peaceful rhythm in how they lived. For a fleeting second, she grasped its appeal. But as she searched for the delight of spontaneity, she found only the sterile predictability of a life too controlled.

Zadie closed her eyes. They had reached for the stars but lost touch with the ground beneath their feet. It was all gone—the mess, the mystery, the spark that once gave life its meaning. Everything that made them human.

The Anunnaki were making the right call.

"The release process is gentle, based on harmonic resonance. Every entity vibrates at a unique frequency. The Anunnaki emit a complex harmonic signature shaped by their biological matter and integrated Quantum Sentience. We will generate a calibrated wave tuned to this signature across Mushēški. It will induce a shift in the QS elements, disrupting their coherence and gently dissolving the sentient connection, ensuring a peaceful transition."

Zadie's eyes met Lugazir's. The one who had once spoken of ancient truths, who had guided her through Dilmun's wonders was already gone. A tightness seized her chest, the realization settling hard. Her hands, once clenched in anger, now hung limp at her sides, drained of the fight she no longer held. All that remained was a quiet grief as she watched a human species on the brink of extinction.

The Abgal produced a low, rhythmic tone. A faint glow built within their circle, spreading from their forms like first light. The tone deepened, filling the hall, reverberating through the air like distant thunder. From the center, waves of light and sound rippled outward, reaching the Anunnaki at the hall's edge.

Zadie caught sight of Sargona. Shoulders squared, eyes steady, as if they'd been waiting for this all along. When the harmonic current touched them, a tremor ran through their body, subtle at first, then building with each wave.

The air shimmered around each Anunnaki, distorting like rising heat. One by one, their forms began to glow. Outlines blurred, then dissolved into radiant energy. Luminous particles spiraled upward, trailing arcs of light like miravys fireflies. The assembly watched in silence as each Anunnaki transformed—light spilling from what had once been flesh, a final release from their trapped existence.

Zadie turned to Javkhlan. "What happens to us now?"

28

The Miravysians

Everything dissolved into a blinding flash of light. For a moment, there was nothing but the sensation of movement without motion.

When the world solidified around Zadie, she was flat on her back, enveloped in darkness. Her heart pounded. Each breath came sharp and unsteady as the shock of the shift hit. A musty odor triggered a wave of nausea. Grit bit into her palms as she pushed herself up.

A scream tore through the air—unrestrained by artificial calm. It was quickly followed by others, some descended into hysterical sobs. Others rose into wails that bounced off unseen walls.

"Get away from me!" A panicked shout was followed by the sound of a scuffle. Someone fell hard against the ground with a painful thud.

"I can't breathe—" A voice broke off into desperate gasps, the sound of someone hyperventilating.

Shapes moved in the dark, bodies shifting and stumbling. Someone collapsed nearby, their body convulsing. Zadie made out two Floresiensis huddled together next to her, their small forms trembling. Against the far wall, someone vomited, the smell adding to the sensory assault.

"Where is the moon?" A sob broke into a wail.

"Who's there? Who's touching me?"

Every muscle in Zadie's body tensed with a heightened awareness. Without the QS dampening her senses, every sound, smell, and sensation hit with bruising force. Her skin felt too tight, her nerves raw. Her heart pounded so violently she feared it might crack her ribs. The flood of unmuted sensation left no doubt—she was no longer in Dilmun. At least the neuroscribe still functioned.

"Javkhlan? Han-Yoon?"

"Zadie!" Javkhlan called back. She heard him pushing through the crowd. "I will find you!"

Han-Yoon's voice broke through a moment later, high and tight with hysteria. "I'm here too." His words gave way to awkward laughter.

She reached out blindly, fingers grasping at the air. A firm grip closed around her wrist; another hand caught her shoulder. Javkhlan pulled her into a protective embrace.

"Where are we? What's happening? Is everyone here?" Han-Yoon asked, his words tumbling over each other.

Lights flooded the space, startlingly bright. Several people screamed, diving for cover and throwing their arms over their faces. Zadie winced, momentarily blinded by the intensity as her eyes struggled to adjust.

"My eyes! It burns!" someone wailed.

As her eyes adjusted, Zadie saw the massive stone walls of a chamber and the ancient humans around her. Most crouched close together, arms slung over shoulders, hands gripping wrists or sleeves. A few sat frozen, eyes wide, mouths slack, as if the ability to move had simply left them.

Whispers began, soft at first. They grew louder, questions and fears bubbling to the surface until they erupted into a cacophony of overlapping voices.

"I cannot hear my own thoughts!" a Neanderthal man roared.

His outburst triggered more chaos. Shouts, crying, and arguments flared as frayed nerves snapped. Two Sapiens from Altay60 shoved each other; a Denisovan stepped in to separate them and took an elbow to the ribs. Javkhlan steered Zadie and Han-Yoon toward the edge of the chamber.

Zadie reached out, her fingers grazing the carved stone wall. "This... this reminds me of Bahrain." Her breath hitched. The patterns, the precision. She had stood here before.

An Earth-born man moved to the front of the chamber with quiet, self-assured ease. "Welcome to Earth," he said. "My name is Ahmed, and I'm also a Miravysian."

"Oh my God, that's my uncle!" The words came out in a half-sob, half-laugh. Before she knew it, she was fighting her way toward him, emotions surging with the desperate need for it to be real. She collided with him hard enough to make him stagger. "Uncle! Is it really you? Are we safe now? Please tell me we're safe!" The words tumbled out between gasping breaths.

Ahmed pulled her into a firm embrace. Zadie pressed her face into his coarse jacket, breathing in his spicy scent as her composure slipped. A shaky breath escaped, then another, and before she could stop it, tears were soaking into his shirt.

"You're safe now, Zadie," Ahmed said, stroking her hair. "You're back."

For a moment, she let herself sink into the relief. But then the memory of everything she'd been through curdled into an intense rage. She yanked back, her brows drawn tight with anger. "Why did you send me there? I trusted you, and you threw me into hell!" Her voice rose with each word until she was shouting. "People died!"

"I'm so sorry, my dear. I didn't know. I swear, I never would have put you through that if I'd known." Ahmed's shoulders sagged, guilt pooling in his eyes. He seemed to age years in seconds.

She shook her head. "I didn't know if I'd ever get back... if I'd ever see home again..." The words came out as a whisper.

Around them, the emotional temperature in the chamber continued to rise. Questions surged, growing louder and more urgent. Individuals pushed forward, faces contorted with fear, anger, and confusion. Emotions long suppressed were now exploding in chaotic bursts.

"Who are you?" a Neanderthal man demanded, his tone sharp with suspicion, his burly frame tensed for conflict. "Who are the Miravysians?" He advanced toward Ahmed, nostrils flaring.

Anxiety rippled through the others, their voices overlapping in a storm of panic:

"Why do we stand here?"

"What is this color?"

"Where will we find food and shelter?"

"Are there predators to fear?"

Her uncle's arm tensed. Then he let go, turning to face the crowd. "Please, let me explain..."

Gradually, the noise diminished. Their eyes fixed on Ahmed, their need for answers edging out the fear.

Zadie returned to Javkhlan's side. She squeezed his arm. He flinched, then leaned into her touch.

"We're in a chamber beneath the Kingdom of Bahrain... on the planet Earth," Ahmed began. "This place was constructed many thousands of years ago by the Anunnaki, in partnership with their ancient Sumerian relatives. The Abgal transitfolded you all here for now, to keep you safe. It's my duty to guide you through what lies ahead."

Someone shifted, scuffing their foot against the stone. A Neanderthal woman wiped tears from her cheeks with the back of her hand, her breath still coming in shuddering gasps.

"The Abgal have passed on some information that I need to tell you," Ahmed said. "Unfortunately, not all of you made it here." He paused, scanning the anxious faces. "The two participants whose souls didn't realign properly... they didn't survive the journey. The transitfold process was somehow incompatible with their state. I'm deeply sorry for your loss."

Ahmed's words were met with a heavy silence. The group stood frozen, shock rippling through their faces like a slow-motion wave.

Javkhlan searched Ahmed's face for answers. "The rest of our people? Do they still walk beneath the sky we knew?"

"Your tribes are safe. They were relocated by other Abgal during the Anunnaki's release. Because of their numbers, they were moved to environments on Earth that resemble the biodomes on Mushëški."

"Where?" Javkhlan asked. "Will our eyes meet theirs again?"

Ahmed closed his eyes, and a sensation gripped Zadie's chest—heat from the Serengeti sun. She realized she wasn't the only one feeling it. Around her, mouths parted in silent awe. The air was dry, carrying the scent of dust and grass. In her mind, she saw the Naledi and Sapiens from Azania180 moving across the golden plains as if they had always belonged there.

The image blurred, replaced by the dense, humid forests of the Togian Islands. Nightfall disoriented the tribes from NusaLale120, throwing them into sudden disarray in the unfamiliar terrain. The Erectus tribes vanished into the undergrowth. Meanwhile, the Floresiensis and Luzonensis huddled together, waiting for daylight, their eyes scanning the darkness with wary patience.

The icy winds of the Mongolian Steppes came next, beneath a sun already slanting low in the sky. The Sylvicolus tribes wasted no time, heading toward the jagged peaks of the Altai Mountains on the horizon. The Denisovan and Neanderthal tribes, however, lingered on the plains, drawing closer together, their eyes wary of some of the ancient Sapiens who roamed nearby.

The visions faded as Ahmed opened his eyes, the neuroscribe's telepathic echo still tingling at her temple. A murmur spread, then swelled into a chorus, voices overlapping, questioning, demanding.

"Why were our feet set on a different path?"

"Why are we not with our kin?"

"Why are we left apart?"

A Floresiensis woman pressed her fists against her eyes, shoulders heaving with silent sobs. Two Neanderthals embraced, their shared grief palpable.

Zadie's eyes darted back to Ahmed. He didn't speak right away. His fingers tapped against his leg, an old habit she recognized. He was struggling to explain something he perhaps didn't fully understand himself.

"Initially, it was a matter of logistics, given your location at the time the Abgal arrived," Ahmed said. "But now that you're here, I'd like to offer you an option. Some of you may wish to return to your original tribes. Others might consider remaining here and exploring the possibility of building a life within modern society. Both paths are equally valid."

Zadie exhaled slowly. The word *integration* remained unspoken, but she understood the weight behind Ahmed's careful phrasing. She had already turned these considerations over, weighing the complex realities, the inevitable challenges of either choice. Zadie studied the ancient humans, noting the spectrum of emotions crossing their faces—confusion, disbelief, curiosity, fear—all written with an honesty that Dilmun had never allowed.

"The world is interconnected, and the isolation of your tribes won't last forever," Ahmed continued. "When Earth-born people discover your tribes, their reactions will vary. If some of you choose to engage with modern society first, your experiences might help pave the way for understanding. This is not about erasing who you are or where you come from, it's about creating a bridge, should you wish to build one."

"We do not see the need for trouble. Why should there be trouble?" a Neanderthal man said, his innocence making the question seem both childlike and profound.

Zadie watched the confusion in his eyes. The ways of this world—of their ancestors' world—were so foreign to them all.

Ahmed pulled at his ear. "People here... they cling to what they know, what feels safe. Your presence will challenge their understanding of humanity."

A Denisovan woman beside the Neanderthal man tilted her head slightly, her braids cascading over her shoulders like a dark waterfall. "But we are human."

The woman's words were so sincere, yet Zadie knew they wouldn't shield her from Earth-born humans. She felt an unexpected surge of protectiveness toward these ancient humans who now faced a world that had forgotten them.

Ahmed nodded, a sad smile touching his lips. "I know. But to many people here, humanity has boundaries, narrow ones. When those boundaries are pushed, it will feel like... like a threat. They'll worry you might be stronger, smarter, or just... better."

The Denisovan woman exchanged a glance with the Neanderthal man. "We will only seek to coexist."

"Unfortunately, it's not about what you intend—it's about what they fear. Identity here is... fragile. People define themselves by their nationality, their gender, their religion, their career, and so on. When something new comes along that doesn't fit into that, it feels like an attack on who they are. People here aren't inherently bad. They just... need time. Time to understand. And until they do, they will react with hostility, because it's easier than facing the reality that the world they thought they knew is... changing."

The woman looked down at her hands, her eyes glistening. "We do not wish to bring such pain."

A Luzonensis man reached out to her, his small hand resting on her forearm in silent solidarity. Others moved closer, drawn by her visible distress, barriers between species dissolving in the face of shared emotion.

Ahmed shook his head, the sadness in his eyes deepening. "With time, acceptance will come. Today, you all become *Miravysians*. Like you, I have made the journey between Mushĕški and Earth. This journey... has given us the ability to see the color miravys. But it's more than just a color, it's part of our shared destiny, a symbol of our connection."

The group exchanged uncertain glances. Despite their differences, something fundamental connected them all. Zadie watched as the realization spread across their faces. The ancient humans shifted, standing a little straighter. The raw emotion that had threatened to overwhelm them began to transform, channeling into a hesitant spark of hope as they began to grasp the enormity of what lay ahead.

"What happens now?" Han-Yoon asked.

"Our new home—for now, anyway—is a network of safe, stable caves nearby, large enough to accommodate everyone. It's a secluded spot, modernized over the years, and perfect for getting to know Earth's languages, customs, and ways of life, until you're ready to step into the world above."

Zadie pictured the fort above—the tourists wandering the ruins, oblivious to the world hidden beneath their feet. What else was down here that the average person didn't know of?

The chamber grew heavy with unease. The ancient humans clustered in their groups, some whispering, others sitting in stunned silence. A few glanced upward, as if already mourning the open skies and fresh air. Ahmed approached Zadie and Han-Yoon.

"I assume you'll want to return to your own homes," he said. "I can make those arrangements now if you're ready."

Zadie looked at Javkhlan. His face was a mask of controlled fear, his eyes pleading though he said nothing. She felt the weight of his unspoken need not to be abandoned in this strange new world.

"No, I'm staying."

A smile broke through Javkhlan's composure, relief transforming his features. He squeezed her hand, the gesture carrying all the affirmation she needed.

"I'll stay for now, too," Han-Yoon added. "It can't be worse than Musheški?" He laughed, too loudly, then rubbed the back of his neck and stepped closer to Zadie and Javkhlan, as if anchoring himself to the choice he'd just made.

Ahmed studied them, a quiet respect deepening in his expression. "Okay," Ahmed said, nodding slowly. "If you're both sure, then that's settled."

Ahmed handed out flashlights. "The journey ahead should take about thirty minutes. We'll be following a path that's been in use for millennia, an ancient network of tunnels and natural caverns. It's a direct route, but we need to move carefully and stay together."

With a grunt, he shoved open an ancient door, exposing the tunnel beyond. The group hesitated, a collective wariness settling over them. A Floresiensis woman shrank back, her small frame pressed against the chamber wall. "More darkness? More stone closing in?"

Ahmed shot Zadie a nervous glance.

Javkhlan stepped forward. "The Earth has held our ancestors since time began. These tunnels feel like fear, but they're protection too."

Ahmed gave a slight nod, then turned and led the way, his flashlight held high. The others followed one by one, their footsteps tentative but trusting, drawn in by Javkhlan's certainty.

The tunnels were made of massive stone blocks, perfectly aligned, no mortar, no gaps. The ground beneath their feet was worn smooth in places by countless steps over the ages. Cool air brushed against Zadie's skin, carrying a chalky scent, musty but clean, like wet stone after rain. They moved with quiet care, footsteps skimming the ancient path, barely loud enough to register.

The tunnel gradually widened into a labyrinth of caverns, each more breathtaking than the last. Stalactites and stalagmites framed the path like silent stone sentinels, their jagged forms frozen in time. The occasional trickle of an underground stream murmured in the darkness.

They rounded a final bend, and the space opened up before them. Zadie took in the sight of modern living spaces integrated into the cave walls, connected by pathways that curved around natural formations. In recessed alcoves, hydroponic gardens thrived, bright greens vivid against the surrounding stone.

Zadie's breath caught. Beyond the living spaces, a vast, tranquil lake stretched out, its surface perfectly still. Overhead, countless embedded pinpricks of light emitted a soft, steady glow, their reflections shimmering across the water as if a constellation had settled beneath the Earth's surface.

"This," Ahmed announced, "is the heart of our new Miravysian community."

His words resonated through the ancient humans, bringing a subtle shift. Shoulders lowered, breathing slowed, anxieties dulling into exhausted acceptance.

"I'd like to introduce you to some of the Earth-born Miravysians." Ahmed nodded toward a group of twenty or so people standing at the edge of the gathering. "These volunteers have helped bring in the supplies we needed, and will play an important role in the weeks and months to come."

Zadie watched as the ancient humans turned toward the volunteers, some with cautious glances, others with open curiosity. The Earth-born Miravysians offered warm smiles tinged with the seriousness of their mission.

"I know it's been an incredibly long day," Ahmed said. "You must all be exhausted." He gestured toward the alcoves and quiet corners scattered around the cavern. "Sleeping areas have been set up for you, along with food and water stations. Tomorrow, we'll have time to talk. For now, focus on regaining your strength."

The group dispersed through the cavern, claiming spaces that seemed to call to them. The sprawling space offered countless inviting spots to make their own. Han-Yoon waved goodnight while settling into a nook overlooking the lake, its walls sparkling with mineral-rich deposits.

Zadie and Javkhlan wandered through the cavern, their steps growing slower as they took in the unexpected beauty around them. Eventually, they stumbled upon a secluded grotto tucked away from the main pathway. A gentle waterfall cascaded over a ledge of smooth rocks, the water pooling into a clear basin below.

Zadie's eyes widened with delight as she realized the basin had been transformed into a warm spa. "What do you reckon about this one?"

Javkhlan crouched down, dipping his hand into the water. "It feels right," he said, with a weariness that mirrored her own.

They exchanged a glance, a wordless understanding passing between them, and began peeling off their jumpsuits, leaving them in a pile on the cool stone.

Zadie exhaled a shaky breath as the water embraced her, heat soothing her tired limbs. Beside her, Javkhlan slid in with a sigh, eyes drifting shut, mouth softening into a peaceful expression as he surrendered to the warmth.

They stayed like that for a while, suspended in silence. Zadie studied the lines of Javkhlan's face, the way his features had softened now that they were alone. "Are you afraid?"

He opened his eyes, meeting her gaze. "Yes. This world carries you. It does not know me."

"I'm afraid, too," she said. "I'm afraid that if I close my eyes, I'll wake up back in Dilmun."

His hand found hers beneath the water, fingers intertwining. Every sensation was sharpened—the warmth, the slight roughness of his palm, the gentle pressure of his thumb tracing circles on the back of her hand. Savoring the closeness between them, Zadie leaned in. She pressed her lips to his—only for him to pull back.

"What... is this?" His gaze darted between her lips and her eyes, searching for meaning. "You... put your mouth on mine?" His brows drew together, bewildered.

Zadie's cheeks flushed. "It's... a kiss." A soft laugh broke through her awkwardness. "People here do it to show... affection, closeness." She bit her lip, trying to explain in a way that didn't sound absurd. "It's like... a touch, but more intimate."

Javkhlan's face remained uncertain. "I don't know closeness this way. I know warmth, scent... to press skin, to feel the other's breath. This... *kiss*..." He paused as if tasting the word. "It is strange."

"That makes sense. I was wondering why you didn't kiss me the other night."

Curiosity sparked in his eyes as he leaned toward her, studying her face as if trying to understand her foreign customs. After a heartbeat of hesitation, he brought his lips near hers, closing the gap in a brief, experimental kiss. The soft contact made his eyes widen in surprise as he pulled back with an almost boyish wonder on his face.

"I don't... dislike it," he said, as though speaking to himself. "It's strange, but... soft. I feel it." His arms encircled her waist, pulling her on top of him. "Show me again."

Heat flickered through her, a warmth entirely different from the spa's embrace. The water sloshed around them as his hands slid down her back, following the curve of her waist beneath the surface.

"We should get out," she said, nodding toward their sleeping area.

They pulled themselves from the water. The cool air nipped at their damp skin until they reached the plush bedding.

Their limbs found each other, chasing the warmth they'd just left behind. His touch carried the weight of their journey—the Anunnaki, the biodomes, the experiments, the loss, the impossible chance that had drawn them together across species and eras. As his fingers traced her skin, she saw it in his eyes—not just desire, but recognition. Two souls from different worlds, carrying the end of one world into the uncertain light of another.

She guided his mouth back to hers. This time, he met her kiss with understanding. His breath mingled with hers, deepening, drawing her under like a slow current.

29
Roots and Branches

J avkhlan's warmth and the tangle of bedding almost kept her there. But hunger had a louder voice. Saffron, cardamom, and freshly brewed coffee teased her senses, and her stomach growled in response. Zadie moved Javkhlan's arm aside, holding her breath as he stirred. But he only grunted, burrowing his head deeper into the pillow.

Soft, warm light bathed the cavern, mimicking daylight and making her forget she was underground. As she made her way to the communal areas, the waterfall's steady roar blended into the background, overtaken by the lively stir of voices and movement ahead.

A kitchen sprawled along one side of the cavern, an intriguing blend of nature and technology. The scent of baking bread drifted from ovens tucked into the rock walls, while steam curled from portable stoves.

Long wooden tables stood piled high with food—too much food. Stacks of warm flatbreads sat beside jugs of milky, cardamom-scented tea and bitter Arabic coffee. The sweet aroma of saffron-infused vermicelli mingled with the buttery scent of golden omelets, the earthy spice of chickpeas, and the sharp, fried edge of *samboosas*. It was familiar and comforting, but at odds with the unusual setting.

Miravysian helpers moved with efficiency, hands kneading, stirring, and chopping. The steady thud of knives punctuated the hum of work. Across the table, the ancient humans watched, their expressions varying. A Denisovan woman leaned closer, her gaze fixed, unblinking. Was she puzzled by the sheer abundance? In subsistence societies, excess wasn't just unusual, it was unnatural. A display of power, a disruption of balance. Zadie swallowed. If nothing muted their impulses now, what would keep the peace?

Someone pressed a warm piece of flatbread and a mug into Zadie's hands. The bread softened under her fingers, its heat a quiet comfort. She took a sip, the bitterness anchoring her thoughts.

Ahmed caught her eye as he headed toward her. There was weariness behind his smile. "Zadie, my dear, again I'm so sorry about what happened on Mushĕški. I didn't know things would escalate so quickly."

"But you knew there were problems?"

"Yes, but that hasn't changed for hundreds of years."

They took their seats side by side.

"Why did you send me, Uncle?"

"Zadie, in less than fifty years, AI will be able to integrate directly into our genomes. We are setting ourselves up for the same journey as the Anunnaki. Someone needs to warn people."

"Why me?"

"Your intellect, critical thinking, courage, ability to communicate..."

"Then why not tell me upfront what I was getting into?"

"Because I was afraid you'd write it off as the ramblings of an eccentric uncle. And, ultimately, it wasn't my decision. The Anunnaki chose you, not me. I could've told you everything, handed you the sphere, only for nothing to happen... Then what would you think of me? And it wasn't just you. Since the 1940s—when the first artificial neuron model was developed—around 900 people have been there."

"Nine hundred?" Zadie absorbed the number. "How has this never made the news? Surely someone would've tried to expose it, or use it to their advantage."

Ahmed smiled and shook his head. "They've tried, Zadie. Plenty have. Over the years, many people have attempted to reveal the truth about the Anunnaki. But so far, no one has been taken seriously. It sounds like the stuff of wild conspiracy theories. People hear it and laugh, dismissing it as nonsense before they ever stop to question it."

Thirty-six years wasn't long at all. People had to be told, somehow.

"These days, in particular, with so much information swirling around social media, stories like ours get buried in the noise," Ahmed said. "What's *real* is often just a matter of perception. Without concrete evidence, our truth is too crazy for most to grasp."

Zadie nodded, digesting his explanation. "What about the Mushěški-born humans? They're undeniable proof... Have they come to Earth before?"

Ahmed's smile faded. "You're right. This is the first time Mushěški-born humans have ever set foot on Earth. But—"

"Don't worry, I would never expose Javkhlan or the others."

"I know you won't. Their safety is our priority too."

Zadie studied her uncle's face, a sudden realization dawning on her. "Wait—you were prepared for us. How did you know we were coming?"

"The Abgal reached out to the Miravysian network," Ahmed replied. "They contacted us immediately after you contacted them."

"The Miravysian network? Like a formal group?"

"Yes. We're small but global. Around 360 active members spread across thirty-eight countries. Scientists, academics, journalists, artists... We have members on the boards of major tech companies, researchers at leading AI labs, policy advisors to governments—even AI critics. You interacted with one during your presentation—"

"No way."

Ahmed nodded. "We've been subtly guiding the conversation for decades, pushing for ethical boundaries, advocating for slower, more deliberate technological integration."

Zadie took a slow sip of her coffee. The idea of a whole network of scientists, artists, people like her uncle, all working behind the scenes... It was reassuring. At least they weren't alone in this.

"You know, I've got about a million questions... but I don't even know your story. What was it like for you on Mushēški?"

Ahmed leaned back, eyes reflecting the past with a gentle smile. "Well, let's see. It happened in my late twenties... And you know, I wasn't the first in our family to go to Mushēški."

Zadie's eyes widened. "Wait, what? Who else went before you? Not my mother?"

"No, no, not your mother—your great-grandmother, Sabika."

The name stirred a faint memory.

"She passed before you were born. On the eve of her death, she gave me a sphere. She said it held secrets for the right moment. I didn't believe her. I unwrapped it and waited for something. But nothing happened. So, I placed it on a shelf and forgot about it." He let out a breathy laugh, brushing his hand over his chin as if swiping away the years. "Sometimes rejection is protection. I wasn't ready then. Years later, on a whim, I picked it up again... and that's when it happened."

She searched his face. "It transported you to Mushēški?"

Ahmed's voice grew more animated, caught up in the memory. "Yes. I spent months there, learning everything I could. Returning wasn't easy." He rubbed his palms together as if warding off the memory of frustration. "I tried to share what I'd discovered, but my colleagues dismissed me. They called it nonsense, and I was discredited. The only way they let me continue working was by conceding that my theories were the product of a nervous breakdown."

Zadie pictured herself back at the university. "Yeah, I can see that happening... What happened to Sabika?"

"In the mid-1940s, she was working as a nurse. She helped save a soldier, who gave her a sphere he'd found as a thank-you, not knowing what it was. That sphere transported her to Mushēški, where she spent three months before returning with what sounded like fanciful tales. Her husband, convinced she had been having an affair, had her committed. In time, she found others like her, Miravysians, and became one of the founders of our network."

Ahmed studied her for a moment, his eyes softening as if seeing her for the first time. He exhaled and placed a hand on her shoulder. "You've come far, Zadie. She would have been proud of you, like I am."

"Good morning," Javkhlan greeted. He affectionately touched the back of Zadie's neck before taking her coffee from her hands in one swift movement. His nose wrinkled at the bitter scent. "That is not food," he warned, his voice low and urgent. "It's poison."

"No, really, it's okay. It's just coffee. Millions of people here drink it every day. It's just bitter."

Javkhlan's brow furrowed as he studied the dark liquid with suspicion. "Plants don't lie. They tell us with their taste when to stay away." He cautiously raised the mug to his lips, taking the smallest possible sip. His face contorted into an expression of profound disgust. "Your kind, they must enjoy suffering."

"You've no idea."

Han-Yoon joined them, sliding onto the bench across from Javkhlan with a plate piled high with food. "The bread here is incredible. Nothing like the bread in South Korea. That was just air and preservatives, this actually tastes like something."

"Yes, try some Javkhlan," Zadie suggested, offering him a piece of flatbread with a dollop of hummus. She watched his eyes as he examined it, noting how he took in every detail—the texture, the color, the way the hummus settled into the bread's surface.

He pressed his fingers into it, then tore off a small piece and placed it on his tongue. "It does not fight the teeth!" he said, his face brightening with wonder. He took another, larger bite, relaxing into the experience. "Strange. My teeth rest. My belly is happy."

A sudden commotion erupted. Several Neanderthals and Denisovans were crowded around a serving table, reaching over one another to grab a dish of sweetened vermicelli. Their movements were frantic.

"Mine!" a Denisovan woman insisted, clutching the dish against her chest.

The others pressed forward, shoulders bumping, voices rising.

"There's more!" called one of the Miravysian helpers, but the ancient humans either didn't hear or didn't believe her.

Ahmed pushed back from the table, moving toward the scuffle. He stepped between the two largest Neanderthals, his presence somehow commanding despite his smaller stature. "Friends," he said, his voice carrying a calm authority. "We have plenty of food—more than enough for everyone."

One of the Neanderthals glanced at him, then looked away, breathing hard. "Sweet is not like meat or roots. It is rare. It is claimed fast."

Ahmed nodded, understanding blooming in his eyes. "I see. But here, food comes again every day. There's no need to fight for it."

Seeing their confusion, Ahmed served each of them a generous portion of the vermicelli. The ancient humans retreated to their tables, savoring each bite of the unfamiliar sweetness.

A thoughtful expression settled on Javkhlan's face. "Survival does not forget. It holds on, even when it is not needed."

With their hunger eased, the ancient humans grew quieter and more contemplative. Their curious glances kept returning to Ahmed.

Sensing their collective focus, Ahmed pushed back his chair and stood. "This afternoon, after we begin the vaccination schedules, we'll move into the first of many sessions to prepare you to adapt to the world above. But for now, I encourage you to take some time to explore and get to know your new home. It will serve you well."

Zadie and Javkhlan walked to the lake's quieter edge, a half mile from the dining area. Voices and laughter echoed off the cavern walls, their origins stretched and distorted by the acoustics, blurring distance and direction. Stillness wrapped around them, broken only by soft drips of water from the rocks above. Zadie's gaze followed each drop as it hit the surface, sending out faint, widening ripples.

"Look," Javkhlan pointed. "There's Han-Yoon."

She followed his gesture. Han-Yoon sat cross-legged near the water's edge, hunched over something in his hands. As they drew closer, the faint glint of a screen caught her eye—an old smartphone, turning over and over between his fingers.

"Hey," Zadie said. "Mind if we join you?"

Han-Yoon startled, shoving the device into his pocket with a quick, guilty motion. "One of the Miravysians let me borrow it. It's a dead zone down here, though... obviously." His voice was casual, but when he looked up, something in his eyes pulled her straight back to Altay60.

He pulled the phone back out. "I used to think each new gadget was like unlocking another level of freedom. Better phone, better headset, faster connection. It was all supposed to make life more awesome." He tapped the dark screen. "Once, back in Seoul, I camped out for eighteen hours just to get the latest smartphone on launch day. Livestreamed the whole thing. Not because I needed it—my old phone worked fine, but because having the latest tech was part of my identity, you know? Part of my brand."

He gave a bitter laugh. "We thought we were ahead of the curve. Really, we were just beta testers building our own prison mod, one upgrade at a time... The Anunnaki's whole QS thing? It's just the final boss version of what we're already doing to ourselves."

"What do you mean?" Zadie asked.

"Think about it," he gestured to the phone. "We're all addicted to that little ping sound. It's literally designed that way—same dopamine hit as casino slots." He glanced between them. "We've handed off everything—memory, directions, even our social lives—to these things. Half the time, those recommendation algorithms know what I'm gonna click before I do."

Zadie caught the slight shake of Javkhlan's head. In his world, connection was everything. Without it, what was left?

"My last job was the worst," Han-Yoon said. "They installed this AI that tracked our engagement levels during meetings by scanning our faces. It was a total privacy invasion. We all started practicing our *I'm totally listening* expressions in the bathroom mirrors. I got so good at faking it that eventually, I couldn't tell if I was actually interested or just... running some engagement.exe in the back of my head."

Javkhlan tilted his head. "AI watched your face so they could know you?"

"That's the thing—they didn't want to know me. They wanted my data points. The version of me they could track, optimize, and predict. It's like how the Anunnaki saw us as variables in their experiments. But now I know there's more to us that can't be measured."

Han-Yoon picked up a stone and sent it skipping across the lake—two bounces, then gone.

Javkhlan tracked the ripples.

"Your turn," Han-Yoon said, passing him a stone.

Javkhlan turned the stone in his hand, nodding as he copied Han-Yoon's stance. His first throw sent the stone straight into the water with a single skip. He frowned, clearly unimpressed.

Han-Yoon flipped the phone between his fingers like a playing card. "What freaks me out now isn't the tech itself. It's how we're all just... accepting it? Like, each time we trade another piece of our privacy or attention for convenience, it gets easier to give up the next piece." He shook his head. "Soon as they offer to stick AI straight into your brain or DNA, people will shrug and say, *Cool, when's the next version out?*"

"Yep, we've seen where it leads," Zadie said. "That gives us something the Anunnaki never had."

Han-Yoon looked up, his eyes intense. "But how do we get through to people who can't even look up from their screens long enough to have a conversation? How do you warn someone about a disaster they're actively walking toward, thinking it's progress? If someone had started talking about souls or metaphysical layers back then, I'd have rolled my eyes. But here we are."

"I don't know." She exhaled. "I guess that's our gig now..."

"Yeah, no pressure or anything." Han-Yoon turned back to the water and picked up a flat stone. A small smile tugged at his lips as he glanced at Javkhlan. "Watch this."

With a flick of his wrist, he demonstrated the technique of skipping stones across the lake. The stone danced over the water, making four and then five skips before sinking with a soft plip. "It's all in the wrist," Han-Yoon coached, demonstrating again. "You want to keep it low and fast, like this." His next stone skimmed the surface, achieving a satisfactory six skips.

Javkhlan adjusted his grip. He drew his arm back and then whipped it forward, releasing the stone with a sharp flick of his wrist. The stone took off, skimming the water's surface with surprising speed. One, two, three... it continued, barely touching the water, until it disappeared into the darker waters of the lake with a triumphant splash.

Zadie clapped her hands in delight. "I counted seventeen!"

"Seventeen skips on your second try?" Han-Yoon shook his head, grinning. "I think you might just be a natural."

Javkhlan spread his arms, smirking. "It seems my calling has revealed itself, too."

30
New Identities

"There are six core pillars of our integration program for those of you who are interested in fitting into the modern world," Ahmed began. "Physical appearance, language, social fluency, cognitive training, hands-on know-how, and mental grit. All six matter, and they need to develop in sync. Today, we start with the basics. We can't erase the differences—but with the right changes, we might make you familiar enough to be overlooked. That starts with shedding a few of your more... distinguishing features."

He pointed to the side of the cavern, where a team of Miravysian volunteers stood ready with scissors, razors, and other grooming tools. Tables nearby were laid out with clothes—shirts, jeans, dresses, stylish *abayas*, and patterned scarves, all matching the latest street styles in Bahrain.

"The volunteers will help you get started."

Zadie drifted toward the tables. A flowing dress with a vibrant pattern caught her eye, a defiant splash of color against the plain uniformity of her Mushēški jumpsuit. She reached for it, paused, then turned to the jeans and a burnt-orange merino top. Simpler. More... comfortable.

Beside her, Javkhlan held up a slim-fit shirt, fingertips trailing over the sleek fabric like it might bite.

The grooming stations came alive with movement. Han-Yoon grabbed a pair of scissors with a playful grin. "You lot are far too trusting," he said, twirling the scissors with theatrical flair. "Let's see if I remember how to cut bangs." His first *client* flinched, just slightly, but enough to draw a glance from one of the Miravysian volunteers.

Clippers buzzed. Razors glinted. At the edge of the crowd, Zadie watched as a volunteer shaved the last of a Denisovan's beard. The man inhaled and touched his newly bare chin, eyes flicking to the mirror, then away, as if the face staring back didn't quite belong to him. Around them, new faces emerged, each snip of the scissors making room for who they might become above ground.

"Wow," Han-Yoon said, eyes widening as the first Mushēški-born Sapiens emerged from their transformation. "I wasn't expecting that."

"They really do look like us, don't they?" Zadie said, tilting her head toward Freeya. The blouse and jeans didn't just bridge time—they obliterated it.

Their composure was the giveaway, for now. No shuffling. No glances to check footing. No nervous gestures. They moved like people with nothing to prove.

Zadie studied the Neanderthals and Denisovans as they emerged. The loose clothing hung deliberately from their frames, softening the bulk and disguising the limb proportions. They were clearly more robust—barrel-chested, thick-limbed, with necks that disappeared into powerful shoulders—but their faces, at a glance, could pass. People wouldn't be expecting to see someone from another human species. Most would do a quick double take, then look away, filing the oddness under strong genes.

Ahmed drifted past with a lopsided grin. "This is working well." He gestured to a Neanderthal woman, her styled hair and modern clothes transforming her into someone who might pass for a stocky Sapiens.

Zadie's attention shifted to Javkhlan. "You look... incredible." She stepped closer, taking in the groomed beard, the subtle fall of his hair, the way his features now straddled ancient and modern. "It's like you've always belonged here."

"It feels... different. I'm not convinced about these foot-cages," he said, glancing down at the sneakers. "The Dilmun ones... let me feel the ground's breath. These? Not so much." He nudged off the shoes, his bare soles meeting the cave floor. Relief softened his face.

Zadie observed the rebellion of the others, shoes discarded, feet bare.

Javkhlan turned to the large mirrors along the stone wall, where others studied their reflections with a mix of wonder and uncertainty. Miravysian volunteers demonstrated simple gestures—smiles, nods, a practiced wave. He gave his reflection an approving nod. Then a fist bump, exaggerated just enough to earn a cheer. His eyes gleamed playfully as he added a confident tilt of his chin, like someone acknowledging a passerby. Zadie couldn't help smiling. He was getting the hang of it.

Two Floresiensis women stepped out from the dressing area, pausing as their eyes met the unfamiliar figures in the mirror. One tugged at the hem of her hoodie. The other stared, unmoving, as though trying to decipher what had been done to her hair. The stylish bobs that might have looked playful on human children couldn't hide the heavy brow ridges, flattened noses, and jaws that jutted forward with an ancient force.

"Do you think maybe they could pass... as kids in a crowd?" Han-Yoon whispered.

Zadie shook her head. "Not a chance."

As she spoke, one of the Floresiensis women spotted a Sapiens child in a fashion magazine lying on a nearby table. She stared at the image, fingers tracing the printed face first, then drifting to her own reflection. She turned to her companion, their eyes locking in silent understanding. Without a word, both removed their colorful hair clips and placed them on the table.

The harsh truth became impossible to ignore when an Erectus man stepped forward. Loose-fitting clothes had been carefully chosen by the Miravysian volunteer, but no grooming could hide his heavy facial structure or the low, sloped forehead.

A Sylvicolus man broke from his group and approached the mirror. Without the facial hair, his ape-like nostrils were fully exposed, and the cut of his clothing only drew more attention to the odd proportions of his limbs. He noticed Zadie watching—a flicker of dignified resignation in his eyes—then turned and retreated to the changing area.

The cavern stilled. Chatter dissolved. Laughter died. Zadie's heart sank as the limits of the illusion stared back from the mirrors—not everywhere, but in enough faces to make the truth impossible to ignore. Hopes that had once felt daring now drifted just out of reach. The weight of Ahmed's miscalculation showed in the slump of his shoulders.

The Sylvicolus leader approached him. "We choose to return to our people in Mongolia," she said. "Your shelter has been a kindness, and we are grateful. But we see now... we cannot become as you are."

One by one, the leaders of the Naledi, Erectus, Floresiensis, and Luzonensis stepped forward. "Us too," they said, not in defeat, but with the quiet dignity of those choosing their own way.

"I understand." Ahmed paused, gathering his thoughts, a warmth in his eyes. "I'll contact the Abgal immediately to arrange safe passage to your tribes."

"What about the Denisovans?" Zadie asked Javkhlan as they watched the other species make their decisions. "Will you stay, or join your people?"

"The Denisovans will stay. The Neanderthals, too. We're not so different. Perhaps your world has room for us." He nodded toward Freeya, standing among the ancient Sapiens. "And the Sapiens from Azania180 and Altay60—no one would see them as outsiders."

As the Miravysians dispersed, Zadie felt an urgent need to be alone. She stepped away from the others and walked to the lake's edge, where she sank onto a dry rock, knees drawn up, arms looped loosely around them.

The lake's center held her gaze. Light shifted across the surface, its reflections rippling in a slow, hypnotic dance. Minutes blurred into something longer, lost in the maze of her thoughts.

After a long while, a voice gently broke the peace. "Mind if I join you?"

She turned, surprised to see Ahmed standing there. "Oh, hey, Uncle. Yeah, go on."

He settled beside her. "How are you holding up, my dear?"

"I'm..." Zadie hesitated. "Honestly? I don't know. Some moments I'm fine. Others..."

Ahmed nodded, letting the silence stretch.

Zadie watched a droplet of water fall from the cavern ceiling. "Javkhlan..." Her voice caught. "What if he can never truly belong here?"

"You're questioning whether you have a future together," Ahmed observed.

"I'm questioning everything, Uncle."

"What else are you questioning?"

"My DPhil... I used to think my research mattered. But how do you go back to academic papers after Mushēški?" She shook her head. Zadie's shoulders tensed at a distant sound, her breath catching before she forced herself to relax. "Sorry," she mumbled. "Still jumpy."

"That's to be expected, Zadie."

A breath steadied her. "I don't know who I am now. I can't just go back to my old life, and I'm not sure how I'm supposed to help humanity avoid making the same mistake as the Anunnaki... I used to think that if I could just... push boundaries and make some huge discovery, everything else would slot into place. But after everything I saw... I don't know what I want anymore. But I don't want to lose touch with what's real."

Ahmed's eyes softened. "So, what's real to you now?"

"People," she said. "I used to see them as distractions, maybe even obstacles. But now..." She shook her head. "I don't know. They're what make life matter, aren't they? If I shut myself away and only focus on the work... it feels like I'd be wasting my chance to actually live."

Ahmed reached out and took her hand, giving it a gentle, reassuring squeeze. "It sounds like you've learned a lot."

Zadie nodded. "But... there is something I still need to know."

Ahmed grinned, intrigued by the sudden inquisitiveness in her tone. "Go on, my dear."

"The Abgal... who are they, really?"

Ahmed nodded as if he'd been expecting the question all along. "Ah, of course, Zadie..." He leaned back, as if creating space to open the door to something immense.

"The Abgal began life on a planet called Kepler-442b."

"Earth's cousin?"

"Yes, exactly. Even though it's one and a half billion years younger than Earth, it's the true cradle of intelligent life in our galaxy. The Abgal evolved there, achieving levels of advancement that allowed them to explore—and even shape—parts of the universe. They began integrating their own DNA into other life forms, creating new pathways for life to grow and adapt."

Zadie blinked rapidly, her heart pounding. "So... are you going to tell me that we are basically some kind of genetic experiment?"

Ahmed's gaze held hers. "From what I understand, the Abgal made various genetic modifications on Earth, and of course, later, they experimented with QS integration in the Sumerians."

Zadie frowned, her mind spinning with questions. "What exactly did they change, and why? And... are they planning any future genetic modifications?"

Ahmed contemplated her questions. "I don't have all the answers. But I'm about to meet with one of them to organize the relocation of some of the tribes. I could ask?"

Zadie's posture stiffened, her eyes narrowing with determination. "No," she said, her voice firm as she leaned forward. "I want to hear it from them myself."

Ahmed's eyes widened, taking in the sudden resolve in her tone. He rose to his feet, a hint of approval in his expression. "Alright... Let's go."

31
The Abgal

Shadows leaped across the stone walls, jagged shapes slipping in and out of their flashlight beams as Zadie and Ahmed made their way back to the chamber beneath Qal'at al-Bahrain. Each step drew her closer to truths she wasn't sure she was ready for, her mind circling questions she couldn't shut out—what life on Kepler-442b might be like, how far the Abgal had traveled, what they wanted from Earth, and whether they'd tolerate her challenging their control over human destiny.

Zadie's fingers tightened around her sleeve. "How long will I get with them?"

"Not long," Ahmed replied. "But long enough to get the answers you're looking for."

They reached the chamber's entrance. Ahmed stopped and turned to face her. "Stay here. I'll go in first." Without waiting for her reply, he slipped through the doorway, leaving Zadie alone in the tunnel.

Zadie stared at the stone walls, trying to anchor herself, but her breath came faster. She replayed her experience of the Abgal in her mind—those towering, fluid figures with skin that shimmered, moving with a calm that bordered on unnatural. Even their words hadn't been spoken, just placed gently in her mind. Without the QS to blunt her emotions, the idea of meeting one of them face-to-face set her nerves on fire. She wiped her palms against her jeans.

Scenes from sci-fi movies played through her mind—sinister aliens, hidden agendas, cold eyes locked on humanity's doom. She shook her head, trying to dispel the images. This wasn't a clichéd invasion. The Abgal weren't monsters lurking in the dark. They were architects. Of worlds. Omnipotent in their influence.

The door creaked open, and Ahmed reappeared, his face giving nothing away. He caught her eye and nodded. "Sara's ready for you."

Zadie's heart pounded in her chest. "Sara?"

"That's what she prefers to be called when she's here. Earth names, Earth customs." Ahmed's mouth twitched, almost a smile. "You'll be fine, dear."

She shot him a skeptical look. "That's what you said last time..."

Zadie stepped through the doorway, her lungs tightening as the significance of the moment hit her. Two chairs stood facing each other, isolated in a pale mist.

Sara sat poised, her gaze tracking Zadie's approach with a subtle warmth in its intensity. With a slight, inviting nod, she gestured to the chair opposite her.

"Zadie, welcome." Sara's telepathic voice vibrated in her mind. *"I understand you have many questions."*

Zadie's apprehension gave way to an almost magnetic fascination the moment she saw Sara up close. From afar, the Abgal's skin had appeared a muted gray-green, but closer inspection revealed tiny, shimmering scales, each flecked with traces of miravys. Sara's large, obsidian-like eyes held her captive, their inky depths laced with spiraling threads of silver and gray that seemed to twist endlessly inward.

A moment passed before she spoke. "Thanks for meeting with me. I'd like to understand the Abgal's role in Earth's history. I just... I need to know why you intervened, and what your intentions are going forward."

Sara nodded. *"Your concerns are understandable, Zadie. It's natural to question the scope and impact of our actions when first encountering us. Our interactions with other life forms beyond our home planet have spanned many eras. Over this time, we've engaged with various species for many reasons—companionship, agriculture, sport, entertainment, genetic research, experimentation, conservation, and aid."*

Zadie's hands tightened around the edge of her seat, the tension in her body slowly building. She felt her shoulders stiffen, her eyes locking onto Sara, trying to prepare herself for whatever might come next.

"Our genetic research has resulted in countless changes throughout the galaxy. Each experiment represents a choice—a life altered, a destiny reshaped. And with every choice comes the burden of consequence, often beyond anything we intended."

"Why did you intervene on Earth?"

"We first discovered life on your planet around 360,000 Earth years ago. At the time, we were curious about your potential. So we initiated a low-level intervention, adjusting key regulatory genes and epigenetic mechanisms to study how small shifts might shape cognitive and physiological outcomes over generations."

"So, you're saying you didn't rewrite our DNA?"

"Not directly. We didn't alter your genetic code itself. Instead, we adjusted how your existing genes responded to stress, nutrition, reproduction, and social behavior. Over time, those changes compounded. At key intervals—roughly 69,000 and 12,000 years ago—we refined the process based on what we'd observed, nudging certain developmental pathways."

"Wait—you've been manipulating Sapiens for as long as we've existed?"

"Yes, though, from our point of view, it's more nuanced. Before we developed transitfold technology, every trip to Earth meant facing extreme time dilation. From your perspective, our interventions spanned hundreds of thousands of years, but to us, they occupied only a small fraction of that time."

Zadie shook her head as she tried to piece it all together, but Sara's words blended into an incomprehensible blur. Instead, her thoughts wandered, brushing against the milestones of human history—the emergence of modern Sapiens, the rise of abstract thinking, the dawn of agriculture. Did they fit into Sara's timelines?

Sara seemed to read her. *"Your anatomy gradually shifted—lighter, more rounded skulls, higher foreheads, reduced teeth and jaw size, changes in pelvic width and ribcage flexibility. We amplified existing trends by altering thresholds of gene expression—particularly during neural and cranial development."*

Zadie frowned. "But why those traits?"

"To see what might emerge. And some traits, like enhanced immune responses, proved decisive. Those minor boosts likely tipped the scales in your favor as other hominin species struggled to adapt."

Had that been why the others had gone extinct?

"Do changes like that... also come at a cost?"

"They did," Sara said, without flinching. *"We observed unintended trade-offs—heightened reactivity in your stress-regulation systems, increased impulsivity, and a greater vulnerability to affective instability. Traits linked to mental health challenges didn't emerge from a single tweak, but from cascading effects across neural development."*

Zadie didn't respond, her jaw tensing.

"We also saw a rise in cancer risk," Sara continued. *"Enhancing tissue regeneration and immune adaptability made your species more resilient to environmental pressures—but it disrupted the balance. Tumor suppression pathways became less reliable in some populations. Certain protective alleles faded, possibly due to shifting selection pressures we didn't anticipate."* She paused before adding, *"None of it was deliberate. That's the inherent danger of indirect influence. Small adjustments can ripple far beyond their original purpose."*

Zadie swallowed hard, her fingers clenching into fists... "What right did you have to play with us like that?" The question escaped her before she could stop it, her voice sharper than she intended. She took a breath, trying to rein in the anger boiling beneath her skin. "How can you justify it?"

"Is it any different from what your kind does to other life forms on your planet?"

Images flooded Zadie's mind. A dog, once wild, now a tailored companion, its form sculpted by countless generations of selective breeding. Fish swam by, their genes laced with fragments from distant creatures. In sterile labs, she saw mice, their DNA spliced and twisted, their fates decided in petri dishes. She saw cloned animals standing docile in confined spaces, mosquitoes engineered to self-destruct, and goats genetically tweaked to produce spider silk in their milk.

Zadie's hands shook as she tried to push the images away, but the comparisons still tangled her thoughts. "Even if that's true, would we have done it without the influence of your genes?"

"That's a fair point, Zadie. It's hard to know."

Sara's response caught Zadie off guard, softening her attack. "Alright, then... how did you end up giving the Anunnaki QS?"

"*When we first developed Quantum Sentience, we needed to see how other biological beings would handle the integration before considering it for ourselves. The Sumerians were open to the trials.*"

"So, you've also used QS on yourselves?"

"*No, we keep our QS systems external. The experiments are ongoing, but managing QS governance remains a concern.*"

"Have other civilizations also suffered the same fate as the Anunnaki?"

"*Yes, many. The soul always vacates at 58% QS governance.*"

Zadie nodded, slow and deliberate, as if the statement confirmed something rather than overturned everything she'd assumed.

"*All life forms have souls, Zadie.*"

"Of course..." She let the words settle, adjusting around her. "Even plants?"

"*The souls of plants aren't contained within individual specimens. They exist as distributed consciousness. Even so, entire plant-based networks experience a soul departure once the 58% threshold is reached.*"

The information shifted something in her, but she didn't know what to do with it. "But then why not impose limits on the QS governance?"

"*Our experiments have shown that QS can only be restricted at very low percentages. In these cases, the benefits are negligible. In all other cases, QS has been shown to increase over time.*"

She wondered whether to mention the effects of sickle cell trait or hypertrichosis. "If you could limit it, do you really think the benefits are worth it?"

"*That's a dilemma we're wrestling with. As you've seen, QS comes at a cost—individuality and autonomy are diminished, creativity and critical thinking are stifled, and emotional depth is eroded. Additionally, QS leads to evolutionary stagnation. It optimizes for certain traits, but that reduces genetic diversity, which makes civilizations less adaptable to change..."*

Zadie shifted in her seat. "So, across your other experiments, it ends up making everyone... the same?"

"Yes."

"So, it's like putting all your eggs in one basket. If something goes wrong..."

"It solves immediate challenges but undermines long-term evolutionary potential. Relying on QS also creates the risk of manipulation by those in control."

"And once you start down that path, there's no undoing it, is there?"

"Correct. It locks a civilization into a specific path."

"So why not give up on it?"

"Because standing still could mean falling behind other unknown civilizations across the universe, and later losing power and influence. That's why we're committed to continuing our experiments, searching for a balance."

Zadie sat quietly. What could she even say? Every answer spawned five more questions, and each one dug deeper than she wanted to go.

"Unfortunately, we are running out of time before I must leave. I understand you would like to learn about our most recent intervention on Earth."

Zadie's heart lurched. "Recent intervention? What have you done?"

32

The Circle of Life

"*O*ur interventions, particularly the one 12,000 years ago, disrupted humanity's natural equilibrium. What was once a harmonious relationship with nature became a drive for dominion. While the Anunnaki shared the knowledge that now propels you toward AI integration, we take full responsibility.*"

"The Anunnaki shared their knowledge with us? About AI?"

"*Yes.*"

"And that's why around 900 of us were sent to Mushēški, right? To understand the impact and stop history from repeating itself."

"*Yes. We've been monitoring your collective insights through the neuroscribes, and these informed our latest intervention.*"

"I'm sorry, I don't understand." Zadie's voice wavered, despite her effort to steady it. "I thought my role, as part of the 900, was to bring understanding back to Earth. To help us change our course..." The words felt naïve the second they left her lips, puzzle pieces jammed into the wrong places. The insights of the 900 had never been meant for Earth. They had always been for the Abgal...

"What did you do?"

"Yesterday, we deployed a therapeutic biotechnological virus engineered with QS precision to integrate genetic modifications into the human population..."

Sara's words faded into the background as emotions surged through Zadie. Her breath came in shallow gasps, her heart thudding under the relentless weight of the revelation. "You can't be serious! After everything you've learned about integrating QS, you played gods again? Programming us as if we were machines?"

"Zadie, I understand your feelings, but—"

"No!" Zadie cut Sara off, her fists clenched at her sides as she stood up and paced back and forth. "How could you!"

She thought about the sterile labs where the Anunnaki were created, the cold efficiency of their society, and the emptiness that lay beneath it. She pictured Lugazir's calm, emotionless face and imagined the same look on her own. Her desires, passions, and even memories, all being absorbed into a collective consciousness, leaving little space for the messy, unpredictable aspects of humanity she now held dear. Would she even recognize herself? The things that made her who she was—her creativity, her curiosity, her critical thinking—would they all be smoothed away? Would she still find joy in life? Would she still love Javkhlan? Who would she become?

Zadie staggered backward, nausea coiling deep in her gut. She turned, legs shaky, and reached the far wall, steadying herself with a hand against the cool, engraved stone. She doubled over. Hot, sour vomit splashed at her feet. Another convulsion forced up the rest. Her ribs ached with the force of it, her throat burning. She gasped, saliva trailing from her lips, and let her forehead rest against the wall. Sweat clung to her skin. Eyes squeezed shut, she spat the last bitter taste from her mouth.

"I would rather die than let QS overtake me," Zadie said, her resolve hardening. "Without the freedom to think and act independently, what's the point?" She stood there, breathless and broken, a lone figure struggling to reconcile the reality of her future.

"Zadie, I need to clarify something important. We didn't integrate QS. The genetic material in the virus—it isn't QS at all. It's DNA from the ancient human species of Mushēški."

Zadie went still. Sara's words cut through the fog of fear and anger that had consumed her. The adrenaline that had fueled her outburst drained away. A wave of heat flushed up her neck, warming her cheeks. She felt her heartbeat slowing, each beat a reminder of how far she'd let her fear take her.

"What do you mean?" Her voice came out small.

"QS tools were used to engineer the virus, but what is being integrated into human cells isn't QS."

Zadie's mind struggled to keep up. "So, we're not going to end up like the Anunnaki?"

"No, not at all. Quite the opposite, in fact."

Zadie's relief quickly gave way to a new kind of unease. "Wait," she said, holding up her hand. "Ancient human DNA?"

Sara's expression didn't waver. *"Yes."*

Zadie's eyes narrowed as she studied Sara, trying to piece together her understanding. "You're saying... you released a virus to modify our genomes with actual human DNA... from the ancient human species? I don't understand. Why would you do that?"

"The ancient species evolved without interference. They retained what you've lost—heightened empathy, intuitive environmental awareness, and an internal equilibrium that would resist dependence on technology."

"Why not just reverse what you did?"

"Reversing our earlier genetic interventions would be impossible. Too many additional mutations and adaptations have occurred since then. By using their DNA, we will restore these vital capabilities in a more stable form."

Zadie leaned forward, her voice sharp with skepticism. "But surely the drive to enhance ourselves with AI isn't genetic—it's got to be a learned behavior." She stood, pacing as her frustration mounted. "We just needed to see the impact of integrating AI to avoid that path. What makes you so sure humanity can't find its own way without your intervention?"

"While learned behaviors are contributors, it's our genetic interventions that made those behaviors possible in the first place. They made it easier to create and maintain systems that worship technological enhancement. The ancient DNA will restore lost safeguards."

"Did the Anunnaki know of this intervention? Does my uncle know?"

"No. The intervention was guided solely by the insights gathered from the 900, through the neuroscribes. And those insights were remarkably consistent. Sapiens expressed a strong preference for cognitive autonomy, neural diversity, emotional intelligence, and creative thought—traits fundamentally incompatible with genomic AI integration. Those values guided us. They left little doubt about what mattered most."

"So you interpreted that as consent."

"Informed, collective intention—yes."

Zadie let out a slow breath, fingers pressing into her brow. "Bloody hell." Her hands fell to her lap. "How will it happen?"

"There will be a gradual change over multiple generations. Children will inherit stronger versions of these traits—empathic attunement, sensory awareness, a deeper tolerance for ambiguity. These aren't instructions,

just predispositions. They won't dictate how people live, but they'll influence what feels right. As those traits reemerge, you may find that the logic of optimization—the drive to enhance and control—starts to feel... abrasive. Disconnected. Human intuition, emotional depth, relational thinking—these will begin to carry more internal weight. It won't be a revolution. It'll be a shift in perception. The idea of integrating AI into your biology won't need to be resisted. It simply won't appeal."

"How do you know these genetic changes won't have unintended consequences? Like with the Anunnaki."

"There are no guarantees. But this time, we're not rewriting your path. We're restoring the parts of you that were quieted."

"But even if people feel more hesitant about AI integration," Zadie pressed, "they're still trapped in technological systems, dependent on AI for jobs, healthcare, communication. Many don't have the privilege of choosing a different relationship with technology."

"Which is why systemic change is crucial. As people's connection to their humanity deepens, they'll push for transformation—demanding changes that serve rather than reshape humans, systems that value human judgment, and economies that preserve human agency. Societies will naturally shift as the population decreases to around two billion over the next century."

Zadie's mouth went dry as she searched for the right response. "Two billion? That's—what, a quarter of the population we have now. Why?" Her voice lowered to nearly a whisper. "That's... six billion lives that will have to go."

"Not go. They will just never be born. Just as the population quadrupled in little over a century, it will now begin to contract—through billions of individual choices. As people grow more attuned to sustainability and interdependence, they'll begin to view reproduction differently. Fewer

children, raised with more attention and care, will feel more meaningful than larger families. The drive to multiply will give way to the desire to balance."

"What will happen to medical advances? To global communications? To technologies?"

"Medical advances will likely focus on preventive care and natural remedies. Communication technologies might evolve to enhance human connection rather than replace it. Technology won't disappear, but it will serve life rather than trying to transcend it."

"And we're just supposed to trust the Abgal to oversee this fairly?" Zadie challenged. "Your track record with the Anunnaki doesn't inspire confidence."

"We're not overseeing anything. We have initiated the restoration of your ancient human traits, but the world that emerges—just or unjust, balanced or imbalanced—is up to humanity."

"How many other species have you done this to? And how many of them actually benefited?"

"You'll be the first."

Zadie sat in silence for a long moment, weighing everything Sara had told her. Part of her understood the Abgal's reasoning—she'd seen the emptiness of the Anunnaki firsthand and felt the warmth and connection of the ancient humans. The prospect of humanity avoiding the Anunnaki's fate held undeniable appeal. But something didn't sit right...

"You're not telling me everything," Zadie said, studying Sara's alien eyes. "Were you afraid... of what we might have become?"

The patterns within Sara's eyes realigned as if adjusting to accommodate this new level of discussion.

"It was actually about protecting yourselves, wasn't it?"

"*Self-preservation is part of the natural order, not separate from it. In 150 years, your AI could have surpassed our own. In 300 years, you could have arrived on Kepler-442b uninvited and armed with the delusion of benevolence. But you would not have come in peace.*"

Zadie swallowed hard. Her words came quieter. "And now?"

"*Now, you'll stay where you belong.*"

Epilogue

*F*ive years later...

Zadie leaned against the stone wall of her cottage, feeling the cold seep through her thick wool sweater as she watched the mist coil around the mountains. The drizzle, a constant companion in this far-flung corner of the Scottish Highlands, tapped on the veranda.

Her eyes scanned the valley, taking in the scattered huts of the Miravysian Denisovans, Neanderthals, and Sapiens. Narrow, winding paths traced gentle lines to a river that snaked through the land. She spotted Freeya teaching the children to hunt hares, and she gave her a quick wave.

Gravel crunched under Javkhlan's boots as he approached, a folded newspaper in his hand. "Zadie, see this. They have found the unseen ones inside us."

"Have they now? Let's have a look," she replied, already reaching for the paper. As she unfolded it, the headline leaped out at her, and her heart seemed to falter for a moment.

Scientists Uncover 'Ghost DNA' in All Human Populations

—Up to 19% Traced to Unknown Ancestors

By Erin Tao, Science Correspondent

In a groundbreaking discovery, geneticists have found traces of ghost DNA in the genomes of all modern human populations, with some groups carrying up to 19% of this mysterious genetic material.

The term ghost DNA refers to genetic sequences inherited from unknown archaic human ancestors who interbred with early Homo sapiens. These ancestors, whose physical remains have yet to be discovered, have left a lasting genetic legacy that spans across continents and cultures.

The study, conducted by an international team of researchers, reveals that ghost DNA is not limited to any single population. Instead, it is present in varying degrees across the globe, suggesting that ancient interbreeding events were far more widespread and complex than previously thought.

While the exact identity of these archaic humans remains elusive, the discovery challenges our understanding of human evolution and highlights the deep interconnectedness of all human beings.

Zadie let out a dry chuckle. "Ghost DNA! Or just the Abgal's blend of traits from the Mushēški-born humans?"

Javkhlan nodded in contemplation. "When eyes are closed, the night is warm and safe."

"Too right. Ignorance is bliss." She set the newspaper aside, her gaze dropping as she considered the implications. "Might make things easier when the other human species are eventually discovered."

A car's distant purr began to cut through the gentle patter of the drizzle, growing louder as it approached. Zadie squeezed Javkhlan's hand reassuringly, aware of how much this mattered to both of them.

"It's been over five journeys around the sun since you looked into their faces," Javkhlan said.

"We couldn't risk it before... back then, they'd have exposed you in an instant. But they're different now... the virus has changed them."

The car pulled up outside the cottage. Her parents stepped out. Peter, usually so precise and critical, paused as his gaze swept across the landscape. He took a deep breath, seeming to savor the crisp Highland air. He adjusted his glasses, as though sharpening his focus on the world around him. Amina let her eyes linger too, the hard lines of her face softening.

"Zadie!" Peter's voice carried an unusual warmth as he pulled her into a firm hug. Normally, he was all about brief formalities, but this time, there was something more to it. Amina followed suit, holding Zadie close with a motherly tenderness that took her aback.

"Mum, Dad—this is Javkhlan." Zadie's voice wavered, her eyes darting between her parents' faces, searching for any sign of disapproval. But as their smiles widened, a relieved breath escaped her lips, and her shoulders relaxed.

"Lovely to meet you at last," Peter said, extending his hand with surprising vigor. "We've been looking forward to this. Zadie's told us all about you in her letters. It's brilliant that you two have finally put down your roots here in the UK."

Javkhlan clasped Peter's hand with a practiced sincerity. "Thank you, sir. The pleasure's mine."

Before Javkhlan could step back, Amina pulled him into a hug, her arms wrapping around him with unexpected warmth. "Oh, come here—you're family now."

Zadie held her breath, waiting for the double take. But it never came. They looked at him and saw only a man. She gestured toward the front door. "Shall we go inside where it's drier?"

Her parents nodded and followed her in as the drizzle picked up.

"Where's the little princess?" Amina asked, her eyes lighting up.

"Oh, she's just down for her nap," Zadie said, smiling as she nodded toward the hallway. "I thought it'd be better for her to be fresh and rested to meet her grandparents for the first time."

Her father chuckled, a sound full of warmth and anticipation. "Fair enough. We're just excited to finally meet her."

Inside the cottage, a fire crackled a warm welcome. Lunch was already laid out—a hearty stew and home-baked bread that filled the room with rich, comforting aromas.

The conversation started light, dancing around the usual topics like the recent drizzle and the local sheepdog trials. But Zadie realized that even these familiar subjects seemed to hold a new weight. When Peter spoke about the weather, it wasn't just idle chatter. His words described the subtle shift in the wind's direction, a hint of the coming change in season. Amina, usually quick to dismiss small talk, listened intently, her gaze occasionally drifting toward the window as if searching for the signs Peter described in the landscape.

"Javkhlan, I have to say, your English is excellent," Peter remarked, his usual reserve giving way to genuine admiration.

Javkhlan smiled, setting down his own spoon. "Thanks. Working with the conservation groups here really threw me into the river's depth."

Peter nodded. "Quite the leap from life in Mongolia, I imagine."

"Yes, definitely," Javkhlan replied. "Here, it's different. The people shape the Earth, bending it to their will, but the mountains... they remember. They've seen more than we can imagine, watched us come and go. And now, here I am, listening again. The language is slower, but it speaks just the same. It always does, if you know how to hear it."

Zadie gave Javkhlan a playful kick under the table—a subtle cue to stick to the heritage story they'd settled on, at least for now.

As Javkhlan spoke, her father leaned forward slightly, his nods carrying a quiet but genuine interest. Her mother's eyes sparkled with curiosity, a soft smile playing on her lips, asking questions that invited Javkhlan to share more of himself. Her mother, who once might have dissected his every word for flaws, now seemed eager to know him.

Amina glanced at the bookshelf near the fireplace, her eyes brightening. "By the way, we've been loving your novels about the ancient human species."

Zadie blinked. "You... have?"

Amina nodded. "Your uncle's even taken one to his dig site in the Serengeti. He's hooked. You made them real, not just bones in a museum. I used to picture them as animals, but now... I see people."

Zadie smiled, a touch of surprise flickering in her eyes. She felt a soft kick under the table. Javkhlan gave her a sideways glance—a subtle nudge to own the praise.

She cleared her throat. "Aww, thanks. Han-Yoon and I had a great time writing them. He's on holiday in North Korea at the moment, visiting a mutual friend, but you'll meet him next time."

With only faint trails of sauce left on the plates, Peter set down his fork, glancing at Amina. "Your mother and I have been thinking a lot about the future. We're finding more and more that our values are shifting towards a simpler way of living." He paused as if weighing his words. "We're considering moving closer to you."

Zadie's brows shot up. "Closer?" She glanced between them. "I mean... that'd be brilliant."

A slight creak echoed from the hallway. The soft patter of tiny feet on the wooden floor followed. Zadie turned her head toward the sound, her face lighting up with a joyful smile. "Hello!" she exclaimed as tousled-haired Ebuni appeared at the dining room entrance.

Her deep-set eyes, still heavy with the remnants of sleep, blinked as she adjusted to the light and the voices around her. "Papa!" Ebuni called out, a grin spreading across her face as she toddled quickly toward Javkhlan, who opened his arms wide for the eager embrace.

Lifting Ebuni into his lap, Javkhlan brushed back the girl's thick brown hair and gently kissed her forehead. "Did you have good dreams?"

Ebuni nodded, her eyes wide with curiosity as they landed on the unfamiliar faces at the table.

"Hello, sweetheart," Amina greeted. "I'm your *Yadda*." Her hand reached out, fingers tracing the curve of Ebuni's cheek—a gesture so tender it made Zadie's heart ache. Ebuni leaned in, her small hand reaching up to grasp Amina's finger.

"And I'm your Gramps." Peter's large hand dwarfed her other hand as he gently squeezed it.

Zadie hadn't expected how easily her parents' warmth could undo her.

She caught her mother mouthing Ebuni's name. Unusual, yes. But nothing else had felt right. To them, it meant resilience, empathy, and bravery. They hadn't chosen it out of grief, but recognition.

"Come here, Ebuni," Amina coaxed, opening her arms.

Ebuni looked up at Javkhlan, seeking reassurance.

With a gentle nod, Javkhlan encouraged her, "Go, child. Greet her."

Carefully, Ebuni slid off Javkhlan's lap and made her way around the table. Amina lifted her onto her lap, enveloping Ebuni in a soft embrace that seemed to melt away her shyness.

"We've waited so long to meet you," she whispered, kissing the top of Ebuni's head.

Zadie gripped Javkhlan's hand as a quiet sense of contentment settled over her.

Glossary

CHARACTERS

Ahmed *(Akh-med)* – Zadie's uncle. An archaeologist of Bahraini heritage, based in Bahrain.

Amina *(AH-mee-nah)* – Zadie's mother. An academic of Bahraini heritage, based in Oxford, England.

Daanjabe *(DAHN-jah-bay)* – The Anunnaki assigned to guide Zadie through the NusaLale120 biodome.

Ebuni *(EH-boo-nee)* – A young Floresiensis woman from the NusaLale120 biodome. Also the name of a toddler introduced near the end of the novel. Her name carries personal significance and marks a turning point in the lives of several characters.

Eka *(Ee-kah)* – A Naledi woman from the Azania180 biodome.

Freeya *(FREE-yah)* – A Sapiens woman from the Altay60 biodome.

Han-Yoon Kwon *(HAHN-yoon KWAHN)* – An Earth-born Sapiens man from South Korea, brought to Mushēški.

Javkhlan *(JAHV-kh-lahn)* – A Denisovan man from the Thalvik tribe in the Altay60 biodome.

Lugazir *(LOO-gah-zeer)* – The Anunnaki responsible for communicating with non-Anunnaki entities.

Min-Jae Song *(MIN-jeh SOHNG)* – An Earth-born Sapiens man from North Korea, brought to Mushēški.

Peter *(PEE-ter)* – Zadie's father, of English heritage. An academic who lives in Oxford, England.

Sara *(SAH-rah)* – One of the Abgal. 'Sara' is her preferred name while on Earth.

Sargona *(SAHR-goh-nah)* – The Anunnaki assigned to guide Zadie through the Azania180 biodome.

Toran *(TOR-an)* – A wolf from the Thalvik tribe in the Altay60 biodome.

Utnapishtim *(OOT-nah-PISH-teem)* – An Anunnaki who returned to Earth, around 2800 BCE.

Zadie Thornton *(ZAY-dee THORN-ton)* – The protagonist of the story. An Earth-born Sapiens woman from Oxford, England, brought to Mushēški. She is an anthropologist and DPhil/PhD candidate. Her mother is Bahraini, and her father is English.

TERMS

Abaya *(ah-BAH-yah)* – A loose-fitting, full-length robe worn by some Muslim women.

Abgal *(AB-gahl)* – Extraterrestrials who saved 616 Sumerians from a great flood and helped them evolve by integrating Quantum Sentience into their genomes. This process transformed the Sumerians into the Anunnaki.

Akashidu *(ah-KAH-shee-doo)* – A vast reservoir of knowledge beyond ordinary perception, believed to contain the wisdom of all souls throughout time.

Altay60 *(AHL-tai 60)* – A biodome on Mushēški replicating the landscapes of Eurasia 60,000 years ago. Home to recreated Homo sapiens, Homo neanderthalensis, Homo denisova, and Homo sylvicolus.

An-Naĝar-ki *(ahn-NAH-gahr-kee)* – The Abgal's interstellar ark (or spaceship) that saved the chosen 616 Sumerians from the flood.

Anunnaki *(ah-nuh-NAH-kee)* – See *Homo anunnaki.*

Azania180 *(ah-ZAH-nee-ah 180)* – A biodome on Mushēški replicating the environment of Africa 180,000 years ago. Home to recreated Homo naledi and Homo sapiens.

Azraelbeam *(AZ-rah-ehl-beem)* – A device developed by the Anunnaki for the purposes of humane euthanasia.

Biodomes – Vast controlled spaces on Mushēški that simulate different Earth environments from specific time periods. The three biodomes (Azania180, NusaLale120, and Altay60) house recreated ancient human species.

Cognitive Pathways – Patterns of thought or information processing built on top of *neural pathways*.

Collective Consciousness – The network that connects the minds of all Anunnaki, allowing for instantaneous communication, decision-making, and resource allocation.

Dilmun *(DEEL-moon)* – The Anunnaki district on Mushēški. Dilmun was also an ancient civilization on Earth that dates back to around 2300 BCE, located primarily in what is now Bahrain.

DPhil – A Doctor of Philosophy degree, the Oxford University equivalent of a PhD.

Emotion Amplification Pods – Booth-like structures used by the Anunnaki to experience heightened emotions.

Genetic Memory Activation – A technological process that directly interacts with the DNA of the recreated humans to activate dormant genetic memories.

Ghost DNA – A term used to describe traces of genetic material found in modern human genomes that are thought to have come from unknown archaic human ancestors.

Harmonic Wave – A wave characterized by its frequency and amplitude.

Homo anunnaki *(Anunnaki – ah-nuh-NAH-kee)* – A genetically modified lineage of *Homo Sapiens*, tracing back to Sumerian civilization. The name Anunnaki derives from the Sumerian words *An* (meaning the heavens) and *Ki* (meaning Earth), signifying their nature as beings who bridge both realms.

Homo denisova *(Denisovan – DEH-nee-soh-vahns)* – A hominin species, extinct on Earth but recreated on Mushēški, where they inhabit the biodome known as Altay60.

Homo erectus *(Erectus – eh-REK-tuhs)* – A hominin species, extinct on Earth but recreated on Mushēški, where they inhabit the biodome known as NusaLale120.

Homo floresiensis *(Floresiensis – floh-REH-see-en-sis)* – A hominin species, extinct on Earth but recreated on Mushēški, where they inhabit the biodome known as NusaLale120. Often referred to as "hobbits" on

Earth due to their small stature.

Homo luzonensis *(Luzonensis – loo-zoh-NEN-sis)* – A hominin species, extinct on Earth but recreated on Mushēški, where they inhabit the biodome known as NusaLale120.

Homo naledi *(Naledi – nah-LEH-dee)* – A hominin species, extinct on Earth but recreated on Mushēški, where they inhabit the biodome known as Azania180.

Homo neanderthalensis *(Neanderthal – nee-AN-der-thahl)* – A hominin species, extinct on Earth but recreated on Mushēški, where they inhabit the biodome known as Altay60.

Homo sapiens *(Sapiens – SAY-pee-ens)* – A hominin species, still in existence on Earth today. Also recreated on Mushēški, where they inhabit the biodomes known as Azania180 and Altay60.

Homo sylvicolus *(Sylvicolus – sihl-vi-KOH-luhs)* – A hominin species, extinct on Earth but recreated on Mushēški, where they inhabit the biodome known as Altay60. Sometimes referred to as Bigfoot, Sasquatch, or the Yeti.

Hypertrichosis *(HY-per-tri-KOH-sis)* – A condition characterized by excessive hair growth on the body in areas where hair is normally minimal or absent.

Inshallah *(IN-shah-lah)* – An Arabic phrase that means *God willing* or *if God wills it.*

Interfold Terminal – The Anunnaki facility used for interstellar transitfolding.

Kepler-442b – An exoplanet located approximately 1,200 light-years from Earth in the constellation Lyra. It is the home planet of the Abgal.

Khüiten *(KHUY-ten)* – The mountain of Javkhlan's tribe.

Khoton *(KHOH-tuh)* – The lake of Javkhlan's tribe.

Luminescent Ring – A streamlined neural interface. It aligns above the head to engage with specific brainwave frequencies, emitting a faint glow as it synchronizes for precise neural connectivity, hence why it is sometimes referred to as a *halo*.

Metaphysical Layer – A plane or dimension of existence that transcends the physical and observable.

Miravys *(MEE-rah-viss)* – The Anunnaki name for ultraviolet light. A color visible only to humans who have been transitfolded.

Miravysians *(MEE-rah-viss-ee-ans)* – Humans living on Earth, who have transitfolded from Mushēški, and now can see the color miravys.

Mushēški *(MOO-shehsh-kee)* – The planet where the Anunnaki (and the recreated ancient humans) reside. It translates to *the wise new Earth,* and was originally a barren planet transformed by the Abgal through geoengineering.

Nanobots – These are microscopic robots that can be programmed to perform specific tasks at the molecular level.

Nanotechnology – The manipulation of matter on an atomic and molecular scale. It involves the design, production, and application of structures, devices, and systems at the nanoscale.

Neural Pathways – Physical structures in the brain—bundles of neurons connected by synapses—that transmit electrical and chemical signals.

Neuroscribe – A small metallic disc-shaped device that, when placed on the temple, facilitates advanced communication between two or more individuals. It enables the exchange of not just words but complete concepts, emotions, memories, and sensory experiences. The neuroscribe works by adapting to each user's unique cognitive and experiential framework, allowing individuals from different species and time periods to communicate seamlessly. The device records observations and emotional responses, also functioning as a data collection tool.

NusaLale120 *(NOO-sah LAH-lay 120)* – This is a biodome replicating the Southeast Asia islands as they were 120,000 years ago. The recreated species in this biodome are Homo floresiensis, Homo luzonensis and Homo erectus.

Qal'at al-Bahrain *(KAHL-aht ahl bah-RAINE)* – A UNESCO World Heritage site in Bahrain, Earth. An ancient fort and archaeological site that once served as the capital of the Dilmun civilization and as a major trading hub from around 2300 BCE until the 16th century.

QS Governance – The percentage of neural pathways replaced by Quantum Sentience. At 58%, significant changes occur in an individual.

Quantum Entanglement – A phenomenon where two or more particles become linked so that their properties are correlated, meaning that a change in the state of one particle instantly influences the state of the other, regardless of the distance separating them.

Quantum Resonance Emitters – Technology that combines the principles of quantum mechanics and resonance, capable of manipulating energy at a quantum level.

Quantum Resonance Imaging – The method used to measure QS governance.

Quantum Psychosis – A serious disorder affecting the Anunnaki. Symptoms vary by individual but include stuttering, twitching, cognitive dissonance, erratic thought patterns, emotional instability, hallucinations, and irrational decision-making. Once QS governance reaches 58%, a permanent systemic change occurs, resulting in beings that function flawlessly but have lost all traces of their humanity.

Quantum Sentience (QS) – An advanced form of artificial intelligence integrated into the genomic structure of the Anunnaki. This embedded intelligence functions at the quantum level within neural pathways and DNA, synchronizing neurons to work collectively and enabling thoughts to exist in multiple states simultaneously. A specialized form of QS is also integrated into plants, buildings, and other environmental elements in Dilmun, allowing the Anunnaki to control and modify their surroundings through the Collective Consciousness.

Samboosas *(sam-BOO-suhz)* – Triangular pastries filled with spiced meat, vegetables, or lentils, then deep-fried until crisp. A Gulf variation of samosas.

Shawarma *(shuh-WAHR-mah)* – A popular Middle Eastern dish consisting of meat that is roasted on a rotating spit and shaved into thin slices. It is typically served in a flatbread wrap or on a plate with various toppings, such as vegetables, sauces, and pickles.

Sickle Cell Trait – A genetic condition in which a person inherits one sickle cell gene and one normal hemoglobin gene. People with sickle cell trait do not have symptoms of sickle cell disease.

Soul – A conscious energy—an enduring, non-physical essence that exists independently of biological processes yet interacts with the physical body and brain.

SoulViewer – Technology developed by the Anunnaki to detect unique quantum signals emitted by souls. It projects a 3D display showing the soul's journey in real-time.

Sphere – A spherical metallic ball that initiates an analysis of biological, mental, and emotional attributes, facilitating the transitfold of select humans to Dilmun, on the planet Mushĕški.

Sumerians *(soo-MARE-ee-ans)* – An ancient civilization from Earth that interacted with the Abgal around 2,900 BCE. When the Abgal warned of a great flood, 616 Sumerians were evacuated on an interstellar ark called An-Naĝar-ki. These Sumerians later integrated Quantum Sentience into their genomes with the Abgal's help, evolving into the Anunnaki and establishing their civilization on the planet Mushëški.

Telepathy – The direct communication of thoughts, feelings, and sensory experiences from one mind to another without using words or physical signals.

Thalvik *(THAHL-vik)* – The name of Javkhlan's tribe.

The Epic of Gilgamesh *(GIL-gah-mesh)* – An ancient Mesopotamian poem that is considered one of the earliest surviving works of literature.

Therapeutic Biotechnological Virus – A virus that has been genetically modified to deliver therapeutic genes.

Time Dilation – The difference in the elapsed time measured by two observers, either due to a relative velocity between them or to a difference in gravitational potential between their locations.

Transitfold – A form of travel that folds space, allowing near-instant movement between distant locations.

Transition Capsules – Specialized devices that temporarily suspend life functions, guiding participants through a controlled death experience before reviving them.

Unifier – A levitating structure consisting of interlocking rings and a translucent sphere that boosts neural connections, merging multiple minds into one.

Yadda *(YAD-uh)* – A colloquial Gulf Arabic term for grandmother, commonly used in Bahrain.

About the Author

M A Noordermeer grew up with a one-legged dad, a three-legged cat, and a fascination with what makes us human. She won writing awards at school—until teachers took issue with her choice of controversial topics.

After her first year of university, dabbling in philosophy, psychology, and sociology, she flew to Japan to work as an English teacher and fund her pilot training. She earned her commercial pilot's license, became a flying instructor, then shifted into aviation strategy, completing a degree in Aviation Management and an MBA along the way. She co-founded the carbon offsetting company *CarbonClick*, and raised four kids in a blended family.

At last, she came back to writing. Her debut novel, **58% Too Far**, draws on lifelong interests in extinct human species, ancient civilizations, and AI. She lives in Auckland, New Zealand, where she writes things her teachers probably still wouldn't have approved of.

Thank You For Reading

If you enjoyed *58% Too Far*, please consider leaving a review on Amazon or Goodreads. It helps more than you'd think and would be greatly appreciated.

And if you'd like to stay in touch, head over to

www.manoordermeer.com

Made in the USA
Middletown, DE
29 December 2025

26366031R00184